A BIOLOGICAL TIME BOMB

It begins slowly.

At first it seems like an unfortunate series of unrelated accidents: a plane crashes into a supermarket, a life-sized robot runs amuck in a toy store, an Apollo capsule is lost in space.

Then the underground transportation system explodes into an inferno of gas and flame and destruction accelerates until—within 48 hours—London is a freezing madhouse without light, heat or communication.

Mankind's nightmare has come true, and it won't be stopped . . .

MUTANT 59:
The Plastic-Eaters

MUTANT 59: THE PLASTIC-EATERS

BY KIT PEDLER AND GERRY DAVIS

A NATIONAL GENERAL COMPANY

This low-priced Bantam Book
has been completely reset in a type face
designed for easy reading, and was printed
from new plates. It contains the complete
text of the original hard-cover edition.
NOT ONE WORD HAS BEEN OMITTED.

MUTANT 59: THE PLASTIC EATERS
A Bantam Book / published by arrangement with
The Viking Press, Inc.

PRINTING HISTORY
Viking edition published February 1973
Literary Guild (Science Fiction Book Club) edition
published 1972
Bantam edition published February 1973

Bantam Books are published by Bantam Books, Inc., a National General company. Its trade-mark, consisting of the words "Bantam Books" and the portrayal of a bantam, is registered in the United States Patent Office and in other countries. Marca Registrada. Bantam Books, Inc., 666 Fifth Avenue, New York, N.Y. 10019.

PRINTED IN THE UNITED STATES OF AMERICA

Mutant 59: The Plastic-Eaters

OBITUARY NOTICE

S. Ainslie, M.B.B.S., M.C.Path.

DR. S. AINSLIE, 53, senior lecturer in microbiology at the Kensington General Hospital, died suddenly on 20th July at his home in Sydenham.

Simon Ainslie was born on 6 December 1919 and qualified at St. Mary's Hospital in 1939. Joining R.A.M.C. shortly after the outbreak of the second world war, he spent considerable time studying the mechanism of bacterial infection in gunshot wounds.

After he returned to civilian life, he decided to train as a research bacteriologist and became deeply interested in the adaptability of bacteria. Over the years he was able to amass a considerable quantity of data regarding the tailoring of bacteria to unusual growth media, and although none of his work had been published, many colleagues have paid tribute to his diligence and single-minded devotion to his work. One writes:

'Simon was a thoroughly charming man. He always gave his expertise willingly to any problem at hand and in the last months it was clear from his notebooks that he had made a series of original observations about *Bacillus prodigiosus* which excited him tremendously. It is tragic he should have died before completing his studies. He will be greatly missed.'

Simon Ainslie is survived by his wife and two daughters, to whom we extend our deepest sympathy.

—BRITISH MEDICAL JOURNAL

1

The switch had cost eighteen dollars and forty-three cents, and although it performed exactly the same task as any other switch on the counter of a general store, it had one difference—unimportant to the houseowner—but vital to Hannsen. In its specification the designers had stated that there was a "P_F of 0.1" that is to say, its likelihood of failure was infinitesimal. For eighteen dollars and forty-three cents, success was in practical terms a certainty. It had two positions, labelled *Attitude Correction—Manual* and *Attitude Correction—Automatic.*

The Apollo commander clicked it over to "manual" and from that millisecond onwards, began to die.

His action should have fired a small pulse of electricity into the intricately woven array of microcircuits behind the control panel. Instead, the current flowed out of a small wire which had once been perfectly insulated but now lay—invisible to his gaze—bare and gleaming. A red warning light flickered once and then lit steadily.

The commander's face showed little reaction. Perhaps a momentary dilation of the pupils and a twitch of an eyelid. He moved the switch again backwards and forwards—each time the warning light went off and on with the switch.

The two crew members followed his actions. No trace of emotion showed on their faces. They were all deadly tired. The fatigue of an almost impossible workload was marked in the dark shadows around their eyes.

All three men were concentrating on the liturgy of

survival imprinted on their memory by the long years of training.

The commander floated back onto his couch and lay quite still. No one spoke. Abruptly their concentration was broken by the voice of Houston ground control, the flat distorted tones filled the cabin.

"Apollo Nineteen—you are one minute forty-five from final T.E.I. course correction, mark." The tone bleeped briefly after the voice.

The commander replied, his voice free of any inflexion, "Copy, Houston. We have switching malfunction on computer severance—repeat, on computer severance, over."

Again the mark tone.

"Roger, Apollo. Running ground check now, over."

"Thank you, Houston."

The ship—a tiny speck in the empty dark of space—lunged faster than any bullet, along its curved trajectory towards Earth. It made no sound as it hurtled onwards—and left nothing in its wake.

"Apollo Nineteen—ground check confirms malfunction on severance control. Reposition control to automatic—repeat, switch to automatic."

The commander replied, "Roger, Houston—time to course correction, please." He moved the switch and the warning light went out.

"Time to correction burn one minute fifteen—on the mark—mark." The tone bleeped.

At the bio-medical console in the manned spacecraft centre, doctors anxiously watched the spiking traces of the commander's body. The flight surgeon made a note on his record sheet. "Command pilot: tachycardia, one hundred and ten, respiration thirty."

In the command module a process never conceived by its designer moved inexorably towards its conclusion behind the control panel.

Two more small components failed abruptly. A cascading series of electrical pulses flashed through computing circuits. There was a soundless flash of flame and smoke billowed out into the confined space of the cabin. In the choking fumes, the three men desperately fought to retain control as the capsule tumbled hopelessly out of control towards the outer limits of the atmosphere. . . .

Out in mid-Atlantic, passengers on board BOAC Flight 122 bound for New York were sleeping in the dim blue light of the cabin. A small boy on the starboard side was fidgeting and sleepless, his face pressed to the window. Suddenly, he shook his mother awake: "Look, quick, Mummy, look!" He pointed out of the window. The mother rubbed her eyes and leant across him to look out.

Spread across the clear starlit sky was a long orange trail of fire; she could see that something at the head of it was moving. It steadily grew larger and then suddenly broke into three separate, flaming points. These broke again and again and spiralled away from the main direction of the fire trail, dying away in the darkness like a Fourth of July firework. She sat back in her seat and cuddled her son down beside her. "Just a shooting star, honey—they don't hurt anyone."

Mrs. Harris finished stacking her husband's books in the loft and, shutting the trapdoor above her, wheezed unsteadily down the ladder to the upstairs landing. Two months, they had told her at the hospital, and it was just three weeks.

In the front hall she passed a photograph of the two of them in its embossed tin frame and wondered tearfully whether to take it back up to the loft and put it with his other things. She thought of her blood pressure and her ankles and instead took it off the wall and put it on the mantelpiece in the front room.

Her concern for her health saved her life.

On the flight deck of BEA Flight 510 from Paris to Heathrow, the captain was relaxed. There were no particular problems ahead on the flight plan except for light ground fog at Heathrow. The door behind him opened, and the co-pilot eased his way past the jump seat and through the congested mass of instruments and controls and sat down. The captain grinned over at him: "I know where you've been—thought she was engaged."

The co-pilot replied, rubbing his hands, "All cabin crew must remain under the instructions of the flight officers."

"In professional matters!"

"This is going to be very professional. What's the latest E.T.A.?"

"Seventeen ten if we don't get stacked."

Rivulets of water streamed up the cabin windows and whipped away in the slipstream, partly obscuring the solid cloud cover beneath the aircraft.

The captain began the routine conversation with Heathrow control, trying to sort out his own ground controller from the jumbled mass of voices he could hear jabbering in the background:

"Alpha Charlie, Flight 510, you are clear to cross and make a right turn as you enter on block 82."

"Thank, you, Alpha Charlie, right turn. . . ."

As he talked, the flight engineer was studying the array of dials in front of him showing, in quadruplicate, the state of each engine; temperature, per-cent thrust, oil pressure. He made notes in a log strapped to the desk as the great aircraft banked on its final turn before entering the cone of signals which would guide it down onto the runway. The co-pilot noted that they were on both the beam transmitter and glide-slope beam. They passed the first vertical marker. . . .

Ena Harris had just finished making tea in the kitchen and was sipping a boiling hot cup and staring glumly out of the window.

In the port wing of Flight 510 there was a small metal box containing a tightly woven mass of wires and solid-state circuitry. Its task, in the almost biological complex of arteries and veins under the gleaming alloy skin of the wing, was to control the flow of fuel to number two engine. It also transmitted information to the engineer's control panel about the fuel feed rate to number two engine, and data about fan temperature in the roaring cyclone of flame inside the thrusting jet engine.

Inside the dull-grey metal skin of the box, two centimetres of wire began to sag away from its contact points.

On the flight deck, the captain made his final communication with ground control.

"Alpha Charlie, Flight 510, you are clear to land on runway four. Good day."

"Thank you, Alpha Charlie. Good day."

He clicked off the trans-ceiver. . . .

In the wing, the control function of the box abruptly failed. Fuel pumped suddenly from the central fuselage tank into number two engine, an event which could only have occurred if the feed line from the port inboard wing tank had previously shut off.

It was still open.

The combustion chambers in the engine flooded and there was a sudden small explosion, a single blade on the turbine shaft sheared away and flew upwards like a projectile. The engine exploded and blew away from its hanging pod under the wing. The streaking blade plunged into the structure of the wing, tearing through pressurized tubes and complex honeycombed sheets like a knife through flesh. It came to rest, wedged into a tightly knotted assembly of pipes, between the inboard spoiler and the flaps. Red hydraulic fluid gushed out like blood from the severed pipes. Both the inboard and outboard aileron slammed into the fully raised position and locked solid. The wing lurched downwards pulling the stricken machine uncontrollably away from the radio cone of safety. . . .

Mrs. Harris finished her tea disconsolately and went out into the garden to fetch in the washing. As she started to unpeg the sheets, grey and dripping with the water and fog, she heard the noise of an approaching aircraft.

For twenty years she had lived in Isleworth only a few miles from the main airport runways, and so at first she took no notice. As the noise grew louder, she began to peer blindly into the fog. The mixed roar and scream grew to an almost intolerable level and then, suddenly, over the two apple trees at the bottom of her garden, an enormous winged shape loomed out of the murk, wings tilted at an impossible level.

Ena Harris stared for a split moment, her mouth sagging in complete disbelief, then she turned and began to run towards the door. She reached it and all light ceased as the sky was blotted out by the enormous spread of the plane. The last image she remembered as she fainted away was the great black doughnut of the wheel suspended by gleaming struts only feet above her head.

From that instant onwards Flight 510 ceased to be a flying machine and became instead a plunging disintegrating mass of machinery. The wheel smashed into the loft, scattering the neatly stacked books, and as the roof timbers and tiles sprayed into the air like matchsticks, the plane slewed around and began to break up. One wing knifed into the houses on the other side of the street and the fuselage, breaking loose like a giant torpedo, tore down the centre of the road, flinging cars and people aside, routing a terrible path of death.

An engine from the starboard wing, its turbine blades still screaming, broke loose and plunged into a crowded supermarket and exploded.

The tail assembly cartwheeled like a giant boomerang and plunged through the wall of a Bingo hall, disappearing in a boiling cloud of dissolving brickwork.

The severed nose section, turning over and over like a giant bullet, bounced once at the end of the road and, in one final gigantic ricochet, spiralled into a tightly packed mass of houses, pulverizing walls and ceilings.

The remaining fuselage began to shatter, turning end over end like a ragged metal stick flung through the air.

The lives of the forty-eight passengers and crew ceased almost simultaneously as collapsing bulkheads and jagged panelling slashed their bodies into a terrible carrion which rained down on the street below.

Finally, in a thunder of collapsing homes and dust, the unrecognizable fragments of the great aircraft spun away from the point of impact and clattered down over the surrounding homes.

A car, flung like a toy onto the roof of a garage, slid slowly off to thump down on its roof in the blackened road.

A street lamp, leaning slowly, began to move like the hands of a mad clock, then snapped and fell.

One man, pulling himself painfully out of the wreckage of his car, began to stagger aimlessly down the street, his face blank of any reaction. As he zigzagged onwards, his senses automatically guided him between the obstacles lying in the road: the scattered airline bags and the chic leather trunks. His eyes failed entirely to comprehend the terrible and pathetic human remains scattered all around him.

Anne Kramer stood shivering in the driving rain. Pulling up the hood of her raincoat, she strained to hear the officer talking through a loud-hailer on the quayside below her.

She was standing on the bridge of a small naval frigate looking down onto the foredeck of H.M.S. *Renown,* a nuclear submarine, carrying sixteen A_3 Polaris missiles. Perforating the black bulbous contours of the foredeck, open to the rain, were the sixteen hatches leading to the missile-launching tubes, running over forty feet down through the full extent of the whale-like hull. Between the two rows of tubes, two ratings were standing on the deck looking upwards.

Above them, hanging from a crane, was the dull grey cylinder of a Polaris missile slowly descending towards one of the open tubes. Gradually the ratings eased its base into the opening and it began to slide down into the body of the submarine. Anne stood among a small group of journalists huddled against the bridgehouse to keep away from the driving rain. One of them came up to her, nudging her shoulder. There was a large drop of water hanging from his nose under a battered hat.

He grinned: "I know what you're thinking."

"You've got a thoroughly dirty mind, Matt," she bantered.

They watched as the two ratings fitted a circular plastic membrane in place over the mouth of the tube holding the missile.

"Complete with maidenhead," he chuckled.

"Bit late," she murmured and turned to listen to the officer's voice.

His voice came metallically through the loud-hailer: "When the missile is launched, high-pressure steam, generated by a conventional cordite explosion, drives the missile up against the plastic membrane. The membrane ruptures and the missile leaves the submarine under the guidance of on-board target computers. . . ."

As the voice crackled on, Anne wondered whether she would be able to remember the exact sequence for her article and hoped that the official handout had enough details in it. Perhaps she could do a first draft in the mess.

The gale drove the rain hard against the picture windows of the officers' mess, obscuring the great sheds of the submarine base down the hill near the lochside. Inside, it was softly lit and warm and there was a relaxed murmur of conversation around the bar. The group was ill-assorted. The uniformed officers looking impossibly well groomed and clean, handing round drinks to the journalists, each wearing a circular orange "press" label in his lapel.

The voice of a senior officer rose above the hubbub: "Can I have your attention please, ladies and gentlemen, can I have . . ."

The talk died away.

"Thank you. Well, first of all, may I welcome you all to Gareloch base. I hope that you are seeing all you want."

There were a few friendly jeers; the officer reacted, smiling: "The Official Secrets Act doesn't cover the systems behind the bar, I assure you, gentlemen, so please enjoy yourselves."

Somebody raised his glass and said in mock accent, "God bless you, governor."

He went on: "Now, as to tomorrow's programme. In the morning, we are to visit the Polaris training school —there are camera restrictions there I'm afraid—and then we were to have gone aboard H.M.S *Triton,* the first Royal Navy Poseidon carrier, in the afternoon. As you've been told, she was to have docked tomorrow morning, but owing to unforeseen circumstances, there has been a bit of a holdup, so intead, we shall take you on to the dry dock where H.M.S. *Resolution* is having a refit. Oh, and one more thing, dinner will begin at seventeen thirty. Thank you very much."

Anne turned to Matt: "What's happened? They're usually as regular as clockwork."

Matt was deadly serious, his eyes flicking round the room for clues: "I agree, they never vary the time schedule without bloody good reason." He looked at Anne intently: "Something is definitely up."

Lionel Slayter's Ph.D. had been in communications theory. The University of Keele had marked him out early in his student days as an unusually gifted mathematician, but one progress report made by his tutor had said that although his math was impeccable, he had a regrettable tendency to speculate well beyond the bounds of reasonable induction. After completing his thesis, he made the usual tour of North American institutions on a travel grant and then returned to England to scan the columns of the science journals for a job. His American tour had been without particular interest or success except for one small event, insignificant in itself.

Spending far more of his grant money than he should have done, he had opted for the short helicopter trip from Kennedy Airport to Manhattan rather than a cab, simply because he wanted to see the city from the air.

Passing west over Brooklyn, he had looked down at the congested lanes of cars in the criss-crossed streets below and saw them briefly as units in a system or, as he later put it, as blood cells in a blood vessel.

He saw that the movement of the shining coloured dots formed a rhythmic pattern as they were influenced by each other and by the traffic signals. In a notebook he started to make simple mathematical approximations, and by the time the helicopter had landed, he was subject to the taut excitement which accompanies the arrival of a good and original idea.

Back in England, after a long, depressing search, he found a job with a systems research unit in the Ministry of Transport and began to develop his ideas to a level of practicability with the aid of highway engineers and electronic specialists.

He found a name for his project; he called it "the learning road system."

Simply stated, his idea was to take a localized system of roads and turn it into an almost biological unit. To provide it with senses in the form of electric eyes, pneumatic counting systems were affixed to the road surface and television cameras. Then, to feed information from those senses into a computer system capable of adapting its performance as a result of past experience, or "learning" as he put it. And finally, to connect the computer output to traffic signals and police who would control the flow through the network of roads.

Where the system differed from others of a similar type was that the computer "learnt" the pattern of traffic through the roads under its control; in this way it could maximize traffic flow on any particular day, week, or month. The only objection to the scheme had been from the police and Atherton.

The police complained on what seemed to him an emotional basis—that they were human beings in thrall to a machine. They felt that it degraded their status as individuals.

Atherton, sitting on the committee which had finally sanctioned the scheme, had kept up a continuous hostility to the whole idea, saying that its limits had not been defined clearly enough and that the performance of the adapting computer could never be predicted sufficiently accurately.

The area chosen for the experiment was limited to the north by Knightsbridge and to the south by the Cromwell Road, west by Gloucester Road, and east by Sloane

Street. It had taken fourteen months to install the necessary road equipment and provide the links to the computer and control room in the nearby Imperial College of Science.

As a control measure, complete estimates of traffic flow through the system had been taken before the experiment started so that the rhythm of flow could be compared before and after the computer was given control of its own "body system." Finally, the system was connected to other centres controlling roads into and out of the area, so that any changes in it could be taken up in adjacent districts.

It took three months for the machine to learn the flow pattern, three months of self-tuition before it achieved total knowledge of its life-function. After repeated tests it was finally given control over its limbs and muscles—the traffic signals and the radio-equipped policemen. Slayter remembered his anxiety when they first relinquished control to the machine.

They had hung the figures of previous traffic flow beside the counters which showed flow under computer control. For long, tense minutes, the counters had shown no change, then slowly—very slowly—began to show an improvement. It was, he remembered, as if the machine had sulked at being given such an anonymous responsibility. Over the succeeding hours, the improvement continued until late in the evening, the jubilant team left the system in the hands of assistants and went off to get suitably drunk.

Since then the performance of the system had continued to improve until it reached its predicted maximum.

But now, Slayter was anxious and fidgeting. He nervously moved around the control room, adjusting a file here, removing a piece of wire there.

In front of him was an array of forty-eight television screens and by the side of each screen an illuminated counter showing the traffic flow at a particular inter-section. By the side of each counter was a card with a number showing traffic flow before the scheme. He looked at the monitors showing the congested, incessantly moving, columns of cars and buses and hoped against hope that nothing would go wrong. He looked at his watch—ten minutes to go. How the hell do you talk to a minister, how many "sirs," how much deference?

The control room was quite abnormally tidy—in fact he had only just managed to restrain his secretary from sticking a pot of flowers on the data terminal.

At last she put her head round the door and said, "They're here."

He heard the approaching murmur of voices in the corridor, then the door swung open and the Director came in, followed by the Minister, two aides, and—Atherton. The Director made the introductions; he was in his professional-charm role.

"Now, Slayter, perhaps you could give us a rundown on your brainchild. I hear it's been going very well."

"Yes, its performance has been quite consistent, sir. Flow rate shows an almost uniform eight-point-four-per-cent increase."

The Minister, trying to maintain a surface interest on his third visit of the day, said, "Flow rate—ah yes. Of course you must treat me as very—you know—about the level of a backward child of three." He smiled, showing yellow tobacco-stained teeth.

Slayter went into his "routine patter for nits" as he called it. The Director looked on paternally and the Minister kept up an intermittent nodding, varying the depth of his nod as if to indicate occasional profound understanding.

The computer in the adjacent room was almost silent except for the staccato groaning noise of the tape heads as they flicked into new positions: its silence giving no indication of the torrent of signals pouring out into the near-by road system. In the arithmetic unit complicated calculations were solved in fractions of a second and logic pulses—the internal language of computers—made exact decisions, all with perfection.

Except one component.

That particular one, known to its designers as "NOR

gate M.13" made two incorrect decisions, then failed altogether.

In the control room, Slayter was coming to the end of his discourse, but as he did so, the result of the component failure had spread out like ripples from a stone in water to the periphery of the machine-controlled road system.

The Minister was talking: "Quite extraordinary, Slayter, most interesting. I do congratulate you. I know you haven't had universal encouragement," Atherton shifted from one leg to the other, "but I'm sure there will be no more problems in the—ah—financial area."

He walked over to the array of monitor screens: "Let me see now, where are we? Ah yes, I recognize that—the Natural History Museum, isn't it? Yes, there's the V. and A. and"—he was moving about like a child with a new toy—"extraordinary, gives one a feeling of being inside a brain looking out." The Minister's voice fell away and the attention of all the men became riveted on the small blue screens.

The component failure had now reverberated throughout the system. At the junction of Exhibition Road and Cromwell Road, traffic lights went from red to green and almost immediately back to red again. A taxi, caught half-way across the intersection, was slammed sideways by a bus.

On the next monitor screen showing the junction of Sloane Street and Knightsbridge, the traffic lights failed and then went totally berserk. Traffic pouring westwards from Piccadilly ground to a fuming halt.

Road counters in Prince Consort Road suddenly added two zeros to their measurements—as a result the Queen's Gate lights went permanently to green at the Cromwell Road. Gradually, over a total time of four minutes, the flow of traffic jerked to a halt. Multiple accidents added to the confusion and in the gathering dusk the blue lights of ambulances could be seen hopelessly flashing in the choked streets.

In the control room, there was complete silence; no one wanted to open the conversation.

Finally, the Director spoke: "For God's sake, Slayter, what's happened?"

Slayter was stupefied. "I'm afraid . . . I don't know, I just don't know." He was near to tears.

The Minister looked at his aides and said a shade too firmly, "Well, gentlemen, I'm very sorry but—eh—we have to get on back to the Ministry." He turned to the Director: "You'll let me have a report about all this won't you?" The Director nodded grimly.

To Slayter he said, "I'm sorry, you know, really sorry."

As they all began to file out, Atherton looked back towards Slayter, his face a mask.

2

Luke Gerrard studied the other three men warily and for the tenth time that day wondered what he was doing there.

Lounging in various attitudes around the room, the members of the Kramer consultancy had spent most of the working week trying to solve the problem of a disposable bottle top. Gerrard was sick of the mental effort and of his colleagues.

It was half past four on a grey December day and the light was gradually fading. The room, Gerrard reflected, looked even more depressing in the dusk. The red-brick Victorian Gothic of the converted school they worked in resisted every effort at restoration. Like the sturdy old spinster it was, it remained resolutely unchanged. It was cold, draughty, ill lit, and uncomfortable with a dais at one end and an enormous roller blackboard covering an entire wall. Most of the board was covered with intricate scientific *graffiti* and the armchairs, tables, and floors were littered with crumpled paper torn from foolscap pads. After some ten days' work they had reached a point of utter stalemate.

The fault lay partly in the curiously ill-balanced quartet of personalities Kramer had gathered together. For a whole week, the patient, introspective Scot, Buchan, had been throwing up ideas with the regularity of a clay-pigeon target machine and Wright, the Englishman, had been studiously shooting them down. Gerrard was sick of both of them. One seemed to cancel the other out, with no advantage to problem solution.

What should have been stimulating and creative usually turned out to be stultified and full of tension. He wondered what had been in Kramer's mind in hiring two such complete opposites in temperament, outlook, and scientific method. They had only been fully successful on one major project: the development of the degradable plastic bottle, a row of which now decorated the farther wall to impress any visitor allowed the privilege of the inner sanctum.

Just how that had been invented, Gerrard felt, was a miracle. He glanced across at the third member of the team, Jim Scanlon.

Scanlon was younger than either of the other two, fresh-faced, a trifle over-eager, a good, rather faceless technician, with very little creativity in his make-up. He would have made a good salesman, Gerrard reflected. As it was, he seemed to delight in stirring up the differences between Wright and Buchan and egging them on one against the other. To be fair, though, given a complex laboratory task, he would do it with complete reliability and precision. A bit of a machine. Gerrard wondered how he made love.

Betty, the secretary, came in with a tray of tea. She put it down on the centre table and completed the routine with her catch phrase: "Anybody for cakes?"

The question, Gerrard now knew, was purely rhetorical. Wright hardly ever seemed to eat and his fastidious concern over his weight would have stopped him from eating the various brands of glutinously creamy cakes imported by Betty. Buchan, a great gourmet, would never have blunted his appetite for dinner by eating at teatime.

The men stared morosely at Betty as she poured out the tea.

"We're not thinking well now, we'd better stop." Wright blinked over through his spectacles at Buchan, as if challenging him to make a reply.

Buchan, deflated and gloomy, merely shook his head and shrugged his shoulders. "No doubt."

Betty handed Gerrard his tea and he took it over to the window to look out at the yellow lights flicking on down the street. It was raining again and Gerrard thought, with a slight twinge of nostalgia, that by now the first fall of snow would be whitening the streets back in his home town in Canada. His mind went back two years to his first meeting with Arnold Kramer, when Kramer had flown up to Canada to start a research project at Gerrard's university.

They had worked together for three months on Kramer's experiments into the spontaneous disintegration of plastic, and the result had been to give Gerrard a completely new perspective on his life. He thought back further, probing into his state of mind at that time.

He had been a doctor, operating a small practice for a mining company in a small northern Ontario township. He had met Sharon, married her, and infected by her restlessness and drive, had started a new career in experimental biology at the age of thirty. After three years, when Kramer arrived, the academic life was beginning to seem a sterile one-way street to nowhere.

Kramer had been first trained at Harvard, by some of the best scientists in North America. A man of colossal intelligence, he also had a driving personality and a fiercely developed critical faculty. At first, Gerrard found him impossible to take. The sheer ferocity of his creative power frankly scared him, and it was some time before he was able to form any sort of relationship with the man. But once this had been achieved, he found the contact with Kramer's mind of tremendous stimulus.

Kramer stayed at Gerrard's house, and Sharon looked after them. It was a time of high excitement for Gerrard, and when Kramer finally left for England to set up his scientific consultancy, Gerrard knew that he would never be able to settle down to the ingrown life of the provincial university, with its Calvinistic power structure.

Tension developed between Gerrard and Sharon, eventually ending with infidelities on both sides and an unpleasantly messy divorce. Gerrard remained at the university for another year, becoming increasingly isolated in the authoritarian atmosphere, eventually leading a revolt against the power regime imposed by the older professors.

The revolt succeeded but in the process, as so often with reformers, he found himself isolated by both factions. It was in this climate that, shortly afterwards, the call had come from Kramer to join his consultancy in London. Gerrard made an instant decision, resigned his post, sold up house, furnishings and car, and, his possessions reduced to the contents of two suitcases, flew over and took the job.

On the surface, the Kramer consultancy was a novel and exciting idea. A group of experts pooling their resources and brains under Kramer's organizing brillance to anticipate and come up with solutions to problems in industry and science.

Eventually stretching themselves beyond the mere solving of problems, they had come up with several highly profitable inventions.

One of these, developed by the team chemist, Wright, was known as Aminostyrene; a new, durable insulating plastic now widely used in industry. The other was an attempt to ease waste-disposal problems by means of a plastic bottle that under the influence of light broke down to a fine dust.

A marvellous idea from a fertile and brilliant stable, thought Gerrard, but lately it seemed to him that something had gone out of the group. It was in some way bound up with the personality of Kramer himself.

Arnold Kramer inspired awe. A compact, powerful man, his heavy-lidded blue eyes very rarely looked at you; instead, he always seemed to be scanning a far horizon slightly above your head. When he lowered his gaze his eyes had an intensity almost impossible to meet. His conversation was brilliant, almost encyclopedic, and yet with a precision and feel for the shape and colour of words that at times verged on the poetic.

But there had been a change since their shared research in Canada. Or perhaps Gerrard hadn't really known him then.

In Canada, Kramer had been "on sabbatical." His erudition and intellect had been turned to research and even, though one hesitated to use the word in connection with Kramer, fun. He had delighted in spending hours, days even, speculating, philosophizing, putting up concepts.

Now all that had gone. The man Gerrard saw before him seemed a totally different version of the Arnold Kramer he had known. The rich flow of his conversation, sparkling with ideas, seemed to have been compressed into an eclectic, terse, even brusque businessman's shorthand. Every remark, every concept, every speculation was now directed towards a profit motive. His one criterion seemed to be . . . does it, or does it not, make money!

If the philosophical Kramer he had known had been intellectually overpowering, then this new one was doubly so. He was also intimidating in another way. His drive burned like a laser beam. He gave the impression of barely holding in check a cold, massive aggression. Before, Gerrard had felt a special intimacy and friendship with the man; now Kramer seemed to be separated from Gerrard and the rest of the team by the aura of a leader. He had turned into a driver who spared no one—himself least of all. There was still a great deal of charm, but it was the direct charm of a man obsessed by a single, driving motivation. Success at all costs.

The room was darkening; suddenly the lights flashed on and Kramer strode across to the middle of the room.

"Well?" he looked around. "Any luck, gentlemen?"

The men looked up. Tired as they were there was something about Kramer which made them sit up from their slumped position and give him their full attention. At the age of forty-five, Kramer with his height, his heavy powerful shoulders, and his slightly stooped, massive head would automatically become the centre of attention in any room he entered.

"Back where we started," said Wright, coming over and standing beside him.

"Exactly," said Kramer. "I fully expected you to end up there."

Buchan stretched his legs out, put his hands behind

his head with a resigned expression. "The last few days have been for nothing, then?"

"You've had the first seven necessary bad ideas," said Kramer, "and now I'd like to have a real session with you if I may."

"Now?" groaned Buchan.

Kramer nodded. "Yes, exactly now. I know you're tired but that's often when the best ideas come out. I'd like to go back over your premises and see why they haven't worked. We may get nothing, but the chances are that we can break out a couple of good ideas you can develop over the week-end."

Kramer looked around at the tired men. "Betty's bringing in a bottle of Scotch, best malt." He nodded over to Buchan. "The best, Jock, an Islay malt. Meanwhile I've got something here that needs looking into."

He looked over and appeared to notice Gerrard for the first time. "Luke, perhaps you can help, it's a bit of leg work."

Gerrard looked up, trying hard not to seem too eager. Any chance to get out of this oppressive building. He'd contributed very little to the debate of the last few days and was conscious of his inadequacies when it came to the chemical side of the consultancy.

"Do you know where Barratt's of Kensington is?" asked Kramer. "Or let's put it this way—do you know *what* Barratt's of Kensington is?"

"The big store near Harrods?"

"That one," said Kramer. "They've had some trouble in their toy department."

"No kidding." Gerrard cocked an eyebrow.

"It looks like some trouble with Aminostyrene."

Wright looked up from some papers he was sorting on his desk. "Perhaps I should go," he said.

Wright's Aminostyrene was their first significant commercial success. An ingenious compound based to some degree on the combined molecular structures of protein and polystyrene, it had proved both cheap and easy to manufacture. Large combines had taken over the mass-production, yielding considerable royalties. Not only was their product the main constituent of the degradable bottle, but it also formed parts of literally hundreds of products from missiles to toys.

"I'd rather you stayed," said Kramer. "Anne's over there now. I don't want to make a big deal out of it. Just want to keep it out of the hands of the press, that's why I want somebody to go over."

Gerrard looked at him inquiringly.

"Some of the plastic in, I don't know, some kind of Christmas toy grotto or bazaar has melted and the guy on the job can't account for it. Probably turn out to be the heat or, more than likely, some joker's poured acetone on it. We don't guarantee it against everything. Anyway, I want you to go take a look and bring back a sample for testing here."

"On my way." Gerrard rose and moved over to the door.

"Will you take your car? I know Anne would be darn grateful for a ride home afterwards."

Betty entered with a bottle and some glasses on a tray just as Gerrard reached the door. He stood aside to let her pass. Buchan stood up for the first time since lunch and went over to help her with the tray, his eyes fixed on the tall green bottle. O.K., don't offer me a drink, thought Gerrard. Anyway, I prefer rye. He passed through the corridor, out of the entrance, and into the rain.

On the way to Barratt's, driving slowly through the jammed pre-Christmas traffic, Gerrard thought about Anne Kramer.

He had met her twice. The first time was at Kramer's home on his first evening in London and the second time at the Kramer consultancy some weeks later. Only two meetings, but they'd been enough for him to know that she attracted him more than any other woman he'd met for years.

He jammed on his brakes and skidded to a halt only inches away from a taxi which had cut in ahead of him. The taxi drove on unheedingly and Gerrard, by now fairly conditioned to the fuming congestion of London traffic, ignored the incident and went on thinking about Anne. She disturbed him.

She was a beautiful woman by any standards. Tall, with thick dark-brown hair, large fine hazel eyes, and a slightly olive complexion. She had an elegant, easy composure which he found difficult to get through and which he attributed to her British upper-class upbringing, as he termed it. There was always a hint of a smile at the corner of her mouth and, perhaps, a hint of a challenge in the way she looked at you. Anyone looking at her could imagine her effectiveness as an interviewer though they might not have guessed that she was one of the country's leading science columnists.

She could certainly handle men, that was obvious. She had the quality of making each man she met feel that she was personally interested in him. It may have been a professional trick of the trade, thought Gerrard, but if so, it was a damn good one.

He was fairly cynical about women. The broken marriage, its aftermath, and a score of fleeting, uneasy affairs had made him apprehensive about any serious involvement. Perhaps he had been looking for a woman rather too eagerly after the break-up. There must have been something hungry and over-anxious about his approach. At all events, his attempts at contact had been notable for their lack of success. A quick roll in the hay with Gerrard, yes, if that was success! He was tall, interesting-looking rather than conventionally handsome, and there was a forceful look about his face which appealed to women. But none of them, it appeared, wanted anything more durable. . . .

With a start, he found that he was at his destination, a small tree-lined square immediately behind Barratt's. There was a Bentley moving out of one of the few parking meter spaces.

He started to edge his Citroën in as the Bentley moved away, not noticing a predatory mini-car which had crept up behind him and was now trying to bypass him by slipping into the space. The mini was driven by a girl with long blonde hair and a flashing smile. Thinking she wanted to pass he waved her forward and she started to slide into the space. Gerrard instinctively jammed the gears into reverse and there was a moment's battle of wills as both cars headed for each other on a collision course. Abruptly the girl jammed on her brakes and backed away frozen-faced. He drove into the space with his tires just touching the curb, got out, put a couple of coins into the parking meter, and headed across the square towards Barratt's.

The store was packed with pre-Christmas shoppers. In the past, Gerrard had enjoyed the pre-Christmas rush and the atmosphere of a store at Christmastime. During his student days he had often helped behind the counter to make some money during the college vacation. He had worked in the big stores in Toronto and Montreal, but the atmosphere here was quite different.

In the big Canadian stores there was a brightness, an innocence about Christmas, despite the gaudy exhortations to buy superfluous presents. Here, everyone seemed tired and jaded; there seemed to be no pleasure in the process. It was a ritual, complied with as any other ritual but without any simple joy or anticipation. Not, Gerrard reflected as he made his way up the escalator towards the toy department, that there was a lot of joy to be found in shopping.

In the toy department the bustle, if anything, was greater, and he put the noise level at well above seventy decibels. Children were yelling, calling to each other, snatching toys, beating drums, and blowing tin horns; there were small record players grinding out last year's pops and metallic screeching nursery rhymes. There was the high-pitched whine of small electric cars and motors mixed with the whirr of clockwork and the disorganized clacking of a hundred tin animals cavorting brainlessly around a large circular table.

At the far end of the department was the traditional grotto and a long queue for Santa Claus. Beside the grotto was a special display of this Christmas season entitled "The Walk on the Moon." Anne Kramer was waiting for him.

"Hello," said Anne. She introduced a fresh-faced, curly-haired, and eager young man in a thick tweed jacket who was standing beside her.

"This is Mr. Aspinall, Dr. Gerrard." They shook hands. Aspinall was tall, gangling, youthful; his handshake was limp and slightly damp.

"Well," said Gerrard, "let's go." Aspinall led the way through into the now closed public exhibition.

Barratt's had really gone to town this year with their special attraction. It must have cost thousands, thought Gerrard. No expense had been spared with a replica of a lunar module, a large expanse of silver moon-sand, and, as the main feature, three life-size figures in space suits, one of which was able, Aspinall explained, to bend down, pick up a lunar rock, and carry it some half a dozen yards across to the waiting space craft. It then loaded it in the space craft and returned to its former position. The trouble had apparently started with this particular figure, which represented the commander of the space ship.

The robot had originally been made for a cybernetics convention as a demonstration machine built by an American university. It had then been partly dismantled and bought up by the company that Aspinall represented. Aspinall and his team had rebuilt the robot including certain gear trains made of Aminostyrene.

In Aspinall's workshop this had worked well. It had made the robot more portable and much cheaper and had been a great success. It had been mounted in the store about a week ago, and Anne Kramer had written a special piece for her column about it and the way it incorporated Aminostyrene and other new plastic materials.

The grand opening of the exhibition had been a success and within two or three days it had drawn a large crowd of adults and children at the inflated price of thirty new pence a head. Then things had started going wrong, and for the last five days, the exhibition had been closed. The trouble apparently lay in the plastic itself.

Aspinall guided them to a small workbench set up behind the space capsule; on the bench were a number of the small gears, back plates, and other components from the robot. Apparently they had softened and lost their shape and were lying in various, rather contorted postures on the bench. They looked as though they had been melted by heat or exposed to a solvent.

"How hot is it inside there?" Gerrard nodded over to the blazing arc lamps reflected on the silver sand which simulated lunar sunlight.

"About seventy-five," said Aspinall. "Not nearly hot enough to have melted these. But you're the expert in that department."

Gerrard felt very far from expert, but he nodded. Anne came up and looked closely at them, picking one up in her hand and looking at it intently.

"Could it have been some form of solvent?" she asked.

"That might account for it, of course," said Aspinall, "but as far as I can make out, nothing like that has been anywhere near it."

"But have you been around all the time?" said Gerrard. "Perhaps a cleaner . . . ?" His weak suggestion embarrassed him.

"Highly unlikely," said Aspinall. "We clean it down ourselves with spirit. The staff here have strict instructions not to meddle. Anyway, it keeps happening. I've replaced these gears three times. Each time this happens. Here," he led them back to the main part of the display. They shielded their eyes from the blaze of the arc lamps.

"Now," he continued, "I have mounted our last set of gears in the robot. I coated them with a protective lacquer so if there's any solvent acetone—or what have you—inside the thing it'll take a while to get through. I've put a thermometer here to give us the temperature. Let's see what happens. If you would like to stand back over here."

He stepped up onto the raised rostrum of the display area and crunched across the sand to where a thin hardboard partition separated them from the main body of the toy department. Anne hesitated in the middle, facing the robot.

Aspinall beckoned to her. "Over here, you'll be in its path there." He looked around and picked up a small radio transmitting set, similar to the type used for model boats and cars.

"Here we go." He switched on and then turned the control knob. They looked across at the robot.

There was a whine of servo-motors, the head slowly moved up, the arms flexed, one of the legs began retracting, and the robot tilted over to one side. Then the legs swung forward purposefully and crunched into the sand.

"It's working again," said Aspinall excitedly.

"Perhaps you've found the answer," said Anne.

The robot came forward with the ponderous motion of a deep-sea diver, heading towards the space capsule. Its arms were outstretched in front of it, as though carrying an imaginary rock.

"He's supposed to place a moon rock into the capsule," said Aspinall.

"And then?" asked Gerrard.

"He turns round and comes back for another rock," said Aspinall.

"Exciting," said Gerrard, not intending it to be too sarcastic.

"The children think so," said Aspinall, a little huffily. "Excuse me." He went over to the space capsule. The robot had now reached it and was stiffly bending down to place an imaginary rock in a container inside the open door. Aspinall climbed past it and disappeared inside the capsule. The robot slowly turned and started lurching back.

Anne, nearly blinded by the arc lamps, turned to Gerrard. "I've got some sand in my shoe," she said. "Would you?" She put out an arm for support and bent down to take off her open-toed shoes.

Gerrard grasped her arm; it was as close as he had been to her and he was aware of a subtle perfume and the rich dark-brown sweep of her hair. She was vitally attractive and he felt a slight tautening of his stomach and an increased flow of adrenalin (he told himself as a medic), something he had not felt for years. She bent down and shook the sand out, holding tight to his arm.

She wore dark-coloured sheer tights and her slender legs were silhouetted in black against the white sand.

A long shadow appeared between them. He glanced round. Above them loomed the huge figure of the robot, its arms stretched up almost above its head, terrifyingly reminiscent of a karate chop.

"Look out!" said Gerrard. He grabbed her round the waist and pulled her away just as the robot's arms swung down towards her head. One of the arms caught Anne a glancing blow on the shoulder as they flung themselves on the sand out of the way of the robot. The robot continued moving towards the screen. Its arms came up again in the initial position, before picking up the moon rocks. As it reached the screen it gradually accelerated the pace of its stiff, piston-like legs. It seemed to hesitate for a moment and then smashed right through the hardboard screen.

One complete panel fell outward and on the other side Gerrard could see the startled faces of the long queue of parents and children waiting for Santa Claus. The next instant the robot was through the space. There were screams, the waiting queue scattered as the giant figure came lurching towards them. A woman with a baby girl fell over in the rush; children scattered, screaming hysterically. Gerrard picked himself up off his knees and ran over to where Aspinall had left the control. As Gerrard reached it, the robot was slowly pacing towards the unconscious woman and her daughter, who was clutching her in a paroxysm of fright. Another moment and the massive boots would be stamping on her body.

Gerrard threw the switch. There was a whirring from the robot, and miraculously, just as the foot was coming up, it creaked and stopped. Its weight could only provide a proper balance while in motion and it slowly toppled over sideways crashing to the ground and shaking the entire floor. The commotion died down and the crying children were led off by their angry parents. Gerrard turned back to Anne.

"You're not hurt, are you?" said Aspinall.

"We're O.K.," said Gerrard. "Get to that goddamn thing." He pointed to the robot and Aspinall hurried through. "And disconnect it," Gerrard shouted after him. "Come on," he said to Anne, "I'm going to get you out of here."

Anne stopped. "No, I'm all right."

"Your shoulder?" said Gerrard touching her shoulder lightly where her coat was torn.

Anne winced: "Leave it—it's only bruised. I want to see what went wrong."

She went over to Aspinall who was now crouched over the figure and opening up a panel on its back.

"We can come back," Gerrard followed her. "I think you need a drink."

"No," said Anne firmly, then she swayed briefly, but was steadied by Gerrard. She raised her hand to her head: "Perhaps I do."

They made their way through the crowds.

"That working now?" Gerrard pointed to her glass. They were sitting with the remains of two large Scotches in a noisy and gaudy Kensington pub near the store.

"I'll say." Anne felt her shoulder gingerly. "This hurts a bit more now, though."

"Where do you live?"

"Just round the corner. We have a flat." She looked up at him. "You know, you've been up there."

"I'd forgotten. O.K., let's get you back home."

"It's really not that bad."

"I'll be the judge of that, O.K.?" Gerrard smiled at her. "I am a doctor," he said in fake, pompous tones.

"Yes, Doctor, I'm sorry. Can we go then?" She stood up and they moved towards the door.

"My car's just across the road," said Gerrard.

Guided by Anne, they drove around what seemed to be a succession of interminable spirals of narrow roads and squares ending up outside a large, ultra-modern apartment block on Cromwell Road.

"All these flats look alike to me," Gerrard said.

"Thanks a lot."

The flat looked different in the daylight. When Gerrard had seen it before, rather dazed from his flight, it had seemed cozy, tasteful, intimate. Now it was different. It must have reflected his mood at the time, thought Gerrard. He had wanted it to look homelike. As they went over to the leather couch and mosaic coffee table by the fire it seemed out of scale, too big, pretentious. The stonework of the fireplace was continued far beyond the actual fire area. Everything was exaggerated, showy rather than merely luxuriant.

"Let's see," he nodded towards her suit jacket and she started undoing the buttons.

Her shoulders were smaller, more slender than they appeared in her clothes. On the left one there was a large purple bruise; the skin was unbroken. He felt her shoulder and the bones of her arm carefully for sign of fractures.

"Does it hurt when you move it here?" he lifted the arm up to an elevation above the shoulder.

"No," she said, "not there."

He lifted it a bit higher. "There?"

She winced. "Yes, that hurts. It's not fractured, is it?"

"I don't think so but I can't be positive about it. You should go for an X-ray, just to make sure." He stood up. "O.K., I'll give up being professional. You can put your coat back on now."

She smiled at him and slipped her jacket back over her light-brown slip. Gerrard had noticed that rather disconcertingly, she did not wear a bra. Her nipples showed dark, and her breasts were full for her slender figure, and firm. He saw a puckered red mark on the side of her neck. She became aware of his gaze and buttoned her coat quickly.

"How did you get that?" said Gerrard.

Anne was confused. She pulled her scarf round her neck and tucked it in. "An old wound."

"Not that old," said Gerrard. Suddenly he became aware of what it could be and cursed himself for being naïve. It looked like a recent love bite. You're badly out of practice in every department, he told himself.

He got up from the settee. "I'd best go back to

Barratt's and collect whatever Aspinall's got. We'll have to take the gears back to the lab. I can't judge anyway, I'm no chemist."

"You will stay for a drink though, won't you?" Anne looked up at him. "I'm very grateful . . . Doctor."

"And leave that poor guy at the store worrying what's happened to you? He'll have you hospitalized by now," said Gerrard. "I'd better go back."

"I must know what it is," said Anne. "Let me know, will you, as soon as you find out? I'm going to put my feet up. I must have walked miles up in Gareloch."

"Sure, but . . . you'll hear, won't you . . .?"

"Through my husband?" said Anne. "He's a very, very busy man. Please don't forget to phone me, I want to know."

"Well, I guess there's a story in it someplace," said Gerrard.

"Not my type of story—'Robot Runs Amok in Crowded Store' "—Anne smiled. "No, I want to know because of our involvement—Aminostyrene."

Gerrard paused awkwardly at the door. "Then I'll phone you. So long." He smiled and went out. As Gerrard went towards the elevator he wondered why she had the power to make him stammer and feel an oaf. He was annoyed with himself, and when the lift didn't arrive he ran down the stairs to work off his annoyance.

As he strode back into the toy department, the shop was on the point of closing, the last shoppers were being politely and impolitely ignored as the staff scrambled to make up their tills.

Inside the display, Aspinall had the huge figure partly dismantled on trestles. "Exhibit A," he said, pointing to the mechanisms he had extracted from the robot. Gerrard looked at them curiously. There was a definite softening of the edges and in one place a plastic surface had become tacky.

"These better go along to the lab." Gerrard opened his briefcase and took out a piece of cloth, being careful to touch the gears only with the points of a pair of tweezers. He placed the bundle carefully into his briefcase. "What will you do?" he asked Aspinall.

"Go back to using metal ones, I suppose. It's a bloody nuisance. I shall have to get it all specially made —take ages."

"Have you seen anything else like this softening?" asked Gerrard.

"Well," said Aspinall, "I don't work here, of course, but I've asked the maintenance chaps. They've not seen it before."

Gerrard nodded, picked up the briefcase, and turned to go.

Aspinall touched his arm, "Do please extend my apologies to Anne . . . Mrs. Kramer."

"Yeah, I will," said Gerrard. "You've met her before?" Gerrard was vaguely annoyed. That was the trouble with Anne Kramer's type of woman. They spread the charm around like flu germs in January.

"She was here at the opening. I read her stuff; it's very good for a woman, you know."

"So they tell me," Gerrard nodded. "I'll be in touch." He went out through the deserted departments accompanied by the hum of the cleaners' vacuums. Dust covers were now on the counters and the place had all the attraction of a stale cigarette butt.

3

Lionel Slayter woke up with a jerk and then pulled the sheets over his head to keep out the chill of the bedroom air. As he lay luxuriating briefly in the warmth of the bed, he was conscious of a vague anxiety—something wrong about the day ahead—something unpleasant . . . maybe the end of a bad dream. . . . His mind cleared with a snap.

The inquiry. Adrenalin surged.

All that work! There was nothing wrong with the idea, nothing at all. Every single step in design and construction was checked and double checked—it couldn't have failed on such a massive scale. There was plenty of circuit redundancy to cope with failure, ample multiplexing—they had all run tests on blank experiments.

He panicked briefly and then began to visualize the reaction of the inquiry board.

Atherton. He couldn't expect any help there; the two of them basically loathed each other, which led to permanent scientific antagonism. First-class mind—no doubt about that—but no originality. Ambitious, hard, completely without compassion, he had always done the right thing at the right time rather than doing the wrong things well. Probably pull himself up to a very senior position in the Ministry and be thoroughly disliked by everyone. Bastard! For a few moments he indulged himself by hating Atherton.

Who else? Professor Starr—he had only met him once after a lecture at the Royal Society. He remembered a large, courteous man, stubbly grey hair cut close to the angles of his skull, gentle but very persistent, probably honest. He would listen.

Holland: road research director. His attitude was unpredictable. A worried little man with an ulcer face. In the end he had given full support to the "learning roads" project, so to some extent he would want to defend it. But if the whole thing was going down the pan, he'd also want a scapegoat. If the facts pointed at project design, then he was cooked and Atherton would slam the bloody oven door.

Hinton: computer man. He remembered their first meeting. An honest industrial con-man, he was out to sell his company's latest product, the D.P.F.6. Incapable of seeing both sides of a problem, he could only behave as an advocate for his product. With a pulse of fear he wondered whether he had kept all the specification sheets of the machine. Any suspicion of computer malfunction or design fault would have Hinton bringing out performance specs on every last printed circuit. He was a professional.

He got out of bed, staggered briefly, and then remembered the pills. The quack had said only two; three had given him a few hours of oblivion, but now his head throbbed and he felt sick. Never get through the day, he thought.

As he scratched the frost patterns on the window with his fingernail and looked out at the bleak December morning, his gloom deepened. Foregone conclusion really: terribly sorry about it all, Slayter, you know we have the highest regard for your ability—it's just that—well, the mistake was too expensive, the S.R.C. are bound to say no. Then back to the journals, back to the Ph.D. queue—probably end up managing a bloody launderette like Matthews.

As he got off the bus in Whitehall, it had started to snow, big wet flakes turning into brown slush as soon as they landed. He felt the cold wetness seeping into one shoe as he went through the main entrance of the Home Office. There was a hole in the shoe.

The effect of the pills had completely worn off and again he felt the panic. It was curtains. He'd never be able to go to any more of the I.E. meetings: "Oh, there's old Slayter—remember that bog-up he made of the road thing? That's what comes of giving grants to science-fiction projects."

No more invitations to lecture—nothing. Once someone went a little way down in research, the academic sons of bitches kicked you all the way.

As he walked down the vaulted corridor smelling of sour paper and old tobacco, he had an almost uncontrollable urge to run. To go back to his flat and feign illness—anything to avoid the humiliation. He felt sick again.

Holland's voice interrupted his anxiety: "Lionel, good morning." Then, seeing his drawn face: "Come on, I don't think it'll be as bad as you think."

Slayter mumbled: "Rubber stamp as far as I can make out, then—chop."

Holland spoke firmly: "Lionel, I'm chairing the inquiry on the basis of *evidence,* not opinion. We're meeting to discuss how, not who."

"But it's going to come down on me in the end, isn't it?"

"Not necessarily. We'll just go by the data."

"Hinton's going to defend his machine to the hilt; Starr's going to sit on the fence, and Atherton wants my guts anyway. What the hell's the use!"

Holland stiffened, his voice took on a formal edge: "Slayter"—the surname hurt—"I'm chairman of this inquiry and I take it a little unkindly that you think it's going to be such a farce. No one's going to be blamed until it can be proved, you can rest assured."

Seeing Slayter's defeated expression, he softened. "I've known Atherton for seven years, and between you and me and the Official Secrets Act, I think he's a shit. Of course Hinton's going to defend his machine. I've been in this trade for a good bit now, you know." He looked at his watch and took Slayter by the arm: "I think we're about ready."

The inquiry room was high-ceilinged and the long mahogany table gleamed and smelt of beeswax. Portraits of long-dead civil servants looked down severely at the intrusion.

Holland drew them to order: "I think it's unlikely that we can reach any firm conclusions today, so first I think we should consider the individual reports—these were all precirculated, I think?"

He looked up; they each nodded their assent.

"If I may summarize their content," he continued. "Dr. Slayter has stated quite firmly that the arithmetic unit in the computer failed and that the disaster stemmed directly from this cause. Mr. Hinton, you have expressed the opposing view that the component failure by itself could not have led to such a widespread disorganization and that, in your opinion," he looked down and read from a document, "there was insufficient—er—fail-safe capacity within the network design."

Hinton looked down at his own copy to check it and nodded.

"Atherton, your view is similar to Hinton's, as far as I can see."

Atherton broke in: "No, not at all. What I didn't make clear in the report is that, in my view, the entire concept was insufficiently quantified and that the available parameters were far below the standard necessary for such a speculative project. . . ."

He spoke almost vehemently and behind the thick glasses there was an unmistakable animosity. Although his face was blank of expression, a close observer could have sensed that to cut a young scientist down was the nearest thing to pleasure he ever experienced.

Holland spoke mildly: "Quite so, this is in fact perfectly clear from your report, Mr. Atherton. Now, Professor Starr, you, I think, made the point that the affair stemmed from an interaction between the component fault and an inherent design instability in Dr. Slayter's control network, is that so?"

Starr spoke with a measured and an almost staccato precision. His eyes took on an inward, contemplative look as he spoke: "Yes, up to a point, but there are still a number of unknowns. I have spoken to Dr. Slayter at some length about this, and as far as I can see, at this stage he made excellent provision for component failure. In many areas of the network design localized failure would have automatically switched in relief circuits. . . ."

Atherton broke in: "Yes, but not in this case. A logic gate fails and produces utter chaos—and, I might add, seven deaths."

Holland turned to Slayter: "What is your view about that, Dr. Slayter?"

"Mr. Atherton is quite correct, there was no relief circuitry designed around this particular unit."

"Oh, and why was that?" Atherton sensed an opening.

"Because we had written assurance that failure probability there was negligible; we couldn't duplicate all the systems because it would have been impossibly expensive."

"Mr. Hinton, how far have you got with your investigations?"

"The unit's back in our clean room; so far there does seem to be a failure in one logic file."

"So there was a fault in the machine?"

"Yes, one gate was on open circuit, but . . ."

Slayter interrupted tensely: "But you told us it couldn't fail."

"You told me it didn't matter if it did!"

"That's absolutely untrue. What I said was that, if the unit failed, we could take up the slack in the adaptive unit but only for a *limited* period."

Hinton flushed with anger; he picked out a letter from his file: "You stated here on—August tenth—that you accepted the design spec of the arithmetic unit and you had—I quote you—made appropriate changes in the control fan-out!"

Slayter broke in: "You know bloody well we talked about it later than that, you told me that we had to compromise, all you want to do is to . . ."

Holland spoke firmly: "We're not making any progress, gentlemen. . . ."

Slayter and Hinton glared at each other furiously.

". . . I suggest we confine ourselves to properly documented fact. Professor Starr?"

"I am running a computer simulation of Dr. Slayter's network on our own machine. We are injecting various artificial faults into the programme to measure their effect on the system as a whole. In a few days I should be in a position to give you more authoritative data."

Atherton grumbled: "I really don't see how that will help when the entire concept is based on speculative math."

As Starr spoke, his eyes gazed calmly away from the group; he appeared to be talking to himself: "I think it's preferable to keep to measurements and data."

Atherton flushed and looked down.

Holland turned to Hinton: "You spoke of a gate on open circuit. Perhaps you could explain."

"Yes, we dismantled the various circuit boards. Only one was affected. For some reason we can't yet explain, there appears to have been a localized, but complete loss of insulation on one of them."

In a near-by office in the Board of Trade building, Tom Myers, an aircraft accident inspector, was correcting the first draft of his report on the Isleworth air crash. He altered a sentence which read: "the initial cause was a loss of reference voltage" to: "the initial cause was a loss of reference voltage following localized insulation failure in a fuel-pump monitor."

Later that evening, in the Red Lion on the other side of Whitehall, there was a noisy cluster of carbon-copy civil servants jostling around the bar. Just time to get two Scotches in before the rush to Waterloo and the long journey home to dull wives, bleak, expensive houses, and a bad replica of the latest *Observer* recipe.

Holland sat by himself, morosely staring into his pint of special keg and wondering what the hell to do with the evening. His ulcer hurt. He reflected that a gaggle of experts, each sharing his own special point of view, was impossible to control peaceably. The day had been particularly weary, particularly with that sod Atherton trying to nail poor Lionel.

"Solitary boozing, that's the beginning of the end!"

He looked up to see the friendly, grinning face of Tom Myers.

"Tom! You're a welcome sight, sit down, what'll you have?"

"Got one, thanks, what about you?"

"No, I'm all right."

"Where's the usual scintillating wit?"

"It's this bloody Knightsbridge business."

"Ah yes, I forgot, you're chairing the technical inquiry, aren't you?"

"Mm."

"What's the problem?"

"Experts!"

Myers belched in sympathy.

Holland went on: "You'd think they could at least agree on matters of fact, but they fall out like schoolboys. I try to make them conclude something sensible and they wriggle back on the fence and come out with some fantastic bit of jargon, which makes them sound wise, but actually just protects their own interest."

Myers laughed. "Yes, I know the routine. They start off by saying 'on the one hand' and you know two minutes further on they're going to say 'on the one hand' and end up by saying 'buggerall.' "

"Right."

"What's the particular issue? Who's the villain?"

"You know the story more or less, don't you?"

"Not really, just what I saw on the box, that's all."

"Well, I've got a systems analyst saying the computer failed, the computer man saying the system failed, and an academic being extremely pure and honest about both sides."

"What do you reckon?"

"There *was* a computer failure, well, a component failure anyway."

"What sort?"

"A logic gate went on open circuit. It shouldn't have

failed at all according to spec, but it did—loss of insulation. All rather strange."

Myers put his beer down slowly. He thought for a moment before replying: "Insulation failure. That's odd, that's extremely odd."

"What?"

"Insulation failure. You know I'm on the Heathrow-Isleworth crash, don't you?"

"Yes."

"Well, we haven't got anything finalized—we know an engine caught fire and probably threw a turbine blade—but one of the control boxes back in the wing, it sensed and controlled fuel feed to number two engine."

"Well?"

"The makers have had it back for dissection. They said although the metal of the box had been subjected to a temperature of over a hundred and fifty C," he paused thinking hard, "inside the box, the wiring showed no sign of insulation!"

"Burnt away!"

"No, the temperature wasn't high enough. The particular plastic—this new Aminostyrene stuff—has a volatilization point of over three fifty C—higher than Teflon!"

Holland frowned: "It's a long one. Can we chat about it?"

Myers raised his beer. "Any time. Cheers."

4

Wright was at his most pedantic, reflected Gerrard. The sort of starchy fussiness he associated with English officers in Hollywood war films. A superb technician, no more. He was getting tired of Dr. Wright.

"It's much the most likely that it's due to some form of solvent action. Heat could never have produced this degree of distortion. It would have caused charring or at least slight carbonization around the rim here. Are we *quite* sure that nobody spilled any volatiles—acetone or whatever—near the robot?" questioned Wright.

"I've only got Aspinall's word for it," said Gerrard. "He was very much on the ball. No one was allowed to go near it except him."

Wright smiled a thin, disbelieving smile. "Well, perhaps, but we'd need proof of that." He bundled up the cloth-wrapped wheels, put them into a metal container, and drew out a paper label and started writing.

"What are you going to do with it?" said Gerrard.

"A few tests," said Wright. "But not right now; we have to get on with this project. Later on we can do rigidity, permeability, and so on."

It was next morning and the sun was streaming through the high arched windows of the schoolroom laboratory, the only advantage Gerrard could see for working in that Victorian folly. The panels of stained glass near the top of the window threw swirling patterns in deep ruby, blue, and yellow onto Wright's desk.

"Suppose it turns out *not* to be an external fault," said Gerrard.

"How's that?" asked Wright.

"I'm not a chemist, but couldn't it be a fault in the plastic which maybe renders it liable to some external influence? A change in molecular structure so that it's susceptible to—well, I don't know—but let's say nitrogen or oxygen in the air?"

Wright looked over his glasses at him. "The Polytad Company are extremely careful in their development testing. They work under licence from us, you know, and I make absolutely certain that each batch goes through a complete specification check. We have it done independently by another firm. Their data is impeccable, they've no reason to make it otherwise—they wouldn't get paid!"

"That wasn't an accusation," said Gerrard.

"Well, I trust my answer resolves your fears, Dr. Gerrard," said Wright. He picked up the box with the specimens and took them over to a large refrigerator, opened it, and put them carefully on a shelf at the back, half-way down from the freezing compartment. Looking back at Gerrard, he closed the door with a bang. "We can finish this later," he said.

"I thought red tape and procrastination were confined to Government departments in this country," replied Gerrard.

"By no means, my dear fellow," said Wright. "You'll find them everywhere, but there is another word you know—priorities." He smiled and left the lab.

Gerrard wandered over to his desk and sat down. Was it any use going to see Kramer? He was sure there was some other factor concerned in the melting plastic. What would happen if plastic insulation started melting . . . ? Wait a minute; insulation melting! It struck a chord somewhere. Hadn't he read something about insulation melting? In connection with what? He thought rapidly and then snapped his fingers.

"Got it," he said aloud. It was the Isleworth air disaster. There had been reports of insulation failure.

Could there have been a connection here? Insulation—plastic—yes. Which newspapers?

He started to his feet and lifted the phone on his desk. "Betty," he said, "the *Post* over the last ten days, can you bring them to me?"

"All of them?" The voice from the phone sounded a bit hesitant. He reflected it takes much more time to gain a secretary's confidence than that of any other person in business.

"Yes, every last one, and pronto." He put the phone down and sat back, his mind racing.

He looked over at the array of shapes on the wall. On the display board were mounted various examples of the use of Aminostyrene: telephone cables, gas pipes, electricity conduits. Suppose there was some fault in the basic plastic, and under certain conditions it all started to break down. What sort of chaos would communications be thrown into? He started to his feet thinking the idea through, then checked himself. He hadn't been there long enough. True, they had not given him anything constructive to do in that time, and part of his irritation towards Wright was based on this. He felt unused, unstretched, unappreciated. Wasn't he now simply looking for some form of competition, something to prove to Wright that he, Gerrard, was a more effective scientist than the older man?

Besides, what would Kramer say if he was able to prove that Aminostyrene, the foundation rock on which the consultancy was based, was defective, and production had to be stopped? It wouldn't exactly enhance the status of the group.

The finances of the group came almost entirely from their one spectacular success: the bio-degradable bottle, made from Degron.

Soon after Wright had joined the group, he gave them a short informal seminar on one of his favourite themes: a plastic with a number of hitherto incompatible properties. High-tensile strength in a single direction, considerable elasticity in the opposite direction, and extreme cheapness. Working from the standpoint of his other, original, success—Aminostyrene—he developed a series of polymers—compounds with tightly cross-linked chains of molecules which, in succession, came nearer and nearer to the required properties.

Eventually one of his experimental compounds seemed to be almost perfect, except for one major and crippling defect. In the presence of oxygen and visible light, it underwent a rapid breakdown, turning, in a space of a few hours, to a grey filamentous powder. He told the assembled group that, as far as he could see, there was no way round these failures in the compound.

Shortly after the talk was over, Buchan became extremely agitated; it was obvious that he was in the throes of some internal struggle. Finally, with a great cry of triumph, he rushed to the blackboard and in a matter of seconds turned the weakness of Wright's compound into what he then called "the self-destruct container." He reasoned that so long as light and oxygen were kept away from the plastic, it would retain its properties, but if it was then exposed to both, it would begin to disintegrate.

Kramer was excited beyond measure, and for a moment returned to his old image of the compulsively creative scientist. He filled in the remaining details: Make the plastic container in an injection moulding apparatus deprived of both air and light, then, under the same conditions, mould on a completely opaque and impervious layer of another plastic. Finally, provide in the outer opaque layer a tear-off strip which it was essential to operate if the container was to be opened. When the strip was pulled off, both light and air were admitted to the surface of the sensitive plastic, and disintegration would begin.

An original and brilliant idea nearly always provokes a hostile reaction in those who hear about it but fail to think of it themselves, and the self-destruct container was no exception.

Everyone produced negative hypotheses to show why it shouldn't work and one by one they fell silent as they failed to refute the idea. Finally, there were no more objections and the group set to work in a fever of activity.

A second-hand injection-moulding machine was installed, a die-maker produced moulds, and Wright set about synthesizing enough "premix" to make a small run of experimental containers. The air in the main laboratory was hot and foul smelling. A smell which was mainly due to complex amines given off by the precursor compounds necessary to make the plastic.

Kramer, meanwhile, had taken out provisional patent rights and negotiated a support grant from the National Research and Development Corporation.

There were many irritating snags to be overcome before the idea worked reliably. The principal problem was to design the molecular structure of the sensitive plastic so that, once light and oxygen had been admitted to the localized area under the tear-off strip, the self-destruct process would propagate itself throughout the container, leaving only the one-thousandth of an inch opaque covering of ordinary plastic.

This covering in itself posed the final problem; it would not undergo spontaneous destruction, as in the case of the main container body, so a compound was introduced into the sensitive plastic which reacted with the residue after self-destruction, releasing a small quantity of solvent for the opaque covering. This converted the covering into a volatile liquid which evaporated, leaving only the carbon particles with which it had been filled to make it black and impervious to light.

The final point to be settled was the self-destruction time of the bottle. Eventually it was decided to make the time two hours and include on the bottle the instruction that the contents were to be transferred to another permanent container directly after the seal was broken.

During the frantic development process, the mood in the group was almost religious in intensity. Everyone worked, often through the night. There was a sustained air of adventure and excitement. Nobody spared himself. Betty became mother and cook providing constant supplies of coffee, food, and whisky. One night, after nearly twenty-four hours of continuous experiment, a bottle passed round and Kramer started to play on the blackboard with names for the new material. As they all relaxed in the glow of the drink, the suggestions became more and more impractical and ribald. Someone suggested "Suncrap," only to be countered with "Oxynure" or "Kramer's Krumbling Krud." Finally, they settled for "Degron."

Then came a press conference in the Central London office hired by Kramer as a selling front for the organization, and, although drink flowed and journalists were freely given information, it was carefully designed so that no one was able to get his hands on any samples to take away for analysis.

Then came interviews on television science-spectacular programmes and finally a flood of manufacturers wanting to mass produce the Degron container under licence from the group.

Kramer conducted a successful auction among the competing firms which would have done credit to a stall holder in the Sooks of Baghdad, finally completing a deal with a nationwide soft-drinks manufacturer who basically wanted a new gimmick to sell the mixture of tartaric and citric acid, saccharin and colouring which he shamelessly called "Tropic Delight."

The sales campaign mounted by the firm was a spectacular success. The public bought the same chemical fraud in the new container, simply because it looked interesting and required a novel operation to open it.

The advertising campaign mounted by the soft-drinks firm was carefully worded. On a hundred hoardings, on the tube, on television commercials, in the newspapers, people were exhorted to buy Tropic Delight.

"Help your environment, drink Tropic Delight. Pull the strip—watch it crumble. Put it on your window box—sprinkle it on your garden. Watch your flowers flourish. If you haven't got a garden, flush it down the sink."

"Every ten intact tear-off strips gets you a bonus gift voucher. Ten gift vouchers can get you any one of a hundred beautiful gifts in your local Tropic Delight shop. Introductory offer until the end of the month only. Hurry, hurry . . ."

So the exhortations went and so the public bought. Bored by the once exciting sexual ritual of rupturing the vacuum seal on the instant coffee jar, they now turned to the equally satisfying ripping sound of the tear-off strip—carefully designed with a serrated edge by media psychologists to give the tearing feel, direct to the fingers. To be able to vent the destructive urge sadistically—to rip to tear. The bottle never cried out in pain.

Throughout the country, the bottles were initiated into their dissolution by a hundred thousand tearing hands, started on their path back towards the earth, flushed without thought down a million lavatories.

Degron became a household word and eager industrialists lined up to buy the manufacturing licence.

In an increasingly pollution-conscious world, it became simply good business to advertise a package which did not add to the garbage-disposal problem. In the first nine months after its announcement, the Kramer group negotiated forty-seven separate deals with container manufacturers. Other soft drinks with names even more transparently dishonest than Tropic Delight began to appear in self-destruct containers. Finally, the Ministry of the Environment stepped in and asked the group to make the process generally available on Government licence.

Everyone was content. Ministers smiled benignly and down into the maze of vaulted echoing sewers in a hundred towns went dissolving Degron. The sewer filtration screens at outfall works cleared of plastic bottles began to be more trouble-free. Councils were pleased.

Profit plus heroism. Kramer was content.

But what had this financial bonanza done to Kramer himself, Gerrard wondered. Was his once global vision now reduced to perfecting financially profitable but intellectually sterile inventions? Suppose a flaw was discovered in Aminostyrene—what then? Would the bonanza dry up? Would Kramer divert the attention of his group back to the study of the world's problems, the careful evolution of the future of science? Or would the whole thing founder?

He remembered Kramer's once deep concern for the future of science, his massive attack on knowledge for its own sake and how much he wanted to reorient the skills of the scientist towards social problems. He compared that image with the profit-seeking obsessional he saw now. He wondered, why the change?

Betty entered with a pile of newspapers and put them on his desk.

"Only the main papers," she said. "I didn't bring the others with the naked dolly birds."

Gerrard smiled: "Party pooper." But there was no response from Betty.

"Nobody else in," said Betty. "You don't want any coffee yet, do you?" She was obviously unwilling to make coffee simply for one, and that one the new boy on the staff.

"That's O.K.," said Gerrard, his smile a bit fixed by now. "Don't bother."

She left the room.

He started to spread out the papers, irritated by her attitude. Goddamn it, he wanted coffee! He would phone her in a minute or two and tell her he had changed his mind. Get her off her fat can. He looked down at the papers.

The air disaster had been about a week ago. He flicked over the pages looking for the accounts of it. Nothing conclusive about insulation failure met his eye. Various causes were suggested by under-employed feature writers looking for a story. It was being investigated, there was an inquiry in progress. He closed the last paper with a sense of frustration. As he pushed the papers away, another headline caught his eye. This one referred to the massive snarl-up of traffic in Central London.

He read it through carefully and then looked through the papers of the next couple of days. In one of them a man called Slayter, the inventor of a new road-control system, had given a press conference in which he had blamed insulation failure in one of his computers for the trouble.

Again, insulation failure! What insulation, Gerrard wondered? He looked up at the wall display. Aminostyrene was widely used as an insulator in a modified form. It would certainly be a feasible assumption that the wiring in both cases would be coated with the stuff. Suppose the same sort of failure had happened here? Aminostyrene and Degron; he wondered about the differences in structure between the two plastics.

What should he do, phone Kramer? He felt the man was getting increasingly remote. The new Kramer scared him. He would probably meet with the same sort of reception as he did with Wright. They had other, more important projects on their plate than to go back and check something that was now passed. He must be very, very sure of his facts first. He looked at the paper again. This guy Slayter was currently under suspension but still occupied an office in the Ministry of Transport. He picked up the phone book.

Slayter was late. They had arranged to meet in a Westminster pub tucked away behind St. James's Street, near the Ministry. He had been cagey on the phone suspecting, from Gerrard's transatlantic accent, another journalist on his neck. Gerrard had also been a little hesitant about stating his ideas over the telephone. If he was wrong, it wouldn't do for one of Kramer's team to show doubts about their own product. Far better to listen to Slayter first without giving too much away.

Slayter arrived rather flustered; a man under great pressure. Gerrard bought him a large whisky. Immediately, he filled it to the brim with soda and began gulping it down like beer.

"You look as though you can use that," said Gerrard, nodding at the Scotch. He was also nursing whisky, a single one. He wanted to pump Slayter and not be too obvious about it. A lager against a double whisky would have seemed as though he was trying to loosen the tongue of the other man.

Slayter paused. "Never work for a big organization. There are too many frightened people about." Slayter finished the drink and insisted upon buying another round. He was beginning to look more relaxed. Gerrard saw a short, compact, strong-looking man with a clean-cut open face. He liked him, and wondered how he'd survive long in governmental research with all its red tape and grinding away of individuality. He seemed far too impatient, nervy, and forthright to survive in civil service science for very long. When he spoke it was in short staccato bursts; he was obviously an intense, rapid thinker. His temporary suspension and the threat hanging over him gave him a caged, paranoid attitude. Each time Gerrard spoke, his reply was oblique and suspicious.

"What exactly is your stake in this?" asked Slayter. "I'd like to know who I'm talking to and why."

"I thought I told you over the phone," said Gerrard.

"You told me who you worked for and what you were but not the why and the how." Then, as Gerrard's face showed his reaction, Slayter went on: "You'll forgive me, but right now I feel like a fox running before a pack of half-starved hounds. It's nice to have someone taking an interest, but right now I'm too hungry for a friendly ear."

Gerrard decided to open out. He gave him a capsule account and told him of the robot in the Barratt's toy department.

Slayter listened intently and then in turn gave Gerrard a diluted version of the inquiry. Again, there was no direct proof that there was anything inherently wrong with the plastic. The breakdown could have been caused by several factors. But with this fresh evidence, it was worth trying anyway.

"I'll try it on Holland for size," Slayter said. "He's the chairman of my so-called inquiry." He rose, glanced at his watch. "He always lunches in his office. If you'd like to wait?"

"I'll wait," said Gerrard. After Slayter had gone, shouldering his way through to the telephone, Gerrard momentarily regretted his action in contacting him. It was like throwing a pebble into a lake—no one knew how far the ripples would extend or what they would wash up when they reached the shore line.

When Slayter returned he was a little less anxious. "He says he'll take it up."

"And?" queried Gerrard.

Slayter shrugged: "Just that! He'll investigate further. Probably a big concession on his part."

"But will he really do anything?"

"Matter of fact, I think he will. He'll probably take it up with Tom Myers. I think we've set the ball in motion, now we can only wait and see."

And that, Gerrard reflected, finishing his drink, was the way things were done over here. Nothing public. Nothing ever on paper—just the right word to the right man at the right time, and if you were very lucky, something got done.

5

Myers pushed the model hovertrain along the length of track on the desk. He studied Holland waiting on the phone, then looked around the cluttered room. On one wall was a faded lithograph of one of the first steam underground trains belching smoke up to the roof of a high, vaulted tunnel. On another was a multi-coloured map of England showing the criss-crossed air corridors covering the land mass.

There were rows of books with abstruse titles: *Systems Analysis of Subway Design, Negative Feedback Theory and the Flow of Rolling Stock.* He looked back at Holland. Poor old Bernard, got the hunted look—too much paper-pushing, not enough time to follow his own nose and be creative. . . . Something about his wife being ill, probably the last straw, poor devil.

He listened as Holland spoke irritably into the phone: "Yes—no I don't want sales—I want Mr. Hinton in R. and D. Yes, I'll hold. Thank you." He gestured impatiently at Myers.

Myers smiled: "Somebody should write a paper on the impossibility of successful communication in large organizations."

Holland raised his eyes: "I remember once . . . Oh hello, Hinton? Bernard Holland here—yes that's right—I was wondering if you'd made any progress on the faulty component. Good, what did you find? Most interesting—you sure? I see. Tell me, do you know who actually supplied the wire? Yes, of course."

He put his hand over the phone. "He's looking it

up," he said. "Hello—yes—it was! Now tell me, was it the new stuff: Aminostyrene-covered?" He nodded over at Myers. "Thanks so much—sorry to bother you—we shall meet on Tuesday when we reconvene—good—yes—good-bye." He put the receiver down.

"The fault was caused by wire covered by Aminostyrene."

Myers shoved the model train violently against the buffers: "Right! One plus one equals a possible three. Who makes it?"

Holland thought for a second. "It's a Polytad product—the plastic whizkids out in Essex."

Myers frowned: "I know them, don't know much about the technology of the stuff, do you?"

"Not a great deal. Apparently it's cheap, doesn't burn, its plasticity doesn't alter with age, and it's foamed with nitrogen. Good insulation. . . ."

Myers interrupted: "I remember, it was Harold Wright. You remember him, don't you?"

"Vaguely. Tall, austere, ascetic character."

"You must be joking! I remember him at Sheffield. Humped practically everything female in his year. Funny, looking at him now he's pure as a priest, wouldn't think he even knew how to do it! Good chemist, though. Didn't he join that professional egghead lot down at Mitcham?"

"That's right, the Kramer group—the American West-Coast idea. You put a lot of bright young Ph.D.'s together, form a company, corner the market in some special technology, and then set up as expensive consultants."

"In their case . . . the bio-degradable bottle."

"Tropic Delight. Don't mind me, I'm just jealous. They made an absolute packet out of it. Now they're searching round for new ideas."

"With the Aminostyrene patent and the bio-degradable bottle, I'd hardly think they need any."

"It'll be interesting to see just how long it takes before Polytad pass it back along the line to Kramer." Holland paused. "Sometimes, you know, I quite enjoy my work."

Kramer was in full swing. "I've got Polytad sitting right down on my neck; they said it's our problem and what are we going to do about it."

Wright's narrow, expressionless eyes watched the snow flakes sliding down the panes of the arched window: "Just what are we being accused of exactly?"

"Nothing specific yet. Look, you know the Isleworth smash."

"I read about it."

"And the Knightsbridge foul-up?"

"I must say I considered that inevitable, it was . . ."

"Forget the details. There was a massive failure in a computerised traffic control experiment, O.K.?"

"I don't see . . ."

"The guy in charge of the air crash rang me. He talked to the Knightsbridge people, and they found that insulation failure was maybe behind both accidents."

Wright went on doodling.

Kramer spat: "Don't say you don't get it! Insulation—wire—death—Aminostyrene! They're saying it's the plastic—insulation failure leading to short circuits. The wires were covered in Aminostyrene."

Wright turned to him: "They'll need to be somewhat more exact than that. What you're saying, as far as I can gather, is that two incidents happen separately and two groups of people, probably absolutely destitute for a good idea, settle for a common factor—any common factor so that they can look intelligent in time for their masters."

"Harold," Kramer was icy, "that's not good enough. I pulled you out of Polytad—I funded you, gave you facilities—you pulled the method out of your head—it worked, we made some money."

"I wouldn't put it quite like that."

"O.K., we've both gained. It became our patent. Polytad bitched about piracy and so on but they knew they couldn't do anything."

Wright glared.

"Now perhaps they can! Just how much of the truth did you tell us? Those Ministry bastards are going to get up and say that we fudged our tests, that we conned them about Aminostyrene. Harold, they're going to sink you unless you've got all the data—unless you can produce all the test sheets—change of resistivity with age, effect of nitrogen foaming on plasticity—every last goddamn fact!"

"Do you doubt it? You saw all the test sheets—everything I reported was true."

"I hope for your sake it was."

Wright eyed him coolly: "You're lashing about, looking for a victim. You know what happened just as well as I do. I didn't cut corners, I didn't need to."

Kramer glanced at him, his mouth pursed; there was sprung menace in every movement of his body. "Don't fool about with me, Harold. What are you telling me?"

Wright's expression was set, immobile. He eyed each part of Kramer's face before replying: "It was you who couldn't wait—'Never mind that,' you said, 'that's enough on that, leave it, I'll do the selling!' You pushed me hard, harder than I've ever been pushed in my life. What was I supposed to do? Calculate standard deviations on every damned titration? Of course I rushed it. *You* couldn't wait!" Wright stopped, frozen, angry with himself at his outburst.

Kramer held his eyes for a moment, then laughed briefly. "Just what I've been trying to tell you. The buck stops here with both of us."

Wright looked at him suspiciously, sensing a new attack, then smiled tightly, the tension slowly going out of him: "There's nothing they can sue us for, even the first batches we made exceeded what we promised. We found no evidence of failure. No depolymerization—nothing. We did have some trouble with the early foaming experiments—low elasticity—but nothing to do with the actual molecular architecture—that's absolutely copper-bottomed . . ."

Kramer interjected: "You'll stand up on that?"

Buchan came in and draped his great angular frame comfortably on a lab bench. He listened in silence.

Wright went on: "You know better than to ask that. You went through the M.I.T. brain factory, didn't you?

Well, I had the same sort of conditioning at Sheffield. For better or for worse, and it's no credit to me, I can't fake a test schedule. Not because I might get found out, not because I think it would be morally wrong, but because I would feel uncomfortable if I did. I'm a technological animal—brain-washed, if you like—but for me the only *bad* technology is technology which doesn't *work.*"

Buchan protested: "I'll take you up on that sometime."

Kramer waved him to silence: "Not now, Buck. You've got the picture?"

Buchan nodded: "I was looking up the total number of sub-contracts for Aminostyrene. There are over three hundred. It's almost everywhere."

Kramer looked up: "What's your point?"

Buchan replied slowly: "Well, if there is any fault in the material, we shall bear an enormous responsibility, won't we?"

"Why?" Wright said. "We develop a product, we produce a specification, we sell the method and the material on the specification as stated."

"Aye, but supposing there *is* some aspect of its ageing we didn't spot? Insulation failure—think of it—you know where it's used, it would be tremendously dangerous. If it can cause accidents, death, and we've missed something, then we're responsible."

Kramer stood up: "What are you trying to say? We made a commercial deal, people buy *after* examining the product, we didn't keep anything back; they got *all* the data. What more can we do?"

Buchan persisted: "I think it's our duty to take a long hard look at it again."

Kramer laughed: "Duty, what's duty? To what? Reckon we call you Buchman, not Buchan."

Buchan flushed angrily at the jibe: "That's a rotten thing to . . ."

"O.K., I'm sorry, but you asked for it. All I meant to say was that we can't afford—and I do mean afford—to do everybody's development work for them. We sold a method at a particular stage—openly and without concealment—we made no guarantees beyond what we had actually measured."

"Well, let me go and talk to them."

"Buck, *not* you, I'm sorry. You'll go into their place wringing your hands with guilt, and we'll be nailed before you've started."

Buchan started to protest, but Kramer turned to the intercom and pressed down the key. Betty's voice answered.

Kramer said, "Is Dr. Gerrard in?"

"I haven't seen him."

"Get him on the phone at home, will you?"

As the phone rang, Gerrard was sniffing the closed lid of the electric coffee grinder, savouring the brown tang of freshly ground blue mountain beans.

The flat had a general air of home-made but elegant comfort. Situated in a Kensington mews over a garage selling vintage racing machinery, it consisted of one large, low room and a bathroom and microscopic kitchen.

The main living-room floor was varnished pine partly covered by a large, hairy white rug. Along one wall were shelves made of thick, chunky wood supported on piles of bricks. On the shelves were piles of books, bits of driftwood, a dark-green glass float from a fishnet, and an alarmingly dangerous looking hi-fi system. Instead of the usual sleek wood modules, there was a large sheet of Perspex with holes cut in it. In the holes were bare printed circuit boards, linked in what looked like total confusion by means of multi-coloured wires. To Gerrard it was beautiful.

On another wall hung two large electrostatic speakers and scattered round the floor were large square blocks of plastic foam, hand covered by coarse woven material. There was only one real chair which had cost him far too much money. It was a satin-chrome and black leather copy of the famous Bauhaus original. The room was lit by home-made spot-lights, made out of aluminium sheet and pointing at the wall, giving a soft reflected glow. In the kitchen were rows of copper saucepans neatly stacked, bottles of herbs, and a fearsome array of steel cooking knives on the wall. There was a faint aroma of black pepper and garlic.

Gerrard put the coffee mill down, walked through, picked up the receiver.

Kramer talked rapidly on the phone: ". . . Yes, that's right, just go and see how much they've got, don't commit yourself. There are two of them, one's called Holland, I don't know him, he's a Ministry of Transport scientist, the other's Tom Myers. Now, Luke, watch that character, he's one of your 'old chap' people—beer and a bulldog face—that's it—but he thinks—he's bright, so play along slowly. Where? Hold on. . . . Room 242, Min. of Tech."

6

The air in the tube train was humid and stale, and emanating from the dense mass of weary homebound commuters was a smell of day-old aftershave and wet clothing. As the train rocked and clattered through the tunnel, the passengers swung from side to side like vertically stacked dolls in a box. There was no room to fall, and confusion was prevented by those lucky enough to have found a roof strap to hold.

The uneven roar of the train almost obliterated conversation; eyes stared into shoulders without seeing.

One tall man, bent down by the roof to the level of the other heads, vainly tried to read the *Financial Times* propped against someone's back jammed against him. An obese woman, breathing stertorously, stood, legs apart, in front of a shaggy, bearded youth sitting comfortably. She glared angrily down at him for not giving up his seat. Farther down the carriage, a young mother sat trying to comfort her baby against the noise.

Gradually, the train groaned down to a halt. Voices raised against the noise died away to an embarrassed whisper as the almost hypnotic rhythm of the train stopped. Then, with a sudden jerk, the carriages started to move again, followed almost immediately by a loud popping noise, then, once again, the train creaked to a halt.

There was a hot, anxious silence.

The minutes ticked by, and the shuffling noises made by the fidgeting passengers began to sound harsh and artificially loud. A pair of young office girls, huddled in a corner near the door, began to giggle, sharing some secret joke.

There was a sharp crackling rustle as the tall man folded away his paper and began to study the advertisements spread out along the panels over the seats. One caught his eye—it told of the advantages of moving offices out of London. He smiled wryly to himself.

The seated youth tapped his foot to a tune he was half whistling and every so often he looked up at the woman standing over him. He winked at her—she glared back.

Suddenly, a compressor motor started under the floor, its cavernous hammering noise providing a momentary relief in the tense silence. It snapped off and once again, in the uneasy silence, there was only the regular clicking of hot metal shrinking as it cooled, somewhere in the mechanism of the coach.

Fifteen minutes went by and passengers began to look at watches, imagining burnt dinners and suspicious wives. A thin, bird-like man took a religious tract out of his pocket and began to read it, mouthing the words to himself. The air grew hotter. The youth pulled out a cigarette and lit it. The fat woman angrily pointed at the *No Smoking* sign on the window. As slowly as he could, staring straight at her, he nipped out the cigarette and spilled the hot ash down the hem of her overcoat.

The glass-panelled door connecting the carriages abruptly swung open and a cheerful, florid motorman in blue denim pushed his way into the packed coach. The tension broke at once and questions came at him from all sides.

"What's going on?"

"How long's it going to be?"

"Want a push?"

He raised his hands placatingly: "Nothing to worry about, ladies and gents, we've had a little signal failure, that's all." Above the groan that followed, he went on: "We're going to get you off down the tunnel into the next station."

"What about the rails? We'll get electrified."

"How far is it?"

"Now, now, now," he was enjoying the role of being fully in command, "there's nothing to worry about, we've turned off the current. A little walk, that's all, it's a bit dusty, that's the worst you'll find. Now come along, just move along into the coach ahead and you'll be all right."

Gently shoving people towards the open door behind him, he moved on towards the next coach as the passengers began to file protestingly out through the doors into the next carriage. As they stepped across the gap, they glanced uneasily into the darkness between the two coaches. It seemed dangerous to be, even for a moment, outside the lit security of the interior. The air in the tunnel smelt of musty damp and hot electrical windings.

In the tunnel, anxious faces peered into the gloom, lit harshly by solitary naked light bulbs. The effect of the black circular ribs of the tunnel holding the great mass of earth away from the frailty of their bodies stopped all conversation.

Somebody whistled a single note, to see whether it echoed. The sound was instantly sucked away to thick silence in the stale air. As they picked their way gingerly along to the bright circle of the station lights, the tall man drawled almost to himself: "On the third day out we struck water." There was nervous laughter from people around him, breaking the tension as they looked ahead and saw the first passengers clamber awkwardly up onto the station platform. There was murder in the eyes of the fat woman as the youth jumped lightly up ahead of her.

Back in the tunnel, the uniformed motorman was speaking into a telephone handset above a signal: "No, it was at green. Anyway the 'train stop' bled the brakes —no, it worked all right. What? Yeah, I'll come up."

He replaced the receiver and trudged along the track towards the station, complaining to himself and scanning the thick cable leashes coursing along the tunnel wall sagging slightly between their supports. He stopped and sniffed, wrinkling his face in disgust. He peered again at the thick knotted wires and then his expression slowly changed to complete disbelief.

In front of him, a section of the cables was covered by a glistening wet mass of multi-coloured viscous slime dripping slowly away on the track beneath. In some places bare copper gleamed red in the dim light, in others the slime was partly covered by a thin rind of wet foam undulating and writhing as the bubbles burst and reformed.

For a minute, he stood staring and then turned and ran stumbling back to the signal telephone.

Holland sat in his office, holding his stomach and wincing. On the table in front of him was a small bottle of white indigestion mixture and a glass of water. He poured some of the liquid into the water, stirred it with a pencil, and drank it down with a single disgusted gulp. After a few seconds he belched and looked anxiously towards the open door to see whether his secretary had heard.

The phone rang, he picked it up.

"Hello, yes. Oh, Slayter? Lionel, how are you? Bernard Holland here. Look, something important's come up, I think it may have something to do with our problem. There's been a signal failure in the tube. No, I'll explain later. I wonder if—what?—oh really?—where? —who did you say I know? Can you come over here right away? Yes, I'm in the office—no reason why not —bring him along by all means—yes, as soon as you can—see you in about fifteen minutes." Holding the phone, he pressed the receiver rest down, let it go immediately, and started to re-dial.

Holland's office was thick with tobacco smoke and empty coffee cups were stacked in a pile on a shelf. Myers was sitting on the window sill, sucking at an empty pipe. Slayter and Holland were intently listening to Gerrard.

"Let's recap on what we've got," Luke said. He tapped off the points with a finger on the palm of his hand: "First, we've got the Heathrow crash: a fuel monitor unit goes and we find insulation failed inside a metal box and there wasn't enough heat to've burnt it off inside the box, right?"

The others nodded, listening cautiously.

"Second," Gerrard pointed to Slayter, "you told us that a computer component failed in your traffic control system and again there was an incomprehensible insulation failure in one component."

Holland interruped: "We don't know that that caused the road disaster."

"Irrelevant," said Myers. "I agree we don't know whether it caused the mess, but we *do* know the component failed, correct?"

Gerrard continued excitedly: "Exactly. We know it failed. Two units, two manufacturers, a common cause."

"No," Myers gestured with his pipe, "I don't think there's much mileage in that. You're indulging in an 'all dogs are mammals' argument. You can't make the assumption . . ."

Gerrard smiled: "I can always try. . . ."

Holland frowned impatiently: "Let me short-cut what you're getting at—Aminostyrene—you're saying the plastic is the common factor, aren't you?"

Gerrard nodded: "So it's long odds but . . ."

Myers snorted: "No odds at all, circumstantial speculation—in any case, whoever heard of a plastic breaking down in that sort of way? Some of them get fatigued —plasticizers evaporate and they crack—but they don't just disappear."

Gerrard persisted: "Supposing there was a change in Aminostyrene. Bear with me for a moment, a change which made it more heat-sensitive."

Slayter cut in: "There wasn't any fire in the computer failure, only in the air crash."

Myers lumbered to his feet, cracking his knuckles with impatience: "Of course! Dr. Gerrard, we're not going to get any more forward with this sort of Sherlock Holmes stuff—sorry, no disrespect—but we must try for a fact or two. You said your people were working on the robot. When can we expect some data?"

"I'm going back now," Gerrard replied. "I should have something in a day or so . . ." He broke off as the phone rang.

Holland picked it up: "Hello, yes, Holland here. Who? Oh yes, I think I do, yes, we met at the Army and Navy—yes—no, I'm not alone, I've got Myers here from the Board of Trade—er—Slayter from M.O.T., and a Dr. Gerrard. What?—yes, Dr. Gerrard, he's representing a private consortium—the Kramer group."

There was a long pause as he listened intently, his face grave. The others were motionless, looking intently at his face for clues.

Finally he said, "How much may I tell them at this stage? I see." He looked at Gerrard directly. "Yes, I'll cope with that. Right. Good-bye."

He put the phone down; they could all feel his embarrassment.

He spoke quickly: "Dr. Gerrard, something very important has come up, I'm afraid we'll have to stop our discussion."

Gerrard looked at his watch. "O.K., I'm going. I'll let you know as soon as we have anything."

"What's going . . ." Myers began. Holland waved him to silence.

"Thank you very much for sparing us your time, Dr. Gerrard. We'll no doubt be in touch in a few days."

Gerrard started to say something but abandoned it, shook hands with each of them, and went out.

Holland immediately took charge: "That was Whiting on the phone—er—one thing I have to clear up, you're both signatories of the Official Secrets Act obviously." They both nodded. "Well, our security ratings are being sent over to Admiralty now—it's only a matter of form really—they need us over there right away."

"You wouldn't tell us just what the hell is going on, would you?" Slayter said irritably.

"I only know what he told me," Holland replied. "It appears that H.M.S. *Triton*—our first Poseidon sub—has been lost with all hands somewhere west of Arran."

If you walk through the centre of Admiralty Arch

down the Mall towards Buckingham Palace keeping to the centre of the road, and if, after you have gone approximately eighty yards, you stop in the centre of the road, you are in fact standing over one of the most secret rooms in the whole of Britain. Not standing directly on its ceiling, because it is eighty-five feet below the surface of the road.

To get to it, you go into an ornate mahogany and brass room in a near-by Admiralty office and present a rectangle of plastic to a rather asexually pretty secretary who, after asking you to wait, takes the plastic sheet to a small data terminal in an adjoining room and allows a distant computer to paw over your personal properties imprinted in ferro-magnetic powder embedded in the plastic. Finally, after a few seconds, the teleprint to one side of the terminal clatters briefly, ejecting a short roll of paper with coded numbers. She compares the numbers with green flickering numeral groups on a read-out screen over the terminal and makes the initial decision to admit you or to reject you. She enjoys her job.

If the computer tells her to admit you, she guides you with her expressionless charm to a dark wooden door and presses a button beside it; a light glows by the button and the door opens. Behind the door are two uniformed Naval Police and you are surprised to see that they are both armed and carrying respirators in bags over their shoulders. As they guide you through the door, the nineteenth-century charm of the office is at once replaced by the bare grey-painted concrete of the war industry. Ahead is a lift door.

While you wait by the lift, there is a soundless flash of light beside a camera lens protruding from the wall at one side of the lift, recording your presence.

Holland, Myers, and Slayter had been taken down by Commodore Whiting, who had arranged emergency computer check-out of their security clearance before their arrival.

Down below, in the white-painted corridor, their footsteps had made no sound on the shining rubber floor. Ahead of them was a large notice reading *Vet. card A holders only*.

Beyond the guards by the notice, they had just been able to catch a glimpse of computers, massive control consoles, and a great wall map showing the oceans in white and the land masses in green.

Whiting had politely diverted them before reaching the guards and they now sat in his office listening intently as he explained: "As you know, the Polaris and Poseidon fleets have a strict list of conditions under which they can break radio-silence while at sea. These are really confined to the weekly crew-to-family transmissions and a number of strategic conditions. . . ."

"What are they?" Myers said.

"Sorry," Whiting said, shaking his head, "we work on the 'need to know' basis here; anyway, they aren't strictly relevant." He stopped, a little put out by his own brusqueness. "Actually, it might surprise you to learn that there are some parts of this operation which I don't know anything about myself—I have 'no need to know.' "

"So the fiendish enemy can't pull your toenails out and make you tell all," Myers joked.

"Something like that," Whiting replied lightly, but he didn't smile. "To go on: *Triton* came through on an emergency low frequency we have reserved for . . ."

"Certain strategic conditions," Slayter put in mildly.

"Er—quite. She gave us a fix—in deep water west of Arran, she was at the end of her fifty-day cruise, going into Gareloch—due to dock the following morning, as a matter of fact—when we received a series of transmissions. I won't bother you with the details, but briefly they reported a cascading series of failures. First, in the hydrovane control system, then in the missile guidance on board computers, and finally in the control room itself. Apparently a fire broke out in the main navigation control console."

"Don't quite follow," Holland said.

"You will in a minute," Whiting went on. "The duty radio officer has a requirement to transmit to land base any system failures. Well, earlier in the day, he had reported a fault in the inertial navigation system due, as he said, and I quote: 'to a number of control loops going on open circuit.' "

Myers sat hunched in his chair. "Open circuit—I begin to see—insulation or switching failure!"

"Almost certainly," Whiting continued. "He also gave a brief account of similar failures in the hydrovane controls and the missile-range computers. The final transmissions are excessively unpleasant, there appears to have been considerable—er—confusion and panic, then nothing—nothing at all."

As he finished talking lamely, he looked slowly round, almost seeking help. They were all imagining the sudden—rending—water-rushing death of 183 officers and men—the great steel hulk—an almost perfectly designed submarine microcosm of warmth and security, plummeting down through the dark, cold water. The implosion of the hull round the nuclear pile and sixteen multiple-warhead Poseidon missiles.

For a long time nobody spoke. It was Myers who broke the silence: "Progressive control failure and then . . ."

"Did the hull implode?" Holland asked.

"Not sure," Whiting replied. "We've three rescue vessels in the area, but it's too deep for on-board rescue chutes to work and there's a force-eight blowing at the moment. All we can do is to wait and take deep-water radiation counts."

"Will you be able to get down?" Holland asked.

"Only with the *Aluminaut* and only if the weather eases off."

"There's no hope?"

"Almost none. No, none at all really," Whiting looked away. "Tony Marsden—the skipper . . . we were at Dartmouth together. . . ." He recovered his manner and went on: "I've heard about the possible mechanisms involved in the road disaster and also in the Heathrow crash."

He nodded at Myers who replied testily: "I don't know how the hell you managed . . ."

Whiting was now fully in command: "Mr. Myers, there is already full Cabinet involvement in this. I assure you, there are fully authorized channels for us to know. As I see it, we have insulation failure in Knightsbridge, at Heathrow, and very probably on board *Triton.*"

After seven years of marriage, Anne Kramer realized that she was still in awe of her husband. In the early years of their courtship and marriage he had been like a friendly giant. In many ways he resembled her father, an austere man with a fierce but desiccated intellect, restlessly trapped in the colonial civil service.

She had been in equal awe of Kramer since they first met, and the fact that this formidable intellect was actually fond of her and wanted to marry her seemed in some way to make up for the past and reconcile her need for the remote dead figure of her father.

During the first year they had been immensely happy. Kramer had turned all his energies towards her and their marriage, illuminating every corner of her existence with his imagination and filling her life completely. Then came the trip to Canada and immediately afterwards the creation of the consultancy in London.

The change had been gradual. At first it was the demands of work and she had been proud to share the load with him. Then, he had been proud of her interest and grateful for her help. They had created the structure of the group together. She had attended all the initial sessions, making coffee, typing reports.

She searched back in her mind to try and imagine the exact moment when the change had begun.

She was lying in bed, the pain in her bruised shoulder now reduced to a dull throb. She had been waiting for Kramer to return home since seven o'clock. It was now two a.m. and there was no sign of him, no phone call, nothing. He had promised to return home early. They had planned a quiet dinner at a new Javanese restaurant and a late visit to the Players' Theatre.

It was not the first time. It had been the pattern of their life together for something like two years now, she reflected. But this was to have been an occasion; it was the anniversary of the first time they had met, under somewhat spectacular circumstances in the hall of the old League of Nations in Geneva, both attending a scientific conference.

When he did get back, she knew he would offer no explanation, no apology. His work came first and his work must never be questioned, nor must he.

She had been trying to probe the point at which the consultancy and, though she couldn't quite say it clearly to herself, the marriage also had begun to lose its initial inspiration. Perhaps it was Wright and his plastic inventions. Until then they had been expecting an exciting but unprofitable future as a small nucleus of scientists thinking out global problems.

They were all, it seemed, dedicated to the idea that science could work for people and not just be an isolated intellectual exercise. The impetus for the development of this new science—a science for people—had mainly come from Kramer, come from his deep erudition and philosophical wisdom.

Now, almost overnight, the chance had come to make the group the immensely profitable and go-ahead concern it was today. Wright had joined them with his new plastic—Aminostyrene. Kramer had seized it as a chance to provide a solid financial base for their other ventures, but gradually the plastic research had overshadowed and choked off practically all the other work of the group. Now his new projects were almost entirely commercial. The new spirit of science which had excited them all had gone.

That evening, waiting up for him, tired, aching, and hungry, she had nerved herself to do something she had never even contemplated before.

She had gone into his study, opened his desk, the Holy of Holies, which even their cleaner was not allowed to touch, and had taken a letter from the top drawer. It was now under her pillow and for the last three hours she had been nerving herself to open it.

She had recognized the writing. After Kramer's last

trip to Canada, there had been a flood of correspondence from various contacts, friends, and acquaintances out there.

Gradually, as the months passed, these dwindled, leaving one persistent correspondent, a woman. The letters had continued for the last two years fairly regularly, and on one occasion she had plucked up courage to ask him whom they were from.

He had laughed and told her that they were from a rather butch professor of chemistry at South Saskatchewan University. A very North American lady with powerful shoulders, and a voice like a bull moose in the rutting season. She had smiled and accepted this. They never showed curiosity about each other's letters or private lives, and Kramer had a vast correspondence from all over the world.

Finally, the letters had started coming from various European capitals, and that morning, by the second post after Kramer had left, this one had arrived, postmarked Cambridge. And that evening, feeling as guilty as Judas, she had taken it into the kitchen, carefully steamed open the flap and placed it open on the table, ready to read.

She could not bring herself to read it. She had sat there looking at it, occasionally pacing the room, but her sense of guilt was too strong. Finally, she had taken it to her bedroom and put it under the pillow. If he hadn't got back by twelve o'clock, she told herself, she'd read it. Twelve o'clock had given place to one o'clock and the ultimatum had been lifted. Now it was two o'clock and still the letter remained unread.

There was a slight noise downstairs in the living room and she started up in bed, twisting her shoulder slightly in the process. She listened intently in the darkened room, but the sound didn't recur.

They had a large, overweight tom cat called Archimedes who still thought of himself as a slim young kitten seeking passage through various objects and ornaments quite unsuited to his middle-age spread.

It was probably him.

She leant back in bed again, her shoulder aching intolerably. Suddenly, almost uncontrollably, she began to cry, feeling acutely sorry for herself. She felt alone and abandoned in the vast bed in the huge empty flat.

Fierce anger began to replace self-pity. She leant over and switched on the light and pulled the envelope out. She unfolded it.

It was a long letter written in a small, feminine, rather cramped hand. At one point she jumped out of bed and, running into the next room, poured herself a drink, bringing it back to her bedside before reading the next page.

It was more than a love letter. It was almost domestic at times. More than that, there was a warm intellectual intimacy between the two of them. The letter was full of little jokes and references to various aspects of science and personalities in the scientific world. Sharon, that was the name at the end, had obviously been on a long tour of Europe sponsored by the Canadian Research Council and had derived much profit from the tour.

She was also, and here Anne felt a sharp pang of jealousy that made her forget about her injured shoulder, undeniably witty and sophisticated. As she finished the last page, the phone's ringing made her jump. Irrationally she bundled up the letter, put it back under the pillow before picking up the phone.

It was Kramer. "Listen, honey, I'm terribly sorry about this evening."

There was a silence at the other end of the line.

"Are you there?"

Anne's voice came across small and strangled: "Yes."

"What did you find at the store?" Kramer didn't pause for reply. "No, honey, you must be tired. I guess I woke you up. I'm sorry. Three o'clock in the morning is no time for scientific reports." His tone was false, jocular, quite unlike the man she knew. "I'm afraid I'm stuck up here. I've just finished a conference. Won't be home tonight. See you later tomorrow. O.K., honey?"

Finally she asked the question: "Where are you?"

"Didn't I tell you?" he said. "I'm up in Cambridge. Now I won't keep you awake any more. Good-night, honey. God bless."

"Good-night," said Anne, and he had clicked off the receiver before she had finished the "night."

She leant back in bed, suddenly feeling weak and drained. She looked at the letter again; it was postmarked the day before and the writer had said that she would be phoning him at the office. The inference was obvious, and somehow, now that the worst was out, she felt much more at ease. She raised the envelope, turned it over, and glanced again at the address on the back: Dr. Sharon Gerrard. Gerrard? That name, of course, the tall, rather shy Canadian who had met her in the toy department that afternoon.

She thought of the man who had so carefully examined her shoulder and who was so obviously attracted to her. There was something familiar about his face, his sloping wide shoulders, his long body. Yves Montand: that was it. He looked something like Yves Montand, not a close resemblance—his hair was lighter in colour—but enough to give one the vague feeling that one had seen him before.

She remembered hearing that his marriage had broken up. Kramer had been very friendly with him out in Canada and had invited him over. Suddenly she sat bolt upright in bed. The letters had started arriving the moment Kramer had returned from his Canadian trip. Wait a minute . . . he had stayed with the Gerrards during his three-month sojourn there.

For the first time Anne felt the real pain of hurt pride. Although they had both been steadily growing away from each other for the last two years, she had never thought that he had been having an affair during the early, euphoric stage of her marriage. It was horrible. It was a betrayal of everything: of their plans, of their ideals, of the future—everything.

And what about Gerrard? Had Kramer broken his marriage up? And then hired him? Her mind was racing round in circles. The large gin she had gulped down was beginning to work and the strain beginning to tell. She drifted off into a broken, restless sleep.

She woke at nine the next morning feeling tired and feverish. Her arm was stiff but otherwise a little improved now that the bruise was yellowing on her shoulder. As she dressed, her doubts of the night before gave place to a firm determination. She would have it out with him that evening. Anything was better than the empty limbo of the last two years. In a way the discovery of his infidelity was almost a relief. It was better to face a flesh-and-blood antagonist than the feeling that he had simply lost interest.

What about Gerrard? Should she tell him? What good would it do? Were they divorced? They were certainly separated and had been for some considerable time. She felt warm towards him. He had been conned, just as she had. For the first time a trace of a smile passed across her lips; if one had to join forces, she could do a lot worse than the tall, attractive scientist.

Later she phoned Gerrard at the lab to ask about the results of the tests on the plastic gears. He told her of Wright's decision to put off the tests. He also told her of the signal failure in the tube and that he was going down to investigate the next morning. She pleaded to go with him, and after a surprised hesitation, he agreed.

Luke wasn't quite sure what his motivation was, perhaps it was to reinforce his position with the group by having the boss's wife down with him. He had no intention of telling any of the group where he was going until he returned with the actual samples taken from the insulation. Or, perhaps, it was the thought of meeting Anne again.

That evening, Anne, braced for the confrontation and with gin bottle to hand, dressed carefully in her best silk lounging suit, waited for Kramer.

Three hours went by. She got quite drunk on the gin, changed into a *négligé,* and then burst into hopeless giggles at the theatricality of waiting for a husband to come home with an accusing letter on the table between them.

Later she grew sober, cold, frightened, and changed into a nightdress and dressing gown. By eleven o'clock she had a throbbing headache and felt sick.

At eleven thirty the phone rang. It was Kramer.

This time his voice was almost brusque, formal: "Sorry, honey, not a chance of getting back." He sounded tired, overworked. "You'll have to excuse me. I'm snowed up here, right over my eyes. Can't come back until tomorrow. You understand, don't you?"

"Yes," said Anne faintly. Earlier in the evening she could have coped, answered him, said something, but now she felt shrivelled, cold, and sick. Her voice was almost a whisper.

"Well, there it is," said Kramer. "I'll see you tomorrow. Now take care of yourself, baby." He rang off.

There was too much to think of, too much to contemplate. Anne went up to bed, and, against the advice of her doctor, took a couple of sleeping tablets. The last thing she thought of before going to sleep was to remember to put on some sensible clothes to go down the underground with Gerrard the following morning.

The next morning Anne rose early. Sleep had sorted out her confused jumble of thoughts. Her mind was clear. She dressed, went into the living room, and sat down at the table and wrote a letter to Kramer.

As always, her upbringing and her lifetime habit of concealing her feelings showed in the letter. It was terse, brief, and to the point. It showed little, if any, feeling. She knew he had been unfaithful over a period of years. It was a betrayal of their marriage. She did not wish to continue that marriage. She was sure that he would find better satisfaction elsewhere, and only in this last sentence did she betray a little sprig of true feeling.

Before she sealed it up, she looked it over hastily. If he'd wanted to use it as evidence in a divorce, she reflected bitterly, it would give a good picture of an unfeeling, cold wife. There was no time to consider that now. The decision had to be made. She sealed the envelope and put it on the mantelpiece.

Outside the front door she flagged down a taxi to take her to her meeting with Gerrard and Slayter.

7

"We go down this way."

Holden, general maintenance manager of the London Underground, jumped lightly off the platform and turned to offer his hand to Anne Kramer. One by one they followed her down from the platform and stood by the electric rail.

Holden glanced at his watch. "It's only a shuttle line for the rush hour. No more trains, are there, stationmaster?"

He turned to the rather squat middle-aged man standing beside him in uniformed cap. His face was a blotchy red from high blood pressure and chronic bronchitis. He was breathing stertorously from the exertion. "Last one was ten ten, sir."

Holden turned back to the others. "Good. Let's make our way then." He was carrying a heavy electric torch which he now pointed into the tunnel ahead. The stationmaster had turned the service lights on from the switch box on the platform and the tunnel curved blackly away from them, the ribs picked out by a succession of pallid naked bulbs.

"Careful as you go," Holden called back, "the current is still on."

"Isn't that dangerous?" Slayter looked across at him.

"Only if you fall between these two rails." He pointed. "That's the conductor rail, the one in the centre here is the earth; you have to span the two in order to get a shock."

Anne grasped rather nervously at Gerrard's arm.

"This way," Holden started leading the way again

along the track, followed by Slayter, Gerrard, and Anne, with the stationmaster bringing up the rear. After a few yards they had left the comforting, familiar brightness of the station with its posters and white tiles and were in the dark, oppressive atmosphere of the tunnel. The air was comparatively cool, cooler than Gerrard expected. Hadn't he read somewhere that deep installations stayed at an even temperature all year round, cool in summer and warm in winter? The air seemed loaded with a dank fustiness. There was a strong, steady draught.

Holden walked ahead, occasionally pointing out obstacles and lighting them with his torch. "Here we are I believe," he said at last, glancing around. "Right, stationmaster?"

The stationmaster nodded breathlessly: "Yes, over there." He pointed at the far side of the tunnel.

They had arrived at a junction where two lines crossed. One line was obviously long out of commission. The tunnel was bricked up to the roof with a strong steel door blocking the way. Diagonally opposite, the line ran into a narrow, obviously disused, tunnel. In contrast to the bright metal of the main lines, the others were rusty. There was an air of crumbling decay about the entrance which made Anne shiver.

"Over here."

Holden led the way across to where the line led up to the blank bricked-in wall. Beside the heavy door there was a large mass of cables and some cast-iron switch-boxes, all covered in a thick mantle of dust. The party crossed from the main line and the stationmaster switched on another light over the fuse boxes.

Slayter stepped forward and very cautiously touched the insulation on the top cables with the tip of a pencil. It pulled away wet and tacky. He raised his fingers to his nose and sniffed. There was a smell reminiscent of decaying meat—with an underlying hint of ammonia.

Gerrard took a haversack from his shoulder, unpacked some specimen jars, and carefully started taking samples of the melted plastic with a nickel spatula.

"How far does it extend?" he asked Holden.

"It's hard to say. We've got a gang of men doing an examination of the entire area. So far it seems to be limited to this particular junction but we can't be sure."

"Listen," said Anne. In the distance they could hear a deep rumbling, steadily growing louder. Anne nervously stepped back a pace.

"Quite all right, miss, you're quite safe here, it's in the other tunnel."

The rumbling grew louder and, looking along the tunnel, they could see the fast approaching lights of a train. The next instant it was upon them, hurtling past with a shattering blast of air. The lights from the carriages flashed in their faces. The tunnel shook to the rattle of the wheels on the rails. Then abruptly it was gone and the noise died away again, leaving the fusty air and the torch beams in the darkness.

"Do you think it'll be progressive?" asked Slayter. "I mean, if the insulation falls away, the wires will begin to short."

"You're the expert, aren't you?" said Holden sharply.

Slayter fell silent and both men looked at Gerrard. Gerrard felt uneasy. Why the hell hadn't he left Wright to clear up his own problems? He was being asked to pronounce on a subject he knew nothing about.

"We'll have to take these samples back to the lab and estimate the reaction rate of . . ." he paused, "of whatever it is that's causing the breakdown. I don't see any immediate danger." He continued gently layering off the softened plastic with the spatula and dropping separate pieces into the specimen jars. These he carefully sealed and put away in his haversack.

Anne brought out a small automatic camera and began to take flash pictures of the melted insulation and the general area around it.

"I'm afraid you can't use those without permission," said Holden.

"We're not going to publish them, we're going to try to solve your problem," said Anne tautly. She adjusted the lens for a close-up and took a picture of part of the cable where the insulation was badly affected, showing the bare copper core. "We'll need them to locate where each sample came from."

"How long will you be then?" asked the stationmaster, looking across at Gerrard.

"I'm finished."

The stationmaster nodded to Holden: "Well, sir, if you don't mind, we ought to be getting on."

"Seen all you want to see?" Holden turned to Slayter.

"Yes, thanks."

"Good, then we'll press on."

The stationmaster, who was becoming increasingly restless, shone the torch back along the tunnel. They followed in single file.

Suddenly, without any warning, the tunnel appeared to move violently up and down. The concrete of the track slapped against their feet, throwing them down on the track.

After this, there was a rapidly growing rumble. Then a series of massive explosions. After each blast, the walls of the tunnel shook. Segments of the concrete and metal lining distorted and pieces crashed down from the roof. The precise circular ribs of the tunnel flexed and whipped as if they were made of rubber.

As they got to their feet in the billowing dust there were a series of more distant explosions and, finally, silence, except for the clattering of small pieces of débris dropping away from the tunnel roof.

"God, what's happened?" said Slayter. As he spoke, there was another explosion, this time slightly farther away. The tunnel shook again and they could feel a deep shuddering vibration under their feet.

"Quick," said Holden, "back to the platform. Come on!" He hurried back along towards the station. As they followed, the lights along the tunnel flickered once and went out.

Ahead, a train was still visible in the station where the dim, flickering emergency lights had automatically come on. They could hear shouts and anxious cries.

As they reached the station, they heard the hiss of compressed air as the conductor released the doors and the anxious passengers began crowding onto the platform. Then came two more distant explosions. Again the station and the tunnel shook and flexed.

A woman screamed. The passengers began pushing through the exit tunnels leading to the escalators.

"We'll have to make our way through the train," said Holden. He leapt up on the step of the cab at the front and started to unfasten the driving-compartment door. As he did so, there was another rumbling crack of thunder followed by a great blast of air that shook the whole train.

From near-total darkness the station flared into brilliant light. Ahead of them the station and the far end of the train were enveloped in a boiling mass of flames.

Holden tore open the second door into the carriage and stumbled out onto the platform, followed by Slayter and Gerrard.

There was total panic. Passengers were running desperately in all directions, clawing past each other as they tried vainly to escape the spurting mass of flames raging out of the tunnel mouth at the far end of the station. Children and the elderly were tramped underfoot in the blind stampede.

A woman stood transfixed in horror as her maxi-coat caught fire and flared up round her body.

An elderly man carrying a polythene container of paraffin suddenly exploded in a ball of flame as the container burst and the contents ignited.

A man in City dress—all reserve gone—hacked and kicked his way into the crowd, his clothes burning on his back.

The dry wooden frames of the old Metropolitan line coaches flared up like tinder, the glass windows cracking and splintering in the furnace heat. People fell like blackened dolls as the flame washed over them. They writhed like ants doused in petrol and then finally lay still in awkward, charred poses.

Anne fell back through the doorway of the coach and cannoned into a group of three people who were huddled against the far side of the coach.

At the far end of the platform, two figures, grotesquely blackened with bright ladders of flame still licking up from their clothing, staggered towards the others.

Shielding their faces against the intense heat, Gerrard and Slayter started towards them. Gerrard put out his hand to grasp the hand of the nearer man who was staggering towards him. As he touched him, he recoiled in horror. The flesh on the man's hand came away from his fingers like a crumbling glove. The man, sightless and blackened, suddenly crumpled and fell forward.

The other figure suddenly disappeared into a gust of flame which licked around Slayter. He darted back, his eyebrows and hair singed.

For a few seconds more, Gerrard dragged the remains of the man farther down the platform but one glance told him it was pointless. He retreated with Slayter to join the others at the far end of the platform.

They leapt back into the train. The leading man, a tall, burly, authoritative figure, went over to the blonde girl and sat on the other side of Anne.

"You all right, Wendy?" he said.

The girl opened her eyes and looked across and nodded weakly.

"Let's get the hell out of here." The man looked across at Anne. "Give me a hand, will you?" He was a man probably used to command rather than request; there was an air of easy authority about his movements. They lifted the girl down the steps back on to the line followed by the others. The stationmaster hung irresolutely inside the front coach of the now furiously burning train.

"For God's sake, come on," said Holden impatiently.

The stationmaster turned. "I don't know," he said. "Harry's lot are in there." He gestured towards the inferno.

"We can't do anything now," said Holden impatiently. "Come on!"

The stationmaster still hesitated. "There's another way up," he said.

"Where?" said Holden.

"Under the escalator," said the stationmaster.

"No good," said Holden. "The steps are made of wood; it'll be like a furnace."

He held out his arm and steadied the stationmaster as he climbed stiffly down from the coach.

"It's our only chance. The next station's way up the track."

He turned to the stationmaster: "How far, Bill?"

"Quite a stretch," said the stationmaster. "About half a mile."

A hot blast of air blew back through the door as Holden shut it. The others were now standing uneasily in the tunnel waiting for Holden to lead them.

"The next train," said Slayter anxiously, "isn't it liable to . . ." He didn't finish the sentence.

"There won't be any next train, the current's off," said Holden shortly.

"O.K.," said Slayter, "but this is a downhill gradient. What if this train takes off after us?"

"The brakes'll hold," said Holden. "We're quite safe."

They started back along the track. The formerly cool air was rapidly warming up as it flowed past them. Behind them, the crackling and roaring of the fire echoed in the tunnel. The front coach was now flaring up and throwing sparks and long flames out towards them along the tunnel, outlining their shadows on the dark ribs. They stumbled along and turned the corner into the junction where they had been examining the damaged wires. The girl, Wendy, and the stationmaster were both badly out of breath. They paused.

Holden looked around. "Wait here for a bit," he said. "I'll go on and check."

"I'll come with you," said Slayter.

Holden shook his head. "Please wait here," he said and set off along the tunnel, taking the main line.

The others sat on a pile of dusty timber and waited. They were out of sight of the fire now but they could still hear it. The air inside the tunnel was now hot and the stationmaster's breathing was getting increasingly laboured. He began to cough.

The big man turned to the others: "My name's Purvis," he said. "I suppose you don't know what the hell this is all about?"

There was something about him, an air of petulant arrogance, that reacted unfavourably upon the others.

Slayter shrugged his shoulders. "You know as much about it as I do." He turned round and took the flashlight from the stationmaster who was now leaning back, visibly ill.

"Here," said Slayter to Gerrard. "You'd better take a look at him."

Gerrard went over to the stationmaster who was starting to droop away from the wall. He was breathing heavily, his face scarlet, gasping for breath, his eyes half closed. Gerrard loosened his tie and bent his head to his chest.

Slayter turned to follow Holden.

"Hey," said Purvis, "don't take that." He pointed at the flashlight. "It's the only one we've got."

Slayter looked down at the flashlight for a moment, then shrugged his shoulders, "I suppose you're right." He handed the torch over, turned, and began groping his way along the tunnel, following Holden.

8

The area around King's Cross mainline railway station is one of the most complex transport communication junctions in the world.

On the surface, there is a vast, intersecting road complex fed with never-ending streams of traffic. Groaning lorries turn up the York Way towards the Great North Road, dense masses of cars and vans pour eastward along the Euston Road towards the city, and at the centre there is an almost incomprehensible mixing of traffic streams. Altogether, six major road systems meet next to the mainline railway station and are further confused by traffic entering the second mainline railway station immediately to the west: St. Pancras.

During the day and far into the night, the noise, vibration, and polluting stench of exhausts never cease. Pedestrians unwise enough to be involved in the clattering racket flinch permanently away from the thrusting leviathans and, as quickly as possible, dive down into the disinfectant air of the underground or up onto the hissing throbbing platforms of the main railway stations. It is their only escape from an area which has long since become intolerable for any real man-machine co-existence.

Underneath the crowded pavements and juddering roadways there is yet another complex of tunnels, walkways, escalators and tracks: the King's Cross underground station.

Those who travel in its brightly lit web of tunnels almost never imagine that they are moving among an interwoven arterial system of tubes: water and gas mains and great vaulted sewers. As they walk, with their senses cut off to avoid having to relate to the intolerable density of humanity around them, they never pause seriously to think either of the thudding traffic overhead or of the complicated mass of conduits and pipes coiling through the ground around them.

It is quite enough to have to face emergent feelings of claustrophobia without having to imagine the pressures above and below the serried lines of humanity flowing, like corpuscles in a vein, towards their destination.

In the whole of a day, there are perhaps two hours when relative peace descends above and below ground. Between approximately one-thirty and three-thirty a.m., the surface traffic dwindles and the wet, empty streets glisten blackly in the harsh light of the overhead sodium lamps.

Down in the tunnels, a small army of cleaners, fluffing gangs, and maintenance engineers move methodically through the stark, echoing system, sweeping the gleaming rails free of oily dust and inspecting the mass of communication and power lines strapped to the spare ribs of the black walls.

Although travellers on the surface and in the tunnels never see each other directly, there are several places where only thirty inches of earth lie between them, a thin membrane of soil preventing a totally unimaginable admixture.

Altogether, there are five main levels of railway tracks at King's Cross. First of all, there are the surface lines of British Railways, then, just under the already overcrowded surface, the Metropolitan Inner Circle line. Then the newly built Victoria line squeezed in under the Inner Circle, followed by the tunnels of the Piccadilly line and finally, deepest of all, the Northern line tube.

Each has its own particular method of construction. The Metropolitan line, for example, is brick lined and has no invert or tunnel material under its tracks.

The Victoria line, on the other hand, bolted together from spun concrete, segments and thrusts its way in between the Metropolitan and Piccadilly and in some places, during its construction, the unsupported tracks of the ancient Metropolitan had to be specially supported on steel plates and giant hydraulic rams to prevent collapse.

Before London became totally covered by its brick and concrete crust of ugliness, several small rivers used to flow freely down from the Northern hills of the town towards the Thames. But as man, the ceaseless builder, spread his artifacts out over the ground, the course of the river was altered, constricted, and finally forced underground into a closed twelve-foot pipe.

One of these was the Fleet. Originally a river open to the sky, it is now an enclosed storm-relief sewer running close by one of the King's Cross underground ticket halls.

Also enmeshed within the intersecting tunnels are a parallel pair of large water mains, two-foot-wide gas mains, and yet another by-pass sewer originally constructed in 1842.

The successful operation of a modern city is now a knife-edge balance between separate and overloaded systems, which just continue to function provided that there are no unwanted inter-reactions between them.

An inter-reaction can sometimes start from an apparently trivial event.

Just such a small event was reaching its conclusion in the Northbound Samson line tunnel leading out of King's Cross towards Hornsey and Islington.

It had, in fact, started some weeks previously, when a minute trickle of water had seeped unnoticed through a faulty seal between segments of a small communications conduit in the Samson line. Ordinarily, this would have constituted no danger at all. But in this particular instance, the water had leaked from the nearby Fleet storm-relief sewer.

Again, this might have soaked away without consequence, had it not been for the fact that the sewage water contained two unique ingredients and that there were plastic coverings over the cables attached to the wall of the tunnel. Also, by a malign chance, the cables were covered by an outer sheath of plastic, but many of the individual wires so enclosed were insulated by synthetic rubber.

Over the following weeks, the outer plastic covering slowly began to soften and decay, to drip away in foul-smelling strips of wet glutinous residue. Since the inner wires were lined by rubber and not affected by the dissolution of the plastic, power and communication systems were almost unaffected, and there were no indications of the developing presence in near-by signal systems and control centres.

The reaction process spread along the conduit in almost total silence, except for a very slight hissing noise due to the development and bursting of bubbles on the surface of the dripping plastic. As the bubbles formed and broke, the tunnel began to fill with a gas. Some of the gas was diluted and sucked away by the ventilation system, but some remained in pockets trapped in track lay-bys and in between staves of the roof structure.

Finally, the component parts of the King's Cross disaster were assembled and related in their proper order.

On the surface, hurrying crowds of home-bound office workers gathered their coats around their faces to keep out the freezing December fog. The tube entrances, like the open mouths of giant primeval animals, were swallowing up the huddled mass of people. They poured down steps and escalators into the brightly lit warmth. In the road, the traffic, slowed almost to walking pace by the acrid fog, fumed and roared impatiently as it waited for the imperious directions of a policeman in a fluorescent orange over-jacket.

Down in the gas-filled Samson line tunnel, two copper cables finally lay bare. One was above the other on the wall of the tunnel and slowly sagged towards its fellow. The upper carried 170 volts of electricity and the lower was at earth potential. They touched. There was a small spark and power abruptly drained away.

In the Coburg Street control room, a duty engineer

raised puzzled eyebrows at an unfamiliar light signal in front of him. In the tunnel came the first explosion as the trapped gas ignited.

It occurred in the space between two northbound trains and so was confined to the cylindrical space of air between them.

A racing wall of flame slammed into the rear of the train ahead and shattered the window of the driver's cab in the train behind.

As the force of the explosion reached its maximum, the bolted-concrete segments of the tunnel split, carrying with them the mass of steel plates and concrete which held the overhead Metropolitan line tunnel from collapse. One of the two twenty-four-inch gas mains embedded in the concrete of the roof support sheared open, releasing a flood of town gas into the shattered tunnel. As it rumbled its deadly contents into the confined space between the two trains, small fires were already burning in the cables on the distorted walls of the tunnel. Finally, the mixture of tunnel air and town gas reached its optimum concentration and exploded.

With a roar heard for miles around, the Samson line tunnel blasted upwards into the Metropolitan line and through the thirty-inch covering of soil into the roadway. At that moment, deep below, Gerrard and the others were thrown to the floor of the tunnel.

On the surface, the road slowly bulged upwards, split, and flung out like a slow-motion mud bubble, bursting into a ball of orange and yellow flame which shot skywards like a small nuclear explosion. Shock waves ballooned out into the fog, sweeping it aside in curved veils of force which flashed through the tightly packed lines of traffic.

Cars spun and crashed, careering out of control, mowing down the hurrying commuters on the pavements.

A giant, articulated lorry carrying a stack of steel pipes jackknifed and broke into two. The cab overturned and plunged into the gaping hole in the road. The load of pipes broke away and rolled through the terrified crowds, crushing and flattening like monstrous pastry rollers.

In the Metropolitan line a packed train hurtled towards the site of the explosion, automatic brakes full on and wheels screeching vainly against the shining rails. Unable to stop in time, the leading coach ran out onto the now unsupported track which bowed crazily downwards into the Samson line. As the tracks snapped, the train plunged to a rending crushing halt, the first two coaches telescoping into a bloody shambles of glass and torn wood panelling.

The shattered gas main in the concrete between the two tunnels was now roaring a thirty-foot jet of flame into the crater. A giant blowtorch, it played on the debris, firing the aged timber of the coaches into a dreadful funeral pyre.

Inside the wreck, those still alive clawed and fought in a blind attempt to escape the heat, only to be incinerated as they managed to crawl clear. One or two who did escape the inferno below were seen to climb over the edge of the crater into the road like insects, their clothes burning on their backs.

Flames were now belching out of the crater, carrying the fog upwards in arches of convection, the air filling with wood smoke and a sickening overlay of burning flesh.

On the pavements, the injured lay in huddled rows, lit by the inferno pouring out of the road. Other shocked groups huddled together and watched silently, blindly trying to understand the impossible scene before them. Practically no one spoke.

Out of the yellow gloom the piercing blue flashes of police cars and ambulances began to appear, sirens baying their ugly warning. Uniformed men jumped down out of vans and moved in quickly and purposefully, shepherding people away from the stricken area. Others, carrying road-block signs, began to close off the area, and firemen, hastily donning aluminium suits, moved towards the flames gouting from the crater.

Gerrard looked around at the others. Anne nodded at the stationmaster: "How is he?"

"He'll probably be all right if we're not down here too long," said Gerrard. "He's got pulmonary edema —left-sided failure."

"That's all we need," said Purvis, turning away. He looked along the tunnel. "How long are they going to take there?" He looked back towards the station. Smoke was beginning to filter along the tunnel. "We'll be suffocated if we stay here."

"Don't know what's happened yet," said Gerrard.

Purvis turned round irritably on him. "Damn it, man, we can't leave this poor bastard here."

Gerrard turned and looked at Hardy who, up until then, hadn't spoken. He was thin, brown haired, and rather bird-like. "O.K.," he said, "if you'll both give me a hand."

Purvis nodded abruptly. "This is Hardy, our company secretary." Again Gerrard felt the absurdity of introductions.

The smoke was curling round them and the stationmaster was coughing violently and gasping for air as Gerrard pulled him to his feet. Hardy went round the other side and put his arm under his shoulder, but couldn't lift the man's almost dead weight.

"Sorry, I can't quite manage," Hardy began.

Purvis brusquely pushed him aside: "Let me." He took the stationmaster's arm and put it round his neck, held on to his hand, and pulled him up.

Wendy was white-faced and holding a handkerchief over her nose. Anne had tied her scarf over her mouth. They started off with Hardy taking the torch and leading the way.

They lurched along the tunnel in the smoke, away from the junction. Anne followed behind Gerrard, who was trying to steady up the stationmaster.

"Luke." She touched his arm.

"What?"

"That train, what happens if it does run away down the tunnel? Can we get out?"

Gerrard turned his head slightly. "I saw one or two

connecting passageways between the tunnels—I think Holden called them bolt-holes—we'll have to get into one."

"Where in God's name have those two got to?" said Purvis. They had now walked some three hundred yards along the curving tunnel but there was still no sign of Slayter or Holden.

"Can't be far off the next station," said Gerrard.

Suddenly Hardy gave an exclamation and stopped, flashing his torch at something ahead.

In the dim light of the torch something was flopping along the rails towards them . . . something hardly human, on all fours. In the light of the torch, as he turned his face up, they recognized Slayter as he collapsed full-length across the rail.

Gerrard and Purvis quickly lowered the stationmaster against the wall of the tunnel, and Gerrard scrambled forward to Hardy who was standing transfixed, staring into the pool of light from the torch. Gerrard snatched the torch and bent down.

Slayter looked dead.

"Quick," Gerrard said, "got to get him breathing."

He rolled Slayter awkwardly onto his back, felt quickly for his pulse, and then started to push his hands up against the lower chest. Rhythmically he began to coax breath back into the unconscious man. After about half a minute, he stopped and bent down listening against Slayter's nose and mouth for the first sounds of spontaneous breathing. Again, he went to work and finally, after about four minutes, Slayter's chest gave a convulsive heave and then started back into the rhythm of normal breathing.

Gerrard sat back, breathing heavily; deeper than usual, he noticed almost subconsciously.

Purvis was at his elbow proffering something. "Any use?"

Gerrard took it. It was a silver-and-leather pocket flask. He held it to Slayter's mouth. For a moment there was no response, then finally he spluttered, choked, and opened his eyes. As he tried to move, he winced in pain.

"Can you talk?" Gerrard cradled him into a sitting position. "What's happened?"

Slayter looked wearily at him. "I don't know. The track ahead, it's blocked . . . partially."

"Where's Holden?" said Gerrard.

"He tried to get through, collapsed—tried to get him out—couldn't." Slayter's eyes closed again and he leant back against the track, breathing heavily.

"I'll go and take a look," said Gerrard.

"Right. I'll come with you." Purvis stood up and moved forward.

They turned and moved along the tunnel. Ahead of them there was a sharp, downward incline. Through the light of the torch they could see the curved, ribbed iron segments of the tunnel flung down across the track. The earth behind had collapsed inwards and the tunnel was blocked except for a narrow passageway between the curved pieces of iron. Water trickled out of the piled debris. The sight of the bare earth bulging in was unnerving.

"God, how deep are we?" exclaimed Purvis.

"According to Holden, about sixty feet," said Gerrard. "There's only one line above us and that's the Metropolitan. The explosion must have been there somewhere."

Both men were beginning to gasp for air, drawing their breath in long, shuddering gulps.

Gerrard shone the torch into the narrow passage formed by the distorted tunnel segments. "He must be in here."

Purvis took something out of his pocket. In the beam of the torch, they could see a trousered leg protruding from the collapsed tunnel.

Behind him, Gerrard heard the scrape of a match. He turned angrily: "Goddamn fool, put it out! Gas!"

But he need not have spoken. As the two men watched, the flame of the match abruptly flickered and snuffed out.

"Can't stay here—probably carbon dioxide."

By now their breathing was heavy and laboured. Gerrard felt light-headed and dizzy and recognized the early symptoms of carbon dioxide poisoning. He started to crawl along towards Holden but the effort was too much. Purvis was swaying on his feet. Gerrard slowly pulled himself up to a standing position. He felt drunk.

"Get out, quick! Move, for Christ's sake!" he gasped, and the two men, swaying like drunks, stumbled along the passage up the incline, supporting each other. They reached the others and flopped down.

"What's happened?" asked Anne, alarmed.

"Gas," said Gerrard, his speech slurred.

Slayter was sitting up, flask in hand, almost himself again. "What about Holden?" he asked.

Gerrard wearily shook his head: "Couldn't get to him. There's no chance. He must be dead."

No one answered, then Purvis spoke: "Where's the gas coming from?"

"Don't know," Gerrard shook his head. "All I know is that we'd better shift and fast!"

"Why aren't we affected here?" Hardy's voice had a slight quaver in it.

"Because," said Gerrard, "being heavier than air, the carbon dioxide has settled in the dip. It could be gradually expanding—up towards us."

From the other side the fire was thrusting long feathery tongues of smoke towards them.

"Now where?" said Slayter.

"I think I saw an inter-connecting tunnel," said Purvis, "about fifty yards back along here."

"We don't know where it leads," said Slayter. He looked round at the stationmaster who was breathing more regularly, his eyes still closed. "We've got to find out. Wake him up."

Purvis went over to the stationmaster and shook him. "Hey!" he said loudly. "Hey!"

Gerrard gripped his arm and pushed him aside. "Give me the brandy." Slayter handed him the flask and Gerrard poured a little on the man's lips. The stationmaster's eyes fluttered slowly and opened. Gerrard leant closer, holding the torch so that he could see his face. "Can you hear me?"

The stationmaster nodded slowly.

"We've got to find another way out. There's a bolt-hole back there, where does it lead?"

The stationmaster gasped for breath and tried to speak. Gerrard gave him a little more brandy.

"There's a ladder." The man spoke in short gasps. "It goes . . . down to . . . Western line below."

"And up to the surface?" said Gerrard.

"No . . . down."

"We're not going deeper," said Purvis.

Gerrard straightened irritably. "What else do you suggest? We've had it here." The smoke was getting thicker. He turned to Slayter: "Can you walk?"

Slayter stretched his legs out and felt them cautiously. "I think so. I'll be all right."

Gerrard looked at the two women. Both nodded. He handed the torch to Slayter. "Lead the way," he said. He nodded to Purvis and they bent down and pulled the stationmaster to his feet.

As they reached the bolt-hole, the others were already inside. Half dragging, half pushing, the men handled the stationmaster through. Inside, to their relief, the air was free from smoke and Gerrard felt a cool fresh draught blowing from a new direction.

They rested for a few moments and then dragged the stationmaster through to a small square opening at the far side. It led into a larger chamber. The others were huddled around an opening in the floor at their feet where an old rusting iron ladder lead downwards into the darkness.

Hardy was shining his torch down. The air blowing up felt fresh and clean.

Gerrard decided to risk an experiment. "Got another match?" He turned to Purvis.

Purvis brought out a box of matches and struck one. It flared brightly; he protected it with his hand and it continued to burn.

"No gas," said Gerrard. "We'll take a chance."

"What about him?" Purvis pointed at the stationmaster reclining unconscious against the wall. "We won't get him down the ladder."

"We'll have to get out and then come back for him," said Gerrard. "He'll be safe here from the fire, and as long as there's a supply of fresh air coming up, the smoke shouldn't get to him."

"You *can't* leave him," said Anne.

"Nothing else we can do," said Gerrard. He looked down. "He's far too heavy to take down that ladder without a rope."

"I've got a belt," said Anne, "so have you." She looked across at the stationmaster. "He's got one too. Can't we tie them together?"

"He's about two hundred pounds," said Gerrard. "It would never take the weight."

Wendy turned away and started to cry, and Anne, to Gerrard's relief, gave up the argument and put her arm around her.

"We need that other flashlight," said Gerrard.

"What?" Purvis turned round. "Where is it?"

Slayter shrugged his shoulders: "Holden had it."

"Why didn't you bring it back?" Purvis snapped angrily.

"I was trying to save the man, not the torch," said Slayter.

Purvis looked at him furiously for a moment and then turned away towards the ladder. "I'll go first," he said, and swung over and started climbing down. He stopped with his head level with the top of the hatchway. "Give me the torch," he said.

"We'll need it up here."

Gerrard turned away from the stationmaster.

Purvis's calm was beginning to disappear. "I'm not going down there without a bloody light. Give it to me!" He held his hand out aggressively.

"I'll light the way down," said Gerrard. The two men glared at each other.

Anne, remembering, opened her handbag. "I've got something here. It's only a keyhole light but it may be useful." She brought out a small key-light attached to a ring of keys and snapped it on. It gave off a dim, yellow beam. She gave it to Purvis who took it without a word and started down.

Gerrard looked round at the others. He nodded to Hardy: "You go next." Hardy clambered over and followed Purvis. "Now you two." The two women and then Slayter followed.

Gerrard turned and took a last look at the stationmaster. He took off his raincoat and bundled it around the unconscious man.

"Can you hear me?" he said. There was a slight flicker of the eyelids. "Now listen." He spoke almost into the man's ear. "We're going to get help. Do you understand?"

There was a faint nod.

"We'll get back as soon as we can. You'll be quite safe here for the time being." There was no answering nod this time, just a flicker of the eyelids. Gerrard turned round, flashed the torch down the hole, swung over onto the ladder and started climbing down. The walls were clammy and damp and there were white limestone excrescences on the ageing, flaking brickwork. It was like the interior of a chimney. He heard a cry from Purvis far below which echoed up towards him.

"I'm down!" There was a pause. "Looks quite clear down here," he said. The others climbed down to join him, Gerrard following, their feet grating on the ancient rungs, flakes of rust falling into their eyes.

At the bottom, Gerrard swung the heavy torch into the darkness. They were in a low, brick-lined chamber with an arched roof. Purvis was trying the massive steel levers on a heavy steel door at the far end. In the middle of the room there were some planks on trestles.

On the planks were some heavy tools and pieces of threaded piping. Against another wall, there was a complete oxy-acetylene welding set, two picks, a crowbar, and some other levers. There was a kettle and two mugs and a packet of tea on the floor. Slayter was examining the tools. Anne picked up the kettle.

"It's warm," she exclaimed.

"Thank God," said Slayter. "That means whoever was here left in the last few minutes. The point is, which way?"

Gerrard turned round and flung the light of the

torch along the other end of the chamber, then back towards the steel door.

"Quite," said Slayter, voicing the thought that was uppermost in the minds of both men. "They must have gone through that door and . . . locked it behind them. Probably standing regulations in case of fire."

Purvis turned on them angrily: "We won't find out waiting here. Let's try the other way." He turned and led the way back to the bottom of the ladder and then started down the other side of the tunnel. It was on an incline and they could feel a steady current of air blowing against their faces.

Anne whispered to Gerrard, "It's warm air."

Gerrard nodded grimly.

"That doesn't mean a way out," said Anne. "It suggests . . ."

Gerrard nodded: "Could come from a deeper level, could be the fire—can't tell." He swung his powerful light into the space ahead.

They had arrived at a short, narrow bolt-hole. On the far side, the beam of the torch picked out a square metal exit.

Purvis was shining his torch downwards. It reflected off a pool on the floor.

"We'll have to go through here," he said.

"Hold on!" snapped Gerrard. Purvis didn't move. "Get out of the way."

Purvis reluctantly moved aside and Gerrard edged closer to the entrance of the bolt-hole and shone the light along the side wall. A thick mass of cables had sagged away from their supports. In one place they almost reached the surface of the water. There was hardly room to pass underneath and get out to the far side.

"Well," said Purvis impatiently, "let's get on."

"Just hold your horses," said Gerrard. "Wait." He slowly and carefully shone his torch back along the tunnel again. "What do you think?" he turned to Slayter.

"It's a hell of a risk."

"Why?" said Purvis.

"If there's juice in those wires and anybody touches

them while they're in the water—they'll go for the chop," said Slayter.

"How can there be any current," said Purvis. "We passed a dozen lights, they were all out."

"They may've been turned off," said Gerrard. "The switches are probably on the other side of that door."

"I'm going through," said Purvis irritably. He started to bend down to get inside the narrow opening.

"I wouldn't." Slayter's voice was calm in contrast to the other's blustering urgency. "You'll never get through without touching the wires."

Now that their eyes had adapted to the darkness they realized that the bolt-hole was illuminated faintly from the other end.

"There's some light on through there," said Purvis.

"Exactly," said Slayter dryly. "That's why I wouldn't advise it."

"Well, what the hell else can we do?" asked Purvis. "You're very good with negative suggestions."

Slayter's voice dropped another couple of tones and grew even more silky and cool. "I do have a more positive suggestion if you're prepared to listen."

Purvis stared sullenly at him.

"Come back and I'll show you," said Slayter.

He led the way back to the chamber and shone the torch on the welding equipment. "I thought so," he said. "We've got the whole works." He looked round at the door. "I reckon we can burn off these locks and bars." He shone the torch up and towards the door and gave an exclamation.

The others followed the beam of the torch and saw a small metal switch-box.

"That's a bit of luck," said Slayter. He went over, opened the case, and pulled down the switch lever. Instantly the chamber flooded with light and they all instinctively put their hands up to cover their eyes.

"Now I think we've got the lot," said Slayter. "We've the means of cutting through that door. We know it leads out, otherwise the workmen would still be here. They certainly couldn't have gone the other way." He looked around. "And, I think . . . ah," he bent down, "there is even food!"

"Food," said Anne. "Where?"

Slayter pointed to a small wooden box: "A lunch-box."

Anne opened it and brought out some cheese, dried milk, sugar, and a tin which, when she opened it, contained biscuits.

Purvis was over by the door examining it, tapping the side of the lock. "There's about half an inch of steel sheet. We'll never get through."

Slayter whipped round in sudden fury, and pushed him back against the wall. "For Christ's sake, shut up," he said. "I've had a gutful of you."

Purvis hesitated for a moment, his eyes narrowed, then he started forward, fists raised.

Gerrard stepped between them: "Don't you think we've got enough problems without wasting energy on a slugging match? Now can it!"

For a moment the two men seemed about to push Gerrard out of the way and fight. Then, finally, the tension drained out of them and they separated. Purvis went sullenly away and sat on the planks by Wendy. Slayter started to check the oxy-acetylene equipment.

After a few moments, Purvis took out his brandy flask, shook it to see how much was left, picked up the kettle, and filled it up with the warm water. He put the cap back on and shook it to mix the contents.

"Not much, but it'll help," he said, passing it to Anne.

Anne took a gulp and passed it around. Finally it got to Slayter who gratefully upended the flask, emptying it.

For about fifteen minutes, they just sat, waiting for the glow of the drink to spread out into their tired limbs. By now they were black with grime. Purvis's immaculate City dress was crumpled and torn. Gradually, they relaxed and began to talk.

Gerrard found himself talking to Hardy, who also turned out to be an expatriate Canadian, his accent flattened out and anglicized after some ten years in Britain. He had a degree in sociology and was a specialist in market research working for Purvis's company. It was no surprise for Gerrard to learn that Purvis made bulldozing equipment.

Slayter was the first to get up. He glanced at his watch. "Time we got started. Give me a hand, will you?" He looked across at Gerrard. Together they dragged the heavy cylinders over to the door. Slayter turned on the main cylinder keys and adjusted the pressure regulators.

"How long do you think it'll take?" said Gerrard, nodding towards the door.

"Can't say," said Slayter. "It's a long time since I've handled these but, at a rough guess, two or three hours, depending on what I find the other side of the metal, of course. Hope to God there's enough gas in the bottles."

They were both breathing more stertorously and there were beads of sweat on Slayter's brow. "You've noticed," began Gerrard.

Slayter nodded. "Yes. It's getting hotter all the time and I imagine the oxygen content in the air is decreasing."

"Right," said Gerrard. "Don't tell the others." He tapped the cylinder of gas. "This isn't going to help much either."

"We're wasting time," said Slayter abruptly. "Look, can you get everybody to move down the tunnel a bit farther. It's not unknown for a blowback to happen on these things and if that happens they go up like a bomb. No point in anyone else being around if that happens." Slayter pulled the goggles down and lit the flame of the torch adjusting the oxygen flow until there was a hard hissing blue flame.

Anne had already gone up the ladder to the stationmaster.

Gerrard walked back to the others: "We'll have to move back a bit," he said, "just in case."

"What do you mean?" asked Purvis suspiciously.

Gerrard nodded back towards the flaring oxy-acetylene cutter. "Sometimes they strike back. Let's move."

They dragged the heavy benches farther along the corridor. It was noticeably warmer and ahead of them was the square metal opening into the bolt-hole and the faint gleam of the water beyond.

Gerrard turned and went towards the ladder. He took his torch and shone it upwards. Anne was coming down. He caught a glimpse of long elegant legs and a flash of white pants between them as she clambered down towards him. Ironic, he thought, fifty-fifty chance of coming out alive and she still raises my adrenalin.

She stepped down and stood beside him and looked up at him curiously. "I was warned about ladders," she said.

Gerrard shrugged his shoulders and half turned away, embarrassed.

Anne smiled: "He's much better."

"Well enough to come down?" asked Gerrard.

Anne hesitated: "Don't know, you'd better take a look at him."

Gerrard nodded and started up the ladder. The air coming down was perceptibly hotter, and by the time he'd reached the top he was pouring with sweat. There wasn't as much smoke but there was an acrid chemical taint in the air which caught at his throat.

The stationmaster was seated in the light which was now shining at the top of the shaft. He was bent over something and seemed to be writing. As Gerrard tapped him on the shoulder, he gave a start and looked up. To Gerrard's amusement he was working on a crossword puzzle in a thumbed copy of the *Daily Mirror*.

"You're a bit better, then?" said Gerrard.

"Much better, sir, thank you," said the stationmaster. His colour had gone down from its hectic red, and he seemed to be breathing more easily. He had rolled up his uniform jacket and was resting up against it. "I'm quite comfortable here. Got my crossword. Don't you worry about me, Guv."

Gerrard bent over and took his pulse, looking at his watch in the light of the one bulb that lit the top of the shaft. Gerrard looked down at him. "Think you can manage the climb now?"

The stationmaster shook his head. "Don't reckon so, and if I got down there I'd certain not get back up again. Besides," he said, "they'll soon have that fire under control and then there'll be a search party coming. I think I'm better off here."

Gerrard didn't feel as optimistic but he nodded his head: "You're the fittest of the lot of us," he lied. He turned and looked along the tunnel. "I'll go take a look." He started back along the now-familiar way through the musty brick room to the main tube tunnel.

As he passed through, he touched the bricks; they were warm to the touch. In the distance he could hear a steady crackling and snapping as the fire raged.

A blast of hot stifling air hit his face and drove him back. He went back to the stationmaster.

"We're trying to open a door down there. When we're through we'll come back and get you out, O.K.?"

The stationmaster looked up and nodded: "Don't be too long then, my missus'll be doing her nut."

"For a bit," said Gerrard, "it'll probably get hotter, but remember that the air circulation should improve soon as we get that door open. You should get a fair draught. It'll cool things down a bit."

As he spoke, he wondered if the man realized the danger. If he did, reflected Gerrard, he didn't show it. He'd got his crossword puzzle and a bit of light to see by and he was warm and reasonably comfortable. He wasn't going to worry further until he had to. Gerrard smiled back at him and started down the ladder.

At the bottom, he went over to Slayter, shielding his eyes against the glare of the flame. The torch had barely made one small circular hole in the metal bar. Slayter stopped for a moment, thrust back the goggles, and wiped his brow. He had already stripped his coat and tie off and his neck was running with sweat. "I don't know whether it's the torch, the metal, or me," he said, "but it's going to be bloody slow, I'm afraid. What's up there?" He nodded up towards the tunnel.

Gerrard described what he'd found.

"This is the only way then," said Slayter, "unless one of the girls wriggles out through that." He nodded towards the other end of the tunnel.

Gerrard shook his head. "Too risky," he said. "One slip and . . ." He shrugged his shoulders.

Slayter nodded, pulled the goggles back over his eyes, and turned back to the door. Gerrard went back to the others. He saw that Wendy was sleeping, utterly exhausted, on Hardy's chest.

Hardy nodded towards the sleeping girl and looked up at Gerrard: "Got a daughter of my own," he said. "Not here, back over in Canada. I sent her back to school in Toronto." He spoke haltingly, breathing a little more deeply than usual.

Anne was sorting out the food on the bench, making neat little piles. She turned and smiled at him, pointing to one pile of two biscuits: "That's your ration," she said.

"All for me?"

"No cheek," said Anne, "or I'll take them back."

"You thrive on this kind of thing, don't you?" said Gerrard, grinning back at her.

Anne smiled: "I hate to say this, but I used to be a Queen's guide. You know the motto, 'Be Prepared!' The trouble is, of course, I never was."

Gerrard looked around for Purvis. He had taken his jacket and shirt off and was striding up and down in front of the bolt-hole entrance.

"Tarzan's feeling the confinement, I'm afraid," said Anne.

"I wish the bastard would keep still," said Gerrard. "He's using up our oxygen. What say we get some rest?" he patted his knee. "Stretch out here."

"I'll have my legs pointing the other way this time," Anne said, smiling at him. She stretched herself beside him and rested her head on his lap. He leant back against the wall and closed his eyes and tried to relax.

Sleep seemed impossible with her head nestling on

his thighs. He looked down at her long brown hair, her oval face, her slightly olive skin, high cheekbones, long dark lashes. It was, he reflected, almost like the personification of a sort of beauty he had always sought after. "Were thine that special face," was that Shakespeare or *Kiss Me Kate?*

There had been a girl once, many years ago, who'd looked something like this . . . very close to that special face. But Anne's was even closer. And she was married to Arnold Kramer! He shook his mind clear and tried to concentrate on the major disaster that must have erupted above their heads, with communications, light, power, gas, water, and transportation cut.

He wondered how widespread it was. Had plastic started breaking down all over? Or was it just in the King's Cross area?

The concept of a London half paralyzed was too much for his tired mind; he became more and more drowsy and then fell away down and down into a deep sleep.

9 Kempton Street, just to the east of the Edgware Road, is nearly always choked with traffic. Along each side of the road there are congested ranks of parked cars and vans which reduce flow to an uneasy single line.

In the centre of the road, there is a pavement island providing temporary refuge for pedestrians trying to dodge anxious, ill-tempered drivers. On the island is a raised concrete block topped off by a black cast-iron grille. It is the exit for one of the ventilation shafts from the Bakerloo tube line. Normally, there is a steady warm updraft from the grille, smelling of tar and disinfectant and voiding a flood of warm stale air into the cold surface atmosphere.

At about the same time as King's Cross station exploded, commuters were jostling in the streets, each on his way to a bus stop or a car tethered to a parking meter.

In the shaft leading to the grille a mindless, groping mass of malodorous corruption was thrusting its way silently towards the surface. Buoyed up by bubbling foam it steadily rose. Single units in an obscene abrogation of normal order divided and made two. Two became four and four, eight. Endlessly supplied with food, each unit absorbed nutrient and in a soft, ancient certainty fulfilled its only purpose—to multiply, to extend, and to multiply.

Eventually, the cylindrical shaft leading to the surface, blocked off at the bottom by the rising foam, filled to the inner surface of the grille.

A nameless commuter reached the island, lit a cigarette, and tossed the match to one side. It fell through the grille.

There was a brief flash, a deep, thumping detonation, and the concrete shaft split open like a hatbox, totally dismembering the commuter. The iron grille flew into the air and crashed down on the pavement, careering madly along like a giant child's hoop cutting down pedestrians and finally smashing through the wall of a delicatessen and coming to rest in a shower of boxes and splintering glass.

In the Coburg Street control room of the London Underground system, there was a full emergency. Transport executives were gathered in the great drum-shaped room anxiously studying the wall plan of the tube system.

Controllers were seated at consoles, hopelessly trying to control the trains represented as red lights on the wall track plans. It was obvious that communication failure was rapidly escalating throughout the whole seventy miles of tunnel complexes.

In a dozen tunnels, trains ground down to a halt. Hordes of terrified commuters made their way anxiously along dark, musty tunnels to the lights and safety of the next station.

There were minor explosions, fires, and the failure of a million wires and cables. As the dissolution of plastic proceeded and accelerated in rate, the elegant order of the system gradually turned into total chaos. Finally, at Coburg Street, the chief transport engineer gave the only instruction possible in the circumstances: Close the underground.

On the surfaces, in the freezing December air, the smell of the rotting plastic began to hang permanently in the air. A cloying wet, rotting smell similar to the smell of long-dead flesh. It filled streets and homes, basements and factories.

Traffic lights failed, causing completely irresolvable jams. The main telephone exchange at Marsham Street gradually developed a series of failures as insulation failed in the main relay-selector room.

The breakdown of plastic spread into Broadcasting House. First, Radio One then Radio Four went off the air. As emergency equipment was brought into action, it failed in turn.

A gas main with polypropylene seals on its pressure regulators erupted into flame in Wardour Street.

A polythene container of concentrated nitric acid in the top floor of an engraving plant in Greek Street softened, bulged, and then burst, releasing a flood of acid through the ceiling of an office below. Young secretaries ran screaming as the acid drenched down over them, bubbling their skin into great yellow blisters.

Plastic cold-water pipes softened, ballooned, and burst, flooding into shops, homes, and restaurants.

Slowly and inexorably, the rate of dissolution increased; failures occurred in increasing succession until, within forty-eight hours, the centre of London had become a freezing chaos without light, heat, or communication.

At the Kramer consultancy, Buchan turned away from the phone in disgust: "I can't get any sense out of anyone; nobody seems to know what's happened."

"How long ago was it they went down?" Wright asked.

Buchan looked at his watch: "It's about eight hours now."

"Surely someone in the head office knows who took them into the tunnel. It was the Samson line, wasn't it?"

"Yes," Buchan replied, "all their communications are absolutely haywire. Last time I tried all I managed to raise was a tape-recorded message saying calls were being transferred to another number."

"Did you try it?"

"Of course. It gave the number-unobtainable tone."

"We'd better go round to their office by car so that . . ."

"Just a minute," Scanlon interrupted; he turned up the volume on the television set.

The announcer was speaking in a heavily contrived calm: "By now you will know about the very serious events in the centre of London. The next broadcast will be seen simultaneously on BBC 2 and ITV. We strongly suggest that you keep your set on, particularly if you live in Central London."

His image dissolved to a pot of carefully arranged flowers on a highly polished mahogany desk. Then, as the camera pulled back to reveal the grave saturnine features of the Home Secretary, the voice of the announcer went on: "The Right Honourable Mr. Justin Bradbury . . ."

The Home Secretary's face stayed immobile for a fraction too long until he received the camera cue, then he spoke: "Good evening. I am speaking to you tonight to tell you of some of the decisions which were made in a special meeting of the Cabinet this morning. All of you will have read of the disastrous events in Central London, which have caused so many tragic deaths and injury, and most of you will know that these are due to some entirely new process which is attacking and dissolving many forms of plastic. It must be clear now that attempts to stem the spread of this terrible breakdown have not been completely successful . . ."

"Why can't he just say they've failed?" asked Buchan.

". . . and unless we take stern and effective measures now, our scientific advisers have told us that much of our city organization may well break down altogether, since the process is rapidly gathering speed. I realize that this may be hard to accept, but the evidence for this statement is now very clear. Therefore I must tell you . . ."

The camera moved up slightly to cut out the nervous picking of his fingers.

". . . that at noon today, Her Majesty, the Queen, signed a state of emergency which gives us full powers to deal with the situation as quickly and effectively as possible.

"Emergency posts are now being set up inside the area by the armed services and since the telephone system has now almost completely failed in the area, all communications must be made through the emergency phones now being installed. If anyone finds any sign of affected plastic, they must go at once to the nearest emergency point and report it. A de-contamination squad will then go to the area and deal with the outbreak.

"Our scientists do not yet know what the breakdown is due to, but one fact emerges, it appears to be contagious. So you must treat any affected plastic as if it were infectious.

"Now I am afraid I come to the most difficult part of my task. I have to tell you that under the emergency powers, the Government have decided to seal off the entire area.

"This has now begun and troops are being deployed around the periphery to close off all exits. As from now, no one in the area may leave except in special circumstances. . . ."

Scanlon got up and switched off the set almost abstractedly, his eyes fixed on some far point: "Good God, just think of it. Take out plastic from a modern city and what do you get—complete breakdown. We're totally dependent on it." He turned to Wright: "Awesome thought, isn't—our product?"

"I hardly think we are to blame." If Wright was rattled, he was determined not to show it.

Buchan looked coolly from one to the other. "Oh, yes you are—we all are, in fact."

"This is scarcely the time for breast-beating," Wright said.

Buchan slapped a file of papers on the desk and jumped to his feet. "My God, you two academics make me sick. The pair of you might have been discussing some obscure point in theoretical chemistry. Don't you *really* see your connection with it all? The whole structure of the city is rotting away and we might just be *fully* responsible!"

Suddenly Wright flared: "And what else can we do? Of course I'm concerned. . . ."

"But you refuse to accept *blame!*"

"I will accept blame if and when the situation arises, but just now we've *got* to think in practical terms. There is no good evidence yet. We simply made a product—we sold it with full test data—we didn't hide anything. You know that just as well as I do!"

Buchan turned away in disgust. Scanlon gestured weakly as if to try and make a peace between the two.

"What defeats me," he said, "is that it's obviously all kinds of plastic. If it was our stuff alone, we could see why it's failing chemically. It could be a light-activated breakdown like our Degron breaking up under the influence of light and oxygen."

"Won't do," Wright said. "Doesn't add up. Look, we make a bio-degradable bottle, you pull the strip on it when you open it, and that admits light and oxygen to the underlying material. It then begins to break down, so you can end up by putting it on your garden or down the loo. But that doesn't make a case. You've no reason to say that the process could spread to other plastics. They're entirely different molecular structures many of them—no reason for them to react in this way."

"Supposing something can be transferred from our stuff to other plastics," Scanlon mused. "Supposing this factor *X* is transferable from one type of plastic to another, what then?"

"If that were true," Wright said, "your mysterious *X* would have to possess stored information, it would have to be either a universally reactable chemical or some entity like a single cell."

"A cell?" Scanlon broke in. "That's an ingenious thought. I agree there's no such compound which would react with all plastics, but a cell, yes, a living cell—that would do quite well. One small crippling snag—there's no such animal, though some bacteria have a pretty odd appetite. Isn't there one which can eat iron rust?"

"Frankly," said Buchan, "I'm more interested in the fate of Anne Kramer at this juncture. Where the devil is Kramer by the way?"

Scanlon looked over at him: "He's still up at Cambridge."

"Well, we'd better contact him, bring him back."

"I find it pretty incredible he's not back here already," said Buchan. "If my wife were down there . . ."

"But that's the point," said Wright. "He doesn't know this, does he?"

10

Gerrard was slow to waken. He had been dreaming of a great furry animal lying across his face and chest. His breathing was impeded by the weight of the animal. It was steadily increasing its pressure.

At last it seemed to him as though it slowly turned its face towards him with round, brilliant-yellow eyes. Suddenly he awoke with a jerk, almost throwing Anne to the floor. She started up with an exclamation.

Gerrard looked around, fully alert. "Where are the others?" he said. The bench alongside them was empty. He felt his shirt wringing with sweat; the atmosphere was thick and hazy in the tunnel and the air was intolerably hot. He found himself gasping for breath as he spoke. As they peered into the gloom, in the distance they could just see Slayter silhouetted in the flare of sparks from the torch. There was no sign of the other three.

Suddenly there was a brilliant flash from the bolt-hole, a loud sizzling crackle followed by a long scream.

Gerrard ran over and swung the torch beam into the bolt-hole. In the entrance, Wendy, the front of her dress charred and ripped, was shaking uncontrollably in the shallow water. Anne bent forward to try and reach the girl but Gerrard pulled her arm away.

"Get back!" He shone the torch farther in.

A body was outlined in the light. It was splayed back against the wall in a grotesque attitude of crucifixion with the arms outstretched; the face a terrible mask of shock; the tongue protruding. Slowly, it began to slide down towards the water. Gerrard shone the torch towards the end of the tunnel. The bare cables were now lying across the exit, one sagging loop under the water. He shone the beam on the face. It was Hardy.

There was no sign of Purvis.

Gerrard gave the torch to Anne and ran quickly back. By the pile of tools there was a coil of rubber hose. He dragged it over to the bolt-hole. Slayter was still so completely absorbed with his work he didn't appear to have noticed anything.

At the entrance to the bolt-hole, Gerrard carefully looped the end of the hose round Wendy's arm and pulled her towards him. He then got a full coil round her body and dragged her clear of the water with its lethal charge of electricity. Finally he laid her gently down onto the concrete floor. She was deadly white but still breathing in short, fluttering gasps. Suddenly she gave a convulsive jerk, a flickering of the eyelids, and the short, pulsating breathing ceased. The body relaxed.

Quickly he straddled the girl's body and began working her arms backwards and forwards. There was no response. He leant forward, pulled down her lower jaw, tilted her head back, and breathed into her open mouth, applying the kiss of life. He looked up briefly to see Slayter standing beside him. Anne explained what had happened as Gerrard worked.

In helpless silence, they watched Gerrard trying to breathe life back into the ashen girl. For long minutes he took deep gulps of the hot, hazy air and blew back into the girl's open mouth. Every few breaths, he stopped to feel for a pulse in the neck.

Then he put one hand over the other on the front of her chest and pushed quickly and hard against her rib cage in a rhythmic series of jerks. He felt again for a pulse.

Finally, after about fifteen minutes, he straightened up exhausted, sweat pouring down his face.

He looked at the others but no one spoke. Then he got to his feet, picked up the girl's slight body, carried it over onto the planks between the trestles, and covered it with his coat.

Anne was shaking, her hands to her face. Gerrard took her gently by the shoulders: "Anne, there's nothing else I could have done. The air down here—there's not enough oxygen."

"What about Hardy?" Slayter asked.

"He got the full force of the shock," Gerrard replied. "He's dead, quite dead." He pointed at Wendy's body on the planks. "He must have acted as a resistance; she got the current through him."

Gerrard walked over to the iron door. Slayter had managed to cut a three-inch slice around the outside of the lock.

"What is it?" said Gerrard. "The pressure?" He looked at the gauges on the cylinders.

Slayter nodded: "It's dropping fast. I'll go on till it gives out, but . . ." He shrugged his shoulders hopelessly and turned back to the door, replacing his goggles. The flare of the torch threw great dancing shadows on the ancient brick of the roof.

Finally, the cut in the sheet steel of the door reached around two sides of the lock. It was big enough to take the end of a crowbar. Gerrard motioned Slayter aside. Slayter snapped off the acetylene torch and took off his goggles.

"Right," said Slayter. "Let's have a go; the gas is just about gone anyway." The two men jammed the chisel end of the crowbar into the gap. It didn't go in quite far enough and Gerrard went back for a hammer.

Then, while Slayter held the crowbar, he pounded the end until the tip was wedged solidly in the gap. They both started pushing against the end of the crowbar. The metal began to bend slightly.

"Once more." This time Gerrard flung all his weight against the crowbar and the lock bent a little farther away from the door. The two men strained and pushed with every ounce of weight and effort. Behind them Anne flung her weight against their backs to no avail.

The crowbar, when the men let go of it, remained sticking out of the door like an Indian arrow in the side of a covered wagon. They sank wearily against the far wall.

Anne pointed to one of the benches; they were made of heavy wood. "Can't we use one of those as a ram?"

Gerrard shook his head slowly. It was becoming difficult to concentrate in the congested atmosphere. All three were gasping and panting, their shirts wringing wet with sweat. Anne's blouse was plastered to her breasts.

"We could drive the bench against the crowbar," said Anne.

Gerrard looked at Slayter.

"Why not?"

Slayter shrugged wearily.

"O.K.," said Gerrard. He led the way over to the heavy bench and the three of them picked it up, staggering a little under the weight.

"Now," he said, "if we get a run from here and hit it at the far end, it might just do it."

They carried the heavy bench back, steadied themselves, and ran forward clumsily towards the crowbar. But the angle of the crowbar to the tunnel was narrow and they misjudged, stumbled ahead, and struck the door, jolting them into dropping the heavy bench and bringing them down into a tangle to the floor. As the bench went down it hit Slayter a glancing blow on the leg. He cried out in pain.

"One more try," said Gerrard. "I'll go in front." He went over to the end of the bench nearest the door and picked it up. Slayter, limping slightly, now took the end position, with Anne in the middle. This time they went back a shorter distance. Gerrard, his chest nearly bursting under the strain, surveyed it. "Right," he panted. "Now!"

They rushed forward, the bench at an angle to the corridor. Its end slammed into the crowbar at exactly the right spot. The crowbar appeared for a minute almost to leap out of the door but held and swung suddenly back against the wall of the tunnel. There was a loud crack, and as they stumbled back, they saw that the door had bent away from the lock and opened one of the riveted seams. There was a gap just wide enough to get a hand through.

Gerrard reached through the gap and felt for the long securing lever. Very slowly, using every ounce of his effort, his body braced against the tunnel wall, he pushed it over. The bolts grated back and the door slowly creaked open.

They were too exhausted to feel any elation. A wave of cool air flowed through the opening and they gratefully opened their clothes to cool down. Ahead of them, only just visible, was a short tunnel ending in a flight of steps leading upwards out of sight.

As they reached the bottom of the steps Gerrard flashed his light up. At the top was a door. Another door, and just as securely locked.

"Oh no," said Anne. "Please don't let it be locked."

Gerrard almost flung himself up the steps, ignoring his aching muscles. He reached the handle and pulled hard. It was locked! Slayter limped up beside him.

"There's got to be a way through here," Gerrard flung himself against the door.

"Not through this one," Slayter wearily shook his head.

"The torch?" said Gerrard.

"No gas left."

"Another cylinder?"

"There aren't any. I looked," said Slayter. He turned away tiredly and slouched back through the tunnel, his shoulders hunched.

Gerrard slumped down to a sitting position, looking at the door which had so cruelly cut off their hope of escape. It was unbelievable. There they were, in the heart of a great city, trapped in what amounted to a subterranean cave. Thus far, there was light, water, even a little food. But how long would they have to remain? What was happening on the surface?

For a moment Gerrard closed his eyes and pictured the London he had seen in old newsreels of the blitz: empty shells of buildings gutted by fire and explosions, cordoned-off roads running with water from burst mains; flares of gas blazing through rubble. He forced his mind to switch away from the prospect, then felt a soft touch on his shoulder.

"Wake up, wake up, Luke." Anne was bending over him, a hand on his shoulder.

"Where's Slayter?"

"Flaked out on one of the benches. Come on back."

"No," said Gerrard. "It's cooler out here."

Anne shivered. "It's like an oven in there now," she said. "Is there really danger of us running short of oxygen?"

"The fire will consume as much oxygen as it needs . . ." said Gerrard. Then he checked himself. If you must speculate, he told himself, keep it to yourself.

Anne looked at him curiously. "Go on," she said.

"It's not important," said Gerrard, wearily shaking his head.

She coloured: "I resent being treated like an empty-headed nit. Please tell me what you mean!"

"I didn't say . . ." began Gerrard.

"Never mind," said Anne. She turned away, chewing her knuckle.

Gerrard stared ahead and shrugged his shoulders.

Anne shifted restlessly. "I'm going back down. It's draughty here."

Gerrard was too weary to argue. She got up and walked back down into the main chamber.

Amazing, thought Gerrard, all through the action she hardly turns a hair. Now it's a matter of sitting and waiting, she takes umbrage at practically everything I say. Draughty? From where? He looked over to the far wall of the tunnel. There was a draught. It was blowing over his hand.

He wet his finger and held it up. It was cold on the side nearest the wall. He picked up the torch and went over to find the source. The wall was rough, probably built around the turn of the century. The bricks were a uniform grey, and the mortar between had crumbled to a powdery chalk. The surface was thickly covered with the dust of years, cobwebs, and a whitish limestone deposit from seepage. He moved the torch along the wall, looking for a chink.

There had been a doorway of some sort. The bricks were a slightly different shade and had obviously been used to seal up an old exit. Near the bottom he found a missing brick. He bent down, shone his torch, and peered through. The bricks were in a single layer, and on the other side he could just make out what appeared to be a passageway. The air felt cold on his eye and fresh compared to the stale air in the chamber. It wouldn't take much to break these bricks down. Perhaps . . .

He became aware that Anne was squatting beside him.

"I'm a cow," she said. "Sorry, it's all this . . ."

Gerrard brushed it aside. "Forget it," he said. "Look!"

Anne bent down and put her eye to the crack. "Can we get through?" she asked.

"There are two picks back there, I saw them. Is Slayter still out?"

"Yes."

Gerrard glanced at his watch. "He's been out for what, twenty minutes?"

"About that," said Anne.

"Give him another fifteen, then we'll wake him. I'll start on this."

Gerrard walked back and took the two picks back to the bricked-up archway. He spat on his hands and looked at them reflectively. It was a long time since he had used a pick and shovel.

He raised the pick, one hand at the bottom of the haft, the other one by the head, and swung it against the wall.

The first blow yielded a cloud of dust which shot back into Gerrard's eyes. Nettled, he swung back and buried the pick into the brickwork with his full force. This time there was a satisfying crash as some dozen bricks parted company from the rest and tumbled inward into the sealed-up tunnel. Behind him Anne was about to attack another section of the wall. Gerrard stopped her as she was about to swing the pick over her head.

"I don't want to have to carry you with a hole in your foot." He took the pick firmly away from her and set it down. "Now stand back and admire my muscles."

"Oh, balls!" Anne stood back angrily and watched him as he swung the pick against the wall. This time such a large section of bricks parted company from the rotten mortar that he almost fell through the hole. Anne laughed loudly.

"Noisy bastard." Slayter was standing behind them. "How the hell do you expect anyone to sleep with this racket going on?"

Gerrard disentangled himself from the débris and stepped back. "Look," he said.

Slayter picked up the torch and flashed it into the hole. It lit up another arch and blackness beyond.

"Quite a labyrinth," said Anne.

Slayter took the second pick, and between them they enlarged the hole until it was big enough to crawl through. The clean air revived them.

"Almost good enough to breathe," said Slayter, drawing in deep lungfuls.

"It's musty," Anne shuddered, "like a tomb."

"Bound to smell like that," said Slayter. "Been shut up for ages," he looked at the brickwork, "might even be prewar."

"Is it safe to breathe? I read somewhere about trapped gas in old lime kilns . . ."

"We've no option," said Gerrard. "Let's get the stuff together." They went back into the chamber. Among the tools was a plumber's basket and Anne filled it with what remained of the food and water.

Slayter took one or two tools, a large screwdriver, and a large spanner and stuck them in his belt. Gerrard turned and made the climb up to the stationmaster again.

As he got to the top of the ladder he saw that the stationmaster was deeply asleep, wheezing heavily. His face was running with sweat. The fire must have been still raging in the first level, but Gerrard saw that the smoke had diminished.

Gerrard briefly felt the stationmaster's pulse, then climbed back down to join the others.

They were waiting at the doorway to the other tunnel.

He glanced at Wendy's body. His coat was missing off the body, which was covered with a sheet of old tarpaulin. As he hurried back, Anne was waiting with the coat. Without a word she gave it to him. Somehow this touched him. To have gone back to the dead girl and taken the coat off her must have cost her quite a bit, but she had probably reasoned that he would be unlikely to do it himself and he needed the coat.

Gerrard switched on the torch and they started through the archway. After they had scrambled awkwardly through the narrow bolt-hole, they finally emerged into a large railway tunnel. In the now dimming light of the torch they could see that there were no rails, just old dusty sleepers. The air felt as if it had been still for years.

"Which way now?" asked Anne.

"There's a slight draught from this side. Come on," said Gerrard. They turned and walked into the draught. The tunnel section was straight but had a steep downhill gradient, and then a curved section. They walked on and came out by a bent and rusting iron grille, like the bars of a prison cage. Gerrard reached forward and tugged at one of the bars. It broke and crumbled away in his grasp. Quickly he broke off three more bars and then shone his torch forward into the dark.

"Can't see anything," he said, then his voice echoed as from a large chamber. "Hey," he shouted; again the echo.

He eased himself through the bars, feeling the way carefully with his feet. The others followed.

"What on earth is it?" Anne whispered. Her whisper echoed. In the torchlight they could see they were in a tube station. But it was old, musty, and deserted.

They imagined the long-gone passengers and the roar and clatter of trains. Now it was empty, silent, and thick with dust. The atmosphere overawed them and no one spoke as they crept forward.

"Maybe there are some switches," said Anne as Gerrard flashed the torch around.

"Let's see which station it is," said Slayter.

Gerrard flashed the torch along the wall, past some posters, and on to the sign. It read: *Gray's Inn.* The enamelled steel of the sign was chipped and rusty.

"Gray's Inn!" said Slayter.

"There's no station called that, is there?" said Anne.

"It's been disused since World War II," said Slayter. "That's why there was no track in the tunnel. They took it up."

They moved warily along the platform. Farther along was a group of posters. The first, badly yellowed and stained and slightly torn at one corner, was clearly recognizable. It was a David Langdon cartoon headed "Billy Brown of London Town." Underneath was a drawing of a natty, bowler-hatted commuter sitting in a railway carriage and restraining a man sitting beside him who was pulling off some lace-like material which covered the windows. The caption read: "I trust you'll pardon my correction, that stuff is meant for your protection." Some long-forgotten wag had added in heavy black pencil: "Thank you for your information, I'd like to see the bloody station."

At another time, reflected Gerrard, it might have been funny. Now there was something horrific about this echo from a long-dead past with its memories of the war and the blitz. He shone his torch farther down the poster; at the bottom it said: "Printed by the Ministry of Information."

"It's a wartime poster," said Slayter. "I read about it; that's the stuff they used to cover tube windows with to stop them being blown out by bomb blast."

"Do you mean the station hasn't been used since then?" said Anne.

"Wasn't there some kind of tube disaster during the war?" Slayter said. "There were hundreds of people killed in a station which had been used as an air raid shelter."

Anne shuddered: "You think it was this one?"

"Possibly," said Slayter. "I think the bomb glanced down a ventilator shaft, blocked up the line. Let's have the torch a minute," he said to Gerrard. Gerrard passed it over and Slayter moved towards the far end of the platform, flashing the light on the walls as they went farther down.

There was a poster showing people in a railway carriage, two of them talking with expansive gestures, the third man, hidden behind his paper, had a moustache and a lank Hitler-type lock of hair flowing over his forehead. The caption was: "Careless talk costs lives."

They reached the end of the platform; ahead of them there was a sign marked *Way Out* and steps leading upwards. As they began to climb, they saw that there was a heavy fall of masonry. The stairs were completely blocked.

"That's were your direct hit was," said Gerrard. "It must have dropped down the shaft and blown in the roof."

"What about this end of the tunnel?" Anne asked. "It must go somewhere."

Slayter shone his torch into the blackness; it picked out a shelving heap of sand reaching from the trackway to the roof.

"Sand buffer!" Gerrard said. "Don't you remember? The stationmaster was telling us. When a line comes to an end they fill the tunnel with sand to stop trains over-running."

Anne was shivering: "Couldn't we rest a bit? I'm very cold."

The two men looked at each other. Slayter pointed: "There's a great pile of wood back there. We could build a fire."

"A fire!" Anne exclaimed. "Wouldn't it—the gas?"

Gerrard thought for a minute, then took out a lighter and, screwing his eyes up, struck it. The flame burned clearly, bending slightly over in the direction of the draught.

Slayter looked at him coolly: "That was an unforgivable risk."

"Yeah," said Gerrard. "And now we can build a fire."

"Won't it set light to everything else!" Anne queried.

"No, it's all stone and concrete," Gerrard replied.

"There's a good draught, the air's clean—it's a good idea. Let's collect up that wood. There's some old newspapers over there, O.K.?"

It took them only a few minutes to break up the wood and pile it over the ancient papers lying in the dust of the platform.

Anne picked up an old yellowed newspaper and read out the headline in the torchlight: "Russians win great victory at Stalingrad." She read the date at the top of the page: "January the sixteenth nineteen forty-three. If I wasn't so damn cold, I could enjoy this."

Soon the fire was burning up brightly, throwing a plume of smoke and sparks up to the station roof. Almost immediately, their spirits improved. They sat staring into the flames, their wet clothing steaming in the heat. The fire threw great dancing shadows on the curved roof of the station.

As the warmth soaked back into their tired bodies, complete fatigue overtook them. Slayter was the first. He was sitting against the wall of the station, his knees hunched against his chest. Slowly his head nodded forward until it rested on his knees; one arm dropped limply to the floor beside him.

Anne had brought a torn and dirty sheet of tarpaulin over to the fire. She was rigging it up on short lengths of plank as a screen against the steady cold air flowing past them.

She unzipped her skirt and took it off together with her blouse, coat, and slip and hung them on pieces of wood, huddling before the fire in her pants completely unself-consciously, as Gerrard noticed, despite the fact that her underclothes were almost transparent. In the bright light of the fire he could easily see the dark shape of her nipples and the dark smudge of hair between her thighs as she squatted forward over the fire.

Anne looked up at Gerrard and then snuggled close to him. He put his arm round her.

Suddenly she turned her face up to him. He kissed her, surprised to find a sudden spring of passion and response. She lay back and he looked down at her. Her hair scattered, her face pale in the firelight, farther down her body a dark gold as the shadows chased each other across her body.

She reached her arms up round his neck and pulled him down. His hand slowly passed down the length of her body from her shoulders, casually brushing over her breasts, over her flat stomach and thighs. Her hands on his body felt cold, almost impersonal, but with a light and delicate touch which he instantly responded to.

Suddenly he laughed and she murmured an inquiry into his ear.

"I don't know" said Gerrard. "It's just, here we are, underneath the middle of this city, lying beside a fire in a cave, half-naked, as naked as our ape ancestors."

"Don't," she said beginning to laugh with him. "Please don't start me off; we'll wake Slayter."

"I can't help it," said Gerrard and he roared and roared with laughter, rolling away from her in the process. Her body was almost bent double with the effort to restrain her giggles, and the two of them, unable to resist, roared helplessly until Gerrard felt the tears streaming down his face.

"You . . . bastard," said Anne, gasping between her laughter. "You unromantic bastard."

Beside them Slayter stirred and jerked upright in astonishment. "God," he said, "that's all we need."

The expression on his face set them off again and, after a moment of astonished bewilderment, Slayter joined in.

"For God's sake, what's so damned funny?" Slayter gasped.

"He wants to play caveman," said Anne. She turned away and started dressing, putting on her now-dry clothes.

"Not a bad idea," said Slayter. "Let me know when it's my turn to play."

"It's time we got the hell out," said Gerrard.

"Quiet," said Anne. "Listen, I can hear something."

"What?"

They fell silent. Gerrard felt his scalp crawl. All

they could hear was the hiss and snap of the damp wood in the fire.

"Not that," Anne said. "It's somewhere else."

She suddenly crouched down and put her ear to the platform. "Yes, there it is. Listen!"

Gerrard bent down and put his ear against the concrete of the platform. He heard a noise which he realized had been part of the atmosphere of the station from the first but which he had been too tired to isolate from the other sounds before. It was a soft hissing and bubbling. It was coming from underneath the platform.

"Let's see if there's a crack, then we can have a look underneath," said Gerrard.

He picked up the torch. Slayter took a burning brand from the fire and followed him. They searched over the surface of the platform. Finally, they discovered a broken iron manhole cover.

Gerrard bent down and put his face closer to the gap. Suddenly, he grimaced, coughed, and drew back. "God, what an awful stench!"

Slayter bent down and sniffed and drew back retching.

"What is it?" Anne gasped.

Slayter thought for a moment. "Why didn't we smell it down the other end of the platform?"

"Draught's going the other way," replied Gerrard. He shone the torch down into the manhole again. "There's a flow, the whole lot's moving in one direction, look!"

The others peered down, hands over their noses. Just visible in the dim light was a seething mass of bubbling, brownish slime. It was moving steadily in one direction.

"This platform must be hollow underneath," said Slayter.

"Right," said Gerrard. "That smell, I know it—somewhere. Where? Goddamn it!" He banged his fist into his palm in concentration. "Of course! The plastic—the decaying cables in the tube and the gears from the robot."

"You're right," Anne said quietly, "you're absolutely

right." She ran back to the fire and disentangled the now-empty canister. She looked at the two men. "Your belt, please," she said to Slayter.

Slayter took his belt off and gave it to her. She tied the end round the handle of the canister and lowered it until it touched the foaming liquid underneath. She let the belt slacken until it submerged, then pulled it up full. The liquid inside was in a perpetual state of movement, bubbling and hissing. Anne carried it back over to the fire, brought out her handbag, and took out a small bottle of cologne which she emptied and shook dry. After cleaning the inside with a tissue on a pencil she then carefully filled it with liquid in the can. Held up against the firelight, the contents were turbid and yellowish. Even in the small bottle it hissed and foamed. She carefully wiped the outside dry with a tissue from her bag. She screwed on the metal cap until it was tight, then unscrewed it by one half-turn.

Gerrard took it from her. "Let's do an experiment," he said. "Let's see what happens."

He felt in his pocket and brought out a cheap plastic ball-point pen. This he placed in the now half-empty canister with the top protruding above the level of the writhing fluid. Slayter remained squatting over the manhole, looking down.

They both went back over to him. "It leads away beyond the end of the platform," he said, puzzled. "The current's quite strong."

"Could it be connecting with one of the underground rivers?" asked Anne. "They have them here, don't they? Doesn't the Fleet run underground at this part of London?"

"Could be," said Slayter hesitantly. "Or it could be the effluent from a busted sewer; smells like it, anyway."

Gerrard went back to the fire and looked into the canister. He shouted out. The others came running.

He bent down and slowly pulled out the pen. The top half was slightly soft and his fingers deformed the plastic slightly but the bottom half had now almost melted away from the metal core. As he pulled it out, its whole shape started dripping away like wet paint.

The liquid in the canister was dyed with the blue colour of the pen.

"I don't understand," said Anne. "What is it?"

"I'm not completely sure," said Gerrard. "But whatever it is it obviously contains the agent that is attacking plastic. This could well be the source of it all."

Suddenly, he plunged his hand in the liquid and held it there.

"Don't! What are you doing?" Anne cried out. "You don't know what's in it."

"Let's find out," said Gerrard.

He held his hand in for another few seconds, pulled it out, and studied it carefully. He dried it off on a handkerchief, which he threw away. He turned to the others: "It feels O.K. I'm going down."

"What! Under the platform?" asked Anne. "You don't know how deep it is."

"It can't be all that deep," said Gerrard. "It's only about three feet down to the level of the track. Anyway, we'll soon find out." He strode back over to the hole, the others following.

"What the hell are you up to?" asked Slayter.

"Tell you in a minute, I hope," he replied. He swung himself over the edge of the hole and lowered his feet gingerly into the angry liquid. It came up just over his waist. The smell almost made him vomit and the current was quite strong. He took the torch from Slayter.

As he ducked down under the rim of the manhole the bubbling and hissing seemed all about him, in his face. He slowly moved forward, shuddering as his feet touched various submerged objects.

Eventually, when he'd walked, as he judged, about half the length of the platform, he found what he was looking for. There was a close mesh grille set low in the wall and the bubbling liquid was streaming through it. It was almost entirely clogged with various bits of débris and the liquid was hissing through into a dark hollow. He steeled himself to put his hand down under the surface and started feeling along the edge of the grille.

The next few minutes seemed the longest of his life

as he brought up various sodden objects and examined them in the light of the torch before discarding them again. His stomach felt gripped by a large hand and he wondered if he could suppress the almost uncontrollable urge to vomit.

Eventually he found what he had been looking for, put it in his pocket, turned round, and began wading back. The level seemed to have risen slightly and was now soaking the front and side of his jacket. When he'd almost reached the underside of the manhole he could hear Anne's voice echoing down: "Luke, Luke!"

The dreadful, cloying smell had now affected him almost to the point of collapse. He was just able to pull himself up onto the surface of the platform only to flop down, exhausted, on the concrete.

Anne bent down beside him and reached out her hand, but he pushed it weakly away. "Don't! I'm a bit untouchable right now. I've got it—two of them." He fumbled weakly in the pocket of his suit and drew out two small, disc-shaped objects. He held them out in the palm of his hand.

"I don't quite . . ." she began.

Slayter craned forward. Anne peered more closely.

"The bottle tops—the bio-degradable bottle tops! Of course! The first people who bought the licence—they had metal inserts made to go into the plastic. They—yes—here it is." She pointed to an interwoven monogram embossed on the metal.

"Couldn't they belong to anything else?" asked Slayter.

"Unlikely," said Anne. She looked at Gerrard. "That's what you were looking for, isn't it?"

"Yes," said Gerrard.

"Then you suspected it all along?" said Anne.

"Logically, there was no other explanation," Gerrard went on. "That bio-degradable bottle was made so that it would break down with light and air to a compound which could be consumed by bacteria. This compound is a half-way structure between plastic and protein, O.K.? Well, I think bacteria fed on this compound and then mutated to feed on other plastics. Each generation growing more efficient and more omnivorous than the last."

"But what kind of bacteria?" asked Slayter.

"I think the answer lies down there," said Gerrard. "It's something that has evolved from the sewage. The bio-degradable bottles found their way into the sewage as intended, and whatever bacteria were in the sewage developed an appetite for this kind of plastic. It then started foraging for other forms of plastic to consume and mutated to the point where it could eat them."

He turned to Anne. "Think now. Do you know of any new type of bacteria that has been used, say, for disposal of sewage?"

Anne nodded. "There was one, I can't think what it's called," she said. "But I know about two years ago I was going to do an article on some bacteria called *B. accelerens*. It was developed at the Reading Sewage Works. It was said to break down sewage faster than any other bacteria. It had an almost exponential growth rate. But it didn't eat plastic. It's impossible surely. Anyway, they gave up the project. But how did the sewage get to," she paused, "plastic wires?"

"Obviously," said Gerrard, "whatever the original channel of the sewage is, it wasn't underneath this platform. Therefore it's found a new outlet. I'm only guessing," he said, "but I imagine that somewhere along the route it came into contact with some plastic cables. Once the stuff gets into the plastic, its growth rate is phenomenal and it wouldn't take long for the degradation to spread right along its length, out of the sewer system, and down here. There are hundreds of seepage points in the underground. Nobody knows where they all are."

"Then from the cables to plastic gas pipes and water mains and . . . eventually to the computer governing my traffic system," said Slayter.

"Right."

"My God," said Slayter. "If that's true, there's no way of stopping it that I can see."

"I don't know," said Gerrard, "and right now I'm incapable of thinking any further. What we've got to do is to take these samples up above ground and fast. God only knows what things are like up there now."

"How are we going to do it?" said Anne.

"The draught," said Gerrard. "That must give us the way out of here. It must be coming from somewhere. We've got to find where."

11

Gerrard's reasoning had been nearly correct, but in one respect he was quite wrong!

He had, in fact, discovered Ainslie's bacillus.

It is usual practice for bacteriologists who discover a new strain to have their names attached to it. It is a minor and rather droll form of immortality and often the only way in which the desiccated ego of a backroom worker can find sustenance.

Ainslie's bacillus had never reached the textbooks. It was, in fact, known only to Ainslie.

Two and a half years before Gerrard and his party were trapped, Ainslie had begun work:

Dr. Simon Ainslie only had one really good idea during the whole of his academic career. It occurred just after the main drain leading from his house blocked solid, and as he was slopping about in gumboots trying rather ineffectually to clear the stoppage with a flexible rod, he found the cause of the obstruction to be a crumpled fragment of polythene sheet, probably flushed down the lavatory by one of his children.

Dr. Ainslie was a bacteriologist.

A mild man by nature, he had never striven particularly hard to climb the academic ladder and was, in late middle age, stuck at the level of senior lecturer in the microbiology department of a London teaching hospital.

Dividing his time equally between routine hospital specimens and giving rather dull lectures to medical students who had begun to scare him with their sense of youth and attack, he often set up rather whimsical experiments in the forlorn hope that he might get enough original material together for a publication.

Poking the polythene sheet out of the drain, it occurred to him that the plastic would have remained in the drain for perhaps a thousand years, that it would never have broken down like ordinary sewage under bacterial attack.

Bacterial attack!

The idea was born. What if bacteria could be induced to attack plastic debris? What if they could be specially tailored by culture and reculture, by genetic mutation with properly designed nucleic acids? What an answer to the problem of garbage pollution. A major world-disposal problem would be solved. His fantasies grew until his carefully acquired critical faculty began to take over.

What about the number of generations necessary? How could he get hold of the equipment? What sort of D.N.A. or R.N.A.?

As he dropped the drain cover back with a clang, his momentary excitement had almost disappeared.

Later on that evening, after his customary glass of dry sherry, the idea recurred and took root. Eased by the drink, he poured himself another—a much larger one—and started to write. Tentatively at first, then with increasing speed, the project sped down onto paper. The idea was valid; it could be made to work.

Midnight came and still he worked on. Finally it was all written and he relaxed into indulgent fantasies of an F.R.S. or even a Nobel Prize.

A week later he still hadn't told anyone, but he believed totally in the idea. He kept it absolutely to himself. If it worked, scientific honour was his at last.

Gradually he began to collect equipment from the lab and take it home. In his study, he started to build apparatus; to set up incubators and tube racks until he had a complete bacteriological work bench. A replica of his hospital laboratory layout on a small scale.

He began to work furiously. Cutting short his lectures at the hospital, he left work earlier and earlier in the evening. He developed a spring in his walk and an air of preoccupation which led his hospital colleagues to suppose that he had acquired a mistress. In fact he sped home on the first available train, and with a cursory word to his wife, locked himself almost immediately into his study laboratory and went to work. Starting with a well-known germ called *Bacillus prodigiosus,* he began experiments to change its nature.

Growing it first of all in its normal culture material, he then began to alter the constituents so that the generations of bacteria began to change their nature. He starved the bacteria of their normal protein food and began to substitute the protein with various materials whose structure resembled the long-chain molecules of plastic.

Every few days, he would secretly take one of the dishes of cultured bacteria with him to the hospital and subject it to radiation from a small radioactive cobalt source which was kept in the hospital laboratory for other experiments.

After the radiation, he would take the treated bacteria back to his home and re-culture them on different media, in the hope that one of the mutations induced by the radiation would be able to adapt to the consumption of plastic.

Like all men wedded to an original idea which means too much to them personally, he began slowly to imagine results. There was no question of fakery, just the nudging of a figure here and the realignment of an experiment there, so that they would better suit his original notion.

As the months wore on, he gave less and less attention to his hospital work and lived only for his small laboratory bench in his house, and although he was not consciously aware of it, his body and mind came under increasing strain. He had no means of knowing, for example, that his left-middle cerebral artery was constricted by a large patch of cholesterol, or atherosclerosis, as his colleagues would have called it. Also, he simply hadn't the time to recongize that his increasingly frequent frontal headaches were due to a steadily rising blood pressure.

One evening, at about eleven o'clock, he had almost finished examining the fifty-ninth variation of *B. prodigiosus* under the microscope. There were, in all, six sample tubes, and as he finished looking at the contents each one, he carefully lowered it into a large beaker of very strong disinfectant.

He did this because he was a careful and highly trained worker and did not want to risk the possibility of accidental release of the mutant bacteria. The results of his investigations were encouraging, at least to his biased eyes. There seemed to be definite evidence of plastic consumption by the carefully tailored organisms.

As he came to the last tube, he suddenly gave a great cry of triumph.

There was no doubt!

The bacteria had consumed a visible amount of the plastic-like material.

His excitement mounted, but as he rose, his already over-stressed middle cerebral artery burst, releasing a fountain of blood into his over-stressed brain tissue.

For an instant, he stood there as his brain function began to stop. As his vision faded and his life ebbed, he was dimly and terminally aware of a terrible pain and a roaring sound in his head.

His body remained poised for an instant more, then crashed heavily backwards against the laboratory bench. The tube of bacteria flew out of his lifeless hand and smashed down on the edge of the sink, a thin trickle of yellowish opaque fluid running down the side of the porcelain and reaching the waste pipe.

Ainslie's body rolled limply off the bench and crashed heavily to the floor, bringing his wife running from the living room.

As she reached the door the fifty-ninth mutant of *Bacillus prodigiosus* had flowed down the waste pipe, past the drain where the blockage had been, and reached the main street sewer. In the flushing water, the hundreds of millions of bacteria which had been present in the tube were diluted and diluted again as the sewage water rushed away to the pumping station.

Ainslie's death was marked in the hospital magazine and in the *British Medical Journal* by short, factual obituaries accompanied by an over-young photograph. He was soon forgotten. But in the months that followed, the fifty-ninth mutant lived a brief existence in the sewers and then began to disappear. Unable to find the specialized food which Ainslie had designed for it, it ceased to be able to divide and died. But not all the individual bacteria was wiped out. Some formed spores.

When bacteria are subjected to hostile conditions they revert to a resting phase called a *spore*. It is really like a seed. So when conditions are favourable once again, the spore germinates and forms a new bacterium which then divides into two, into four, into eight, and so on, forming a new generation. Spores can last for hundreds of years and are almost totally resistant to drying and quite strong heat or cold.

Deep in a storm-relief sewer near King's Cross Station, about a hundred spores lay in a dried patch just above the water line. Each one only two thousandths of a millimetre in diameter, each containing a perfect biological blueprint for the fifty-ninth mutant of *Bacillus prodigiosus*. A silent and microscopic testimony to Ainslie's one original thought, they lay embedded in a dried patch of sewage, waiting with all the mindless patience of suspended life. Waiting for specialized food which would never come. Waiting for the infinitely small possibility that another molecule of similar size and shape to the food they needed would eventually find its way into the dark fetor of the sewer and so give them energy to start into full life once more.

Two years after Dr. Ainslie had passed into obscurity, the Kramer group's bio-degradable bottle had gone into general use by the public. Down into the sewers went the fragmenting containers. Down into the rushing effluents from a million drains floated the specialized molecules of Degron.

One evening, after a heavy rain storm, the water in the storm-relief sewer at King's Cross rose rapidly to an unprecedented height. The molecules of Degron, almost exactly similar to those of Ainslie's special culture medium, splashed over the dried spores.

For almost twenty-four hours, the spores remained dormant. Then, in a blind but totally efficient way, they began to recognize the properties of the material outside their desiccated shells.

The spore cases broke and the fifty-ninth mutant of *Bacillus prodigiosus* emerged and expanded into life.

Conditions were to its liking. It burgeoned and spread. Everywhere it flowed, it found food. Degron was everywhere. Each generation became more versatile and more omnivorous. Man had been good to mutant 59. He had provided it with food for a millennium.

The Kramer laboratory was dark except for neon indicator lights glowing on the congested blocks of electronic equipment lining the walls. The only sound came from a single refrigerator pump softly whirring in one corner. Buchan walked over and pulled the main switches. The room flooded with light, helping to dispel the tension they both felt.

"Where are they?" Scanlon asked.

Without answering, Buchan opened the door of an incubator and took out a rack of clear glass flasks, each one labelled with a felt pen symbol. He was tense and clumsy: "May not have been long enough. I had to do it in a hurry."

"Perhaps you'd tell me what you *have* done. Anyway, what about Wright?"

"Never mind about that, bear with me." Buchan held each flask in turn up to the light and made short notes on a desk pad. He appeared not to notice Scanlon's presence at all.

"Buck!" Scanlon complained. "It's two in the morning. I said I'd come down; now tell me what the hell you're doing?"

"Aye, I treat you badly, but I've put a lot of money on this. Let me show you what I've done." He pointed to the flasks in turn: "This is an aqueous suspension of the goo Gerrard got from the bits out of the robot, number two here is the same, except it's been sterilized in the autoclave."

"Sterilized, why?"

"You'll see in a minute. Number three is a standard broth-culture medium and I put some of number one—the unsterilized material—into it. Number four is the same broth culture, but I added some of the sterilized material. Now look!"

He held up the rack against the light. The first two flasks contained a slightly yellow fluid, the third was an opaque brown colour and was topped by a thin layer of foam. The fourth was clear and light brown.

"Remember, number three got the unsterilized stuff and number four the sterilized, O.K.?"

"Yes."

"Don't you see, man, number three got the raw stuff—it's grown?"

"That's just not a complete experiment," Scanlon complained. "When he took the original specimens he must have collected hundreds of different bacteria. There could be any one of a hundred different species in number three there."

"Very well, I agree." He went back to the incubator and took out a stack of circular flat Petri dishes, each one like a glass ashtray with a close-fitting lid containing a thin layer of coloured jelly. He laid them out in a row. The lid of each dish was marked in red wax pencil.

"So far you're right, of course, so I did these. My technique's a bit rusty, it's a long time since Edinburgh."

He opened the lid of the first dish. Scanlon peered forward. On it he could see dozens of small round colonies of bacteria. There were many different shapes, sizes, and colours.

Buchan went on: "This is a sub-culture of the original specimen. You can see about four different species of colony." He was pointing with a small platinum-wire loop, fused on the end of a glass rod. "These are coliforms, these are probably staphs, those are probably diphtheroids, and these," he paused for a moment, "are interesting."

"It's what I told you," Scanlon persisted. "We've got a complete spectrum of bugs out of the original specimen."

"Yes we did, but plating out a mixture like this is a way of separating a lot of different bacteria. Once you can see different colonies, you can take a tiny bit of each one and identify it on a slide in a microscope."

"Not just by looking, surely?"

"No, by using gram-staining—various logically selective methods and media—it's like a crossword puzzle really—finally you end up with a clear case of identity!" He was excited, enjoying the description of the chase.

"Look," he continued, "I'll show you." He picked up another dish. "Finally I isolated this one." He pointed to a small group of wrinkled, glistening discs on the layer of jelly in one of the dishes. "This was the character I was after."

"Buck, it's very late, I'm losing the thread."

"Wait—all will be revealed. If you look carefully, the edges of each colony show little dried-up specks."

"So?"

"So, our wee friends here don't like the medium they're growing on—it's blood-agar by the way."

"They don't like blood?"

"Different bugs like different food, it's as simple as that. Anyway I identified all the sample bacteria except this one which wouldn't grow on conventional media: plain agar, blood-agar, McConochie's, and so on."

"So what did you do?"

"I made up my own medium."

Buchan walked over to an incubator and took out a larger beaker. On the bottom of the beaker, there was a small, squat, conical flask plugged with cotton wool. The top of the beaker was sealed with metal foil. He placed it gingerly on the bench underneath the light. Buchan looked down in amazement. Around the edges of the cotton wool, there was a slowly moving rim of foam pouring outwards and sliding stickily down the outer surface of the flask and collecting on the base of the beaker.

"God, what did you use?"

Buchan paused for several seconds before replying: "I chopped up some Degron—made it into a paste together with some salts and one or two amino acids, mostly tyrosine. . . ."

"This is pretty damning. There must be some other explanation."

"Such as?"

"Well," Scanlon was hesitating, frantically trying to find a logical way round the evidence. "All right, you've grown bacteria, some like blood, others like sugar . . ."

"Scanlon, there's one more experiment necessary for a proof situation. If you suspect a bug as the cause of a condition—a clinical condition anyway—you must be able to recover the bug in pure culture from the patient. Now the patient in this case is the plastic—O.K., you don't believe it, but it's true. So I took a culture from the muck in that flask there and put it up on more plastic." He opened the last of the Petri dishes. "And here it is." He showed him the surface of the gel in the dish. It was covered by wet, glutinous foam. "This time I used larger fragments of Degron and some ordinary polystyrene. Look, you can see the bits with the naked eye."

"How do you *know* it's bacteria? Couldn't it be—a chemical—some substance which carries through all these samples?" Scanlon felt the weakness of the suggestion even as he said it.

"It could just be. So there's still one more experiment. We can do it now if you'll help."

"What experiment?"

"The electron microscope. We can look and see what's in there. Come on." He got up and went towards a door labelled with the international radiation clover-leaf sign and a notice stating *Danger, High Voltage. No Unauthorized Admission.*

Inside, in the dim yellow light, the eight-foot-high column of the high-resolution electron microscope towered over them. From the apex of the column a thick high-tension cable led away to a six-foot cube of complex electronics.

From another unit came the soft, squashing, flapping sound of vacuum pumps, keeping the space inside the column of the instrument at a vacuum harder than outer space.

Buchan began to operate the controls. Lights sprang up on the control panels and the noise of the pumps changed to a more urgent, hard-working note.

Buchan got up. "We'll leave it pumping down, while we get the specimen ready."

In the lab he laid down a glass plate on the bench top and put the Petri dish containing the plastic medium on the glass. Then he cleaned a glass slide and waved it briefly through a Bunsen flame. With a small glass hand-dropper, he put one drop of distilled water on the glass plate.

Then, with a small platinum wire, heated first in the flame and allowed to cool, he carefully opened the lid of the Petri dish and took a small sample of the contents. This he mixed with the drop of distilled water on the slide until the whole drop turned milky, finally passing the platinum wire through the flame to sterilize it. He was talking as he worked. Scanlon looked on, fascinated by the almost priest-like ritual of the technique.

"What I'm doing now is to make a diluted sample of whatever's in that culture dish. Then, like this, I'm going to mix it with phospho-tungstic acid.

"So now I've got sample plus water plus phospho-tungstic. Now here I've got a wee copper grid—it's just three millimetres across. It fits into the microscope. Now I'm putting a small drop of the mixture on the grid."

He got up, carrying the grid on a filter paper. He opened a glass bell-jar attached to pumps; put the filter paper and grid inside, sealed the bell-jar on its base, and switched on the pumps. He sat carefully watching the vacuum gauge as it indicated the pressure of the atmosphere inside the jar.

"The vacuum inside there will dry off the water in

the drop. When the water's gone, the phospho-tungstic acid will dry down around whatever solid bodies are in the sample. Now, the electron microscope shows all biological objects to be almost transparent, but substances containing heavy metals look black."

"So everything biological will look like—let me think it out—like a clear area surrounded by a—yes—a black halo."

"Aye, you're a good visualiser, Jim. Now it should be about ready." He opened a valve, letting air back into the bell-jar. The hissing sound gradually died away. Lifting the bell-jar on its counter-weights, he took the filter paper with the grid and moved methodically over to the microscope room. Scanlon followed and closed the light, tight door behind them.

Buchan opened the specimen lock and inserted the grid. Then, deftly moving over the complex of controls, he ran the machine up to operating condition.

Finally, the screen inside the radiation-proof glass on the base of the column glowed green, under-lighting their faces as they peered at the image on the screen. Buchan turned the remote controls to the specimen high up on the column. The lines on the screen wavered and vanished, then hardened and fixed. For a long minute, the two of them sat quite silent, without speaking.

In front of them, on the screen, were hundreds of thousands of clear, rectangular spaces, each one surrounded by a dark halo. Each space the unmistakable electronic image—of bacteria.

"We'd better get Wright," Scanlon said.

Buchan reached for the telephone.

12

The emergency control room had been built in 1945. Over sixty feet down, beneath Horse Guards Parade, it formed part of an underground complex of tunnels, communication centres, and living quarters stretching as far north as Trafalgar Square and to the east under Whitehall to the War Office. An underground city from which an entire country could be run without anyone ever going to the surface.

Its walls were heavily buttressed by re-inforced concrete beams painted white and the floor was Government-issue green linoleum. At one end, almost the whole wall was covered by a back projection screen and in front of it was a jumble of desks littered with phones of different colours, scrambler controls, and closed-circuit television links. The rest of the room was occupied by hastily arranged rows of stacking chairs.

The air was now thick with smoke and filled by a loud excited buzz of conversation from about fifty people, some uniformed and others in the neutral anonymity of civil service grey. There was an atmosphere of suppressed tension and excitement.

Most of the faces were on the wrong side of fifty. Faces used to power, influence, and privilege. Men who would, rightly or wrongly, not flinch from taking grave decisions.

In the front row, a stocky man in the uniform of a Brigadier stood up and turned round, tapping his knuckle on a desk-top to gain attention. The conversation died away to silence almost reluctantly. He spoke in the relaxed manner of easy authority, hands deliberately in pockets.

"Gentlemen," he looked briefly at his watch, "I think we should begin." He walked over to a desk in front of the screen and pressed a buzzer.

"Most of you are more or less in the picture, I think, but first I want to introduce you to each other. You've all been brought here in great haste and for this I must apologize, but we have done our best to provide you with some quarters. Mr. Riggs over there"—he nodded to a civilian standing by one of the exits—"will provide you with a room card and instructions as to how to get there. The tunnel system is rather complex and I must ask you please to comply with the directions on the card, our—ah—security services are—enthusiastic." He smiled bleakly. "Now, you should all have a lapel badge, so if I may I'll kick off.

"The medical side of the operation is under the control of Sir Frank Dale," he pointed to a grey-haired, austere man in the second row, who half got to his feet in an embarrassed attempt to introduce himself. The Brigadier indicated each person as he spoke:

"Police matters and traffic control are in the hands of the Assistant Commissioner. Underground transport, Mr. Holland. Troop movements are under the command of General Fenwick here, assisted by myself and the decontamination centres are controlled by Dr. Fanning, Chief Medical Officer to the Greater London Council.

"You will have already seen the control suites; these run and inter-communicate according to the procedure laid down in the 'regional seats of Government' paper which I take it you've all read."

He looked up for assent; heads nodded.

"Now with your permission, sir"—he half turned towards General Fenwick, who waved a pudgy hand briefly—"we'll consider the region involved."

He pressed the buzzer on the desk, and behind him, the back projection screen filled with a green outlined map of Central London.

"Our reports indicate that most of the outbreak—whatever its nature—is confined to quite a limited area." He picked up a white pointer. "It seems to be bounded by the Euston Road to the north, as far west as the junction with Portland Place, and east as far as Woburn Place. These limits, of course, are only approximate. Again, southwards down Southampton Row around the Aldwych to the river, which forms the south perimeter. An area in all of some one and a half square miles.

"There have in fact been other outbreaks outside the area but these are few and far between and we believe that these can be dealt with without serious risk.

"According to the recent reports we've had, the process is spreading rapidly inside the area and it is now of the greatest urgency to contain it. To some extent we are helped by the weather, since the cold appears to slow down the rate of—er—reaction time . . ." he paused and looked over at the yellow parchment face of Sir Frank Dale for approval of the words, then continued: ". . . as it reaches the surface.

"Our whole aim," he tapped the desk for emphasis, "must be completely to isolate the area—on the surface, in the air, and underground. I don't need to remind you that if this plastic-destroying agent gets out into the world at large it could well bring things to a halt altogether. We must treat the area as a deadly plague zone.

"Now, from the point of view of troop movement. Since the state of emergency was signed at midday by Her Majesty, we have begun to deploy men around the perimeter.

"The First Battalion Scots Guards are in the process of sealing off the northwestern sector—here—and linking with three companies of the armoured division of the Horse Guards to the northeast—here." He tapped the screen for emphasis.

"Perimeter control of the south sector is under the over-all command of Colonel Sethbridge, who is bringing mobile units of the Parachute regiment into the area at this moment.

"At approximately twenty-three hundred hours, sealing of the zone should be complete and we shall be in a position to begin evacuation. As to support facilities, these are in the hands of the Service Corps, and the Royal Corps, of Signals." He paused for a moment surveying the audience for evidence of complete attention.

"As you know, electrical and gas power have failed in some sectors so emergency generators are being moved to the perimeter and cables run in to provide some emergency power supply—mainly for heat. Warm-air turbine generators are also being brought in as quickly as possible to provide heat. There are many old people resident in the zone who are entirely without any heating. Now that's basically the situation and now, if I may, I'd like to hand you over to Sir Frank Dale. He will explain the background to the affair. Sir Frank."

Dale got awkwardly to his feet and moved forward to the screen as the Brigadier sat down. He turned and surveyed the audience in silence for a moment, his expression suggesting some distaste at having to explain such elegant scientific matters to a lay audience. He spoke in a meticulous monotone without preamble.

"So far we have got very little specific information about this agent and its effect. From the practical standpoint, we know that through an intermediate substance of semi-proteinaceous nature in sewage it has evolved the increasingly widespread ability to attack a variety of plastic materials."

The audience settled back anxiously, trying to concentrate.

"Normally, bacteria grow relatively slowly, but in this case the lag and decline phases of growth have been—ah—replaced by an accelerated log phase. . . ."

A voice came irritably from the audience: "Sir Frank, I am sorry but I haven't understood a word of that. Could you please defer to our ignorance?" A muted murmur grew to support the objector.

Dale replied: "Mm? Oh, I see—yes—well, what it amounts to is that there has been a change in the rate of growth coupled with a truly extraordinary increase in rate of reproduction. Moreover, as each new generation strain appears, it seems able to attack a wider variety of plastic materials. As it feeds upon the plastic it produces large volumes of gas—an inflammable and explosive mixture as it so happens, mainly sulphuretted hydrogen and methane—this has been the root cause of the disastrous series of explosions we have experienced.

"I have advised the Home Secretary that my council have already taken over two disused wards in St. Thomas's Hospital—across the river from the south part of the affected zone—and these are being converted into research laboratories. We are already working on a twenty-four-hour basis to establish a means of destroying this quite fascinating organism.

"Immunology—that is to say serum use or inoculation—is obviously of no value, since humans and animals are not—as yet—infected, or affected, whichever way you like to look at it.

"We shall probably have to rely on widespread use of antibiotic sprays, but up till now we have been unable to find an antibiotic to which the organism is sensitive. In the meantime, we think that the best way of checking the underground spread is to fill the tube tunnels and sewers with an inert gas. So far we have found that reproduction can be diminished in rates by an atmosphere of nitrogen and carbon dioxide, and I understand," he looked over at the Brigadier, "that supplies of these gases are being assembled at all the main tube and sewer outlets. I must tell you that we have had to proceed on an entirely empirical base of experiment, since we have no precedents to go by. I hope to have more positive news for you in a day or so." He turned to the Brigadier. "I think that's all, thank you."

The Brigadier got to his feet. "Thank you, Sir Frank, and now, Commissioner, perhaps you could give us a brief rundown on the arrangements you have made."

The Assistant Commissioner, a slow-moving, ponderous man, walked slowly up to the desk carrying a small sheaf of papers. He spoke in an only slightly disguised cockney accent; an accent which his detractors said had grown broader as his rank grew higher. They said he used it to remind people of his beginnings as a constable, on the beat in Hackney. . . .

"Our main responsibility is to evacuate all people from the area as soon as possible. The procedure we shall use is, I think, fully described in the War Emergency Plans, which should have been circulated." He looked up as people nodded, looking among their papers to check. "You'll see from your photostats, there are three main de-contamination centres, these are being set up at Charing Cross, Euston, and St. Pancras railway stations.

"Dr. Fanning will tell you about these in more detail in a moment. I shall confine myself to the actual plans for moving people. Briefly we have residents and non-residents. As the barriers go up around the area, a lot of commuters, visitors to London, tourists, and so on won't be able to leave and so we have decided to get them out first.

"The Emergency Powers Act gives us full authority to requisition property and so we are telling all hotels in the area that we require them to set up as many beds as possible to accommodate people who don't live here —at least until we can get them out.

"The most urgent task is to move as many of the patients in the two main hospitals—University College and Charing Cross. Ambulances are in the area now and we hope to have as many of the—er—walking-wounded out by midnight tonight.

"A special decontamination centre is being set up here," he pointed to the projected map, "at Regent's Park Square, so that the patients can be treated separately. This gives us, according to the Emergency Bed Service, about two hundred and thirty empty hospital beds. If the emergency continues for any length of time, we expect to have to deal with a number of cases of sickness—hypothermia in the elderly and so on.

"Once the sick and the non-residents have been moved, we shall start on the residents. Everyone, of course, will have to go through the full de-contamination procedure before they're allowed out and our loud-hailer vans are touring the streets now, telling people what to do and distributing leaflets of instructions. This won't be complete for about sixteen or eighteen hours, and there is bound to be considerable confusion at first, I'm afraid.

"The most important single thing we can do at the moment is to make sure that people stay where they are. First of all to go to one of the emergency posts—get shelter and stay put. Sir Frank told me earlier that the more people move around, the more likely they are to spread this thing, whatever it is, so my people have been told to clear the streets. Obviously some folk will have to be about—doctors and so on—and we are arranging to provide them with some form of identification.

"The whole situation, I'm afraid, will be an extremely attractive proposition to the criminal fraternity, and we are bound to have an increase in various sorts of crime.

"As to crowd control, we don't anticipate much trouble but to be forearmed, so to speak, we have arranged with Brigadier Powell for an adequate supply of riot-control apparatus. This has already been issued to the 'Teeth' arms on the periphery, and we ourselves are bringing in protective shields, rubber bullet projectors, and C.S. canisters. These will be stockpiled at the emergency posts.

"Now, Dr. Fanning, I believe you have some data on de-contamination?"

As the Commissioner stepped down, there was an excited murmur of conversation as the various specialists began to compare notes and papers.

Fanning, a tall athletic man in his thirties, jumped easily up onto the dais and cleared his throat to gain attention, waiting impatiently for the noise to die down.

He talked fluently in an easy, extrovert style: "Well, de-contamination is really terribly simple. All you need to do basically is to sterilize everybody.

"Our problem in de-contamination is really similar to barrier nursing of a dangerously infective case in a hospital. Basically each unit is like a valve. As people go through it one way, they have to be parted from their clothing; they have to shower and have to be given new clothes. Unlike a valve, though, this is a two-part process. People coming out have to strip completely, shower down, and wait while their clothes are sterilized in an autoclave—that's a high-pressure steam oven. Now, in this case, we shan't be able to do this in time, so people are being asked to come in old clothes, which will be labelled and sterilized, and after showering they will be given new—that is—new-old clothing on the safe exit side. We are asking people outside the area to bring old clothes they don't want, and—er—Oxfam have said they will help in this respect.

"We chose railway stations for the de-contamination centres because this gives us a highly controllable form of transport to take people away from the area. Also, trains are easier to keep separate from unaffected parts of the city. Now perhaps if I can give you a little more detail about . . ."

The Brigadier glanced impatiently at his watch and said firmly, "Well, thank you—er—very much, Dr. Fanning, I am sure that's helpful. Now, time is getting on so," he looked briefly at a list of names, "Mr. Holland, have you anything to add from the transport angle?"

Holland sat nervously picking his thumb and trying not to think about the rising acid in his stomach.

"Er, nothing at the moment," he replied, "except to say that this sealing-off will obviously have a very serious effect on traffic elsewhere. In fact, our computers are already showing jams as far out as thirty miles." He paused.

"Effectively we have taken the centre out of a radial flow system, and although diversions are being set up, our estimate is that they will only carry fourteen per cent of the normal load. There's nothing else we can do at the moment. All tubes are stopped in the area, of course, and all we can do is to run to-and-fro shuttle services to the periphery of London.

"If you look at this underground map," he pressed the buzzer and the tube map flashed up on the screen, "you can see that the area cuts through every major line except the Bank branch of the Northern. Since the source of the infection seems to be centred in disused sections of the track, we have thought it better to close off the whole system except at the periphery.

"The military, I understand, are sending men down to work in towards the centre of the area, using flame-throwers to sterilize as they go. This may not of course be possible in some areas, since accumulations of gas may provide too great a risk. I think that's all for the moment." He stepped down.

The Brigadier looked at a paper and said, "Now Mr. Hantrey from the G.L.C. Sanitation will tell us about the position regarding sewage."

A small, dapper man got neatly to his feet behind Holland and started talking quickly as he walked up to the dais: "A few essential points. The affected area lies over the west-east middle-level sewer feeding northeast-wards into the Abbey Mills pumping station at Stratford. Now, you've already been told that all sewage from the area will stop. That's because everybody inside has been told not to use their drains or lavatories. But we still have to pump sewage from parts west of the area up to the northern outfall at Beckton."

He pressed the buzzer and a map showing the main drainage system of Central London replaced the picture of the de-contamination centre. It showed a fantastic inter-woven complex of lines almost as dense as a street map.

He wielded a pointer and went on: "The only north-south sewer under the area is the Savoy Street branch. This is quite small and can easily be closed off at the Euston Road end. The problem really is the diversion of material from the west. We thought first of using the Fleet storm-relief system and the Northern high level, but this is impracticable for reasons due to the power of the pumps at the Lots Road.

"Another possibility was the Piccadilly branch and the Ranelagh storm-relief system, but once again we are in trouble with branches from the affected area which we shall be unable to close off."

He paused for a moment, almost savouring the effect of what he was going to say.

"So we have concluded that, since we can't be sure that people in the area won't put some contaminating material down the drain, we shall have to close the main middle-level system completely. This means, I'm afraid, that material from the north and west will have to be diverted into the storm-relief system and—voided direct into the Thames."

Above the immediate burst of conversation which followed, Sir Frank Dale's voice could be heard protesting: "But, good God, man, you can't do that; the health hazard will be enormous, don't you realize? There are dozens of communicable diseases—we'd have a dozen epidemics. . . ."

Hantrey replied patiently: "Sir Frank, we have *no* alternative; there is just nowhere else we can put the material. . . ."

"Aren't there storage ponds or something?"

"Yes, but these couldn't possibly handle more than about ten per cent of the volume. We simply have to pump it into the river—there's no alternative."

Sir Frank spoke almost petulantly. "I warn you, we shall have serious outbreaks of . . ."

The Brigadier hastily got to his feet; he spoke placatingly: "Thank you, Mr. Hantrey, that's most helpful. Sir Frank, I think it would be best if we continued this particular discussion after we break. I think we need more data and I understand"—he turned to an aide who nodded—"that a Port of London officer will be here shortly to give us some data about tidal flow and so on —so may we do that?"

Dale nodded impatiently.

"Now, if I may tell you a little more about our underground system here . . ."

As the Brigadier spoke in the brightly lit warmth of the underground complex, far above on the surface a bitterly cold north wind was sweeping light flurries of snow down Portland Place outside Broadcasting House. A police van, parked in the centre of Langham Place, was harshly barking instructions through a loudspeaker on its roof to bewildered pedestrians gathered round.

"All residents are advised to go back to their homes and stay indoors. Non-residents must go as quickly as possible to one of the centres marked on the map where they will be passed through to the outside as quickly as possible. Maps showing the location of these centres are available here and from any uniformed constable. There are bound to be some delays, and to avoid hardship a list of requisitioned hotels is also available. These will supply temporary shelter and food at no charge. . . ."

An elderly woman huddled in an ill-fitting tweed coat was grumbling testily, looking at the rough-printed map handed to her by a policeman.

"I ask you, 'ow can I walk all that way, I got bunions, I wouldn't get a 'undred yards."

The policeman, a large man with a friendly farmer's face, looked down at her, grinning: "Never mind, dear, I'll give you a piggyback."

For a moment she glared back at him and then crackled wheezily: "Wouldn't mind, either."

Two elegantly dressed businessmen were listening to the voice from the speaker. One turned to the other: "Calls for a brandy or two, don't you think?"

The other grinned: "The Saville?" "Right."

They both turned abruptly and walked away.

Police were moving through the crowd, handing out the maps and the emergency instructions. Then, over the dry sound of the wind from the north end of the road, there was a growing rumble.

Round the crescent of Park Square a long black line of Army lorries swept into Portland Place, outlined harshly against the snow. Motorcycle outriders tore up and down alongside the column, like attendant insects.

Finally, as the leading troop carrier reached Langham Place, the whole column screeched to a halt. Almost immediately, tail-boards went down and soldiers jumped out unloading wooden barriers and coils of rusting, barbed wire.

Red-capped military police from one carrier spread out quickly along the west side of the street, and began halting traffic trying to get into the road. Car drivers were curtly told to reverse and go back the way they had come.

There were many angry arguments with drivers who refused both to accept the situation and to take orders from soldiers. The troops worked at a furious pace erecting bars on cross-shaped supports. Finally, all side-access roads were sealed off.

Along the great sweep of the embankment to the south, the river formed a natural barrier, and only Waterloo Bridge was closed. Just by the "egg-in-a-box" shape of the Festival Hall on the south bank, two half-track armoured vehicles were parked across the road. A police land-rover was between them, and two traffic police were setting up flashing light beacons and *No Entry* signs. To the north, angry pedestrians trying to cross the Hungerford foot-bridge were being turned away from the long flight of stone steps leading up to it from Villiers Street.

Slowly, as troops and police spread out with their barriers and equipment, the great complex of streets, shops, and squares was sealed off like some ancient ghetto. Along Euston Road and Southampton Row, barriers were dragged across access roads. Multiple road jams built up as drivers hurried to get out.

Accidents multiplied as anxious commuters jostled with each other in the fumes and the noise.

Gradually, as the last cars left, the area began to fall silent. The habitual roar of the traffic was replaced by the sound of footsteps as pedestrians gathered in frightened groups studying the maps and instructions given out by the police and then hurried for the nearest shelter.

In the dry, freezing air, the snow began to pile up in small drifts against the pavements.

In his luxurious flat overlooking the untidy, cosmopolitan spread of Old Compton Street in Soho, Harry Menzelos was listening intently to the radio as the announcer read out the emergency plans. As it finished, he switched off, walked over to the window, and looked thoughtfully down at the delicatessens in the street below. He stood for a long moment, tapping his finger on the glass, his rather sad face completely expressionless. Then he turned away and took a long cigarette from a gold case.

Menzelos was a professional.

He had learnt the hard facts of life and death as a company sergeant-major with the British military mission in Salonika. Operating in the mountains of Khortiatis to the north, he had easily established a reputation—among ally and enemy alike—as an efficient killer. To his own men he was respected as an operator who made things work but demanded in return total loyalty.

After the war, he left his home town of Piraeus and made his way to England, drifting through various minor rackets in London without ever making any serious money or getting caught. His first success was a major snatch in Hatton Garden, netting a cool ten thousand pounds' worth of small saleable diamonds.

An intelligent and sensitive man, he had planned and carried out several major robberies, investing the spoils in legitimate business enterprises. He currently owned two clubs in Paddington and managed a string of shoe shops in London and the Home counties.

He also paid income tax.

He poured himself an inch of Fourneaux's special reserve cognac, picked up the phone and dialled, studying the growing ash on his cigarette as he waited.

"Solly? Harry—yes. Heard the radio? Bad, isn't it?" He laughed briefly. "It's given me a very good idea, Solly, you want? Well, why don't you come over—yes —make it quick, Solly, it must be now—yes—you'd better bring Alford—yes, that's right. Where does he keep the lorry? Good, good, that's inside, isn't it? Bring it over and park it in the mews—yeah—see you."

He put the phone down and went into the bedroom and pulled the large double bed to one side on its castors. Then he folded the carpet back and pulled up three of the narrow floor-boards beneath the underfelt.

Reaching down, he brought up a heavy bundle of oily rags and unfolded them.

The wall lights reflected dully on a Sten gun, two Army-issue revolvers, and a bundle of loaded magazines.

In the street below, shops were closing down; barrels of cucumbers and preserved fish were pulled in as shopkeepers began to tidy away empty containers.

Brewer Street was dark and deserted as the three men huddled in the doorway, listening. The snow was beginning to lie on the pavement and they looked anxiously at the jumbled line of black footprints leading up to where they stood.

Finally, satisfied that no one was about, Solly Ackerman took a small battery-drill out of his holdall, screwed in a long carbide-tipped tool, and started to drill just above the centre keyhole of the heavy deadlock in the main door. Above his head the snow was beginning to gather over the tops of the large, embossed letters stating *A. Bonnington. Jewellers Merchants.*

The angry whine of the drill seemed dangerously loud in the quiet of the deserted street.

Finally, he pulled out the drill and poked a long, threaded rod down the hole in the lock. On the far end of the rod was a weighted cross-bar which sprang open across the hole as soon as it reached the inner side of the lock, holding it in position against removal.

Then, onto the threaded outer end he screwed a heavily built fly-cutter—a precision version of a schoolboy's compass—and then attached a ratchet brace to the cutter. As he swung the brace to and fro, the fly-cutter turned in jerky segments, cutting a circular swathe into the steel of the door surrounding the deadlock. The others looked on impatiently as he worked, sweating in the cold air. Shiny blue curls of hot steel shavings fell into the snow and hissed briefly as they cooled.

Ten feet below the street outside the jewellers, in an

old brick-arched Victorian sewer, mutant 59 was inexorably following out its life pattern. Feeding greedily on the broken-down constitutents of the bio-degradable bottle, the generations of bacteria grew, divided, and died, each one contributing its own small quotient of gas. Gas which filled the wet tunnels, rising slowly up into waste pipes, into basements, and into houses.

Ackerman led the way across the floor of the shop, past glass cabinets empty of their contents and down the heavily carpeted stairs, his torch beam picking out the plush furnishings and the line of Crimean prints on the curving wall of the stairway. Finally, the beam of light fixed on a fuse box and an array of cast-iron switches. Silently, he handed the torch to the third man, Alford, who kept it trained on the switches. He opened the cover of one of the switches, first breaking the lead electricity-board seals. Taking a small meter with wire leads out of his holdall, he touched the metal prods on two of the gleaming copper bars inside the switch. The meter needle stayed at zero.

"O.K., no juice in the main switch," he whispered.

"Let's go to work," Menzelos said.

As they crept forward in the dark, Alford complained: "Somebody must have crapped down here. God, what a stink."

"Come on, come on," said Menzelos irritably, snatching the torch from Alford and sweeping it round the room. "There it is, that's it." The beam picked out the squat, black safe in one corner.

In the semi-darkness, none of them saw the small, pouting mass of foam rising through the drain in the sink in the opposite corner.

Alford was examining the safe in the torch beam: "Won't need bottles for this lot, it's a Parkstone superior. Look, four lock bars, two on the key side and two on the hinge side. Putty'll do that lot all right, no bother."

Twenty minutes later, Ackerman finished drilling four three-eighths holes in the casing of the safe. Each hole lay close to the four lock bars.

Menzelos was setting up wires leading to a cylindrical

stack of nickel cadmium high-discharge battery cells, and Alford had taken the carpet from the stairs and had piled it up on the floor in front of the safe.

Ackerman took a cocoa tin out of his holdall and began digging out the plastic explosive inside it, rolling it into long sausages and stuffing it into the holes he had drilled. Then he took four small copper-tube detonators and pushed each one into the putty-like explosive protruding from the holes. Each detonator had two wires hanging from the outer end. Finally, he took a ball of modeller's clay, divided it into four equal lumps, and tamped it carefully round each detonator with his hands, leaving the wires protruding.

Menzelos took each pair of wires, connected them up to the fly nuts on a crudely made junction box, and trailed the lead back up the bare stairs, carrying the batteries. Alford carefully packed the stair carpet around the front of the safe, holding it in position with two tilted office chairs.

The foam was spreading out from the drain across the bottom of the sink.

Menzelos called down the stairs to the others: "Right, come out of the way."

Alford and Ackerman took a last look round with the torch and went back upstairs to join Menzelos. The three men huddled down in a corner of the shop.

"Have a look out, Lennie," said Menzelos. "Make sure nobody there."

Alford made his way to the window, looking up and down the street to make sure it was empty. He came back: "O.K., nobody."

Menzelos carefully attached one lead to the batteries and the other to a switch strapped on the side with black tape. Closing his eyes, he threw the switch.

Down in the basement, the four charges blew with a sharp cracking thud, flinging the carpet and the chairs across the room and releasing a momentary flash of flame from each hole. As the three men started to rush down the stairs, the gas trapped in the sink ignited.

It flashed down the waste pipe, whipping along the branching underground pipes leading to the sewer.

Then, with a tremendous roar, the trapped gas in the sewer tunnel exploded. A heavy iron grille in the surface of the street blasted into the air, followed by a volcano of flame. Windows in surrounding buildings shattered and the grille spun through the air, turning over and over like a giant discus and finally smashing down onto the pavement with a ringing metallic clang.

The three men peered into the shattered basement room, coughing and wheezing in the fumes, the beam of the torch barely penetrating the murk. There was a complete shambles. The plaster and some of the brickwork on one wall had collapsed. Where the sink had been there was a gaping hole in the floor. The distorted safe door was open on one remaining hinge.

"Christ!" Alford whispered. "What the hell did you use?"

Ackerman was aghast: "Just the putty, that's all."

Alford was beginning to panic: "Let's scarper. That'll bring the law, quick as that." He began to move towards the stairs.

Menzelos held him back by the arm: "We ain't got the stones, Lennie, we ain't got the stones."

Ackerman was already at the safe door raking out blackened files and jewel boxes. Finally, he got three labelled velvet bags out of a small metal box. "They're here—quick." He threw one over to Menzelos and pocketed the other two.

From over their heads there was a brief sound of screeching tires in the street outside, then the thump of car doors and muffled voices. They all strained to hear what was being said. There were grating footsteps on the skylight over their heads.

Menzelos snapped off the torch: "Not a sound, not a sound."

"The bloody door!" Alford whispered. "They'll see the hole in the door!"

"Shut up," Ackerman whispered. The three waited in total silence. There was a muted click as Menzelos cocked the breech mechanism of the Sten gun. After what seemed like an age, the voices and the footsteps receded; there was the sound of car doors again, an engine starting and accelerating away into silence.

"Now we wait," said Menzelos, switching on the torch again. "We stay here, then we walk out nice and slow and go back to my place."

"Not supposed to be anybody on the streets, Harry," Ackerman said.

"Everybody's trying to get somewhere, that's why we had to do it today. Later we'll have the place to ourselves. Even the troops won't be out."

13

The fifty-ninth mutant now held the centre of London in its grip.

In the freezing December cold, it steadily evolved, adapted, and divided—each generation learning to attack and dissect new molecular structures. As each outbreak began, fresh supplies of plastic softened and then bubbled as the foraging bacteria invaded. Each time the bacteria took hold in a confined space where there was a spark or naked flame, gas built up to an optimum concentration and exploded.

The great complex of systems—the vascular and nervous systems of normal city operation—broke down. Underground tunnels—the so-called subways—containing gas, water, and electricity mains—fell into a shambles. Everywhere there was a plastic junction and infecting spores or live bacteria, there was a fresh breakdown.

Aggregations of infected foam were carried by the wind to cause new outbreaks. People unknowingly acted as vectors or carriers of the plastic disease, carrying small specks of infected material on their clothing or hands.

One outbreak became two, two became four, four, eight, and so on in rigorous geometric progression.

As the full emergency regulations took hold, people hurried to food shops to stock up for the emergency. There were queues at every shop. The delicatessens of Soho were emptied as people who had never eaten a pickled herring or garlic sausage in their life bought them by the pound.

Without any warning, the ring subway encircling the Aldwych blew up like a Bangalore torpedo, setting fire to Bush House and wrecking the front of the television building.

A surgeon, performing an emergency orthopedic operation in University College, watched helplessly as the plastic drip-tube leading into the patient's vein began to soften and balloon out under the pressure from the hanging drip-bottle.

In the Coburg Street control room of the London Underground, the wall map of the tube railway was silent and dark. Engineers sat over cold cups of coffee, staring morosely at lifeless banks of instruments.

At Scotland Yard, the radio-car control centre failed suddenly as insulation in its main relay room failed.

Although most of the more serious outbreaks were confined to the sealed area, people who had left the zone before de-contamination had started carried small patches of infection with them to the world outside.

At Heathrow, an air traffic controller watched in horror as one of the knobs on his control console came stickily away in his hand.

A long-distance lorry loaded with polythene carboys of liquid industrial cyanide was roaring north up the M.1 motorway. At the base of one of the carboys, there was a small bulging patch of softened plastic where a loader had lifted it onto the lorry in London. The patch slowly ballooned outwards under the weight of the deadly poisonous liquid it contained. The patch split and the poison began to dribble out of the hole, down under the tail-board of the lorry and onto the road.

An industrialist away from his flat in Westminster, fly-fishing in the Wye valley, watched in amazement as his plastic wading boots softened as he stood knee-deep in the river.

In the silence of an almost deserted city, Jack Bailey trudged wearily through the snow along Shaftesbury Avenue, an old Navy melton pulled up round his face. Still wearing his commissionaire's peaked cap to keep out the cold, he was carrying two paper bags bulging with food. As he turned off into Newport Street, he wondered dully whether Mary had been able to cook anything on the paraffin heater. He walked round the back of the car park, still half-filled with the white-humped shapes of abandoned cars, and let himself in through the door of their ground-floor flat.

Inside, the air was warm but smelt strongly of a badly adjusted paraffin stove. The only light came from two candles on the cheap varnished sideboard, giving out just enough light for him to see his wife sitting curled up in a blanket, warming her hands over the heater. She shivered at the breath of cold air from the door as he closed it behind him.

"They just said on the radio we can't go out no more," she said in a complaining tone.

"I know, we heard it in the club before it closed. I got the instructions—tells us what to do. Got any tea? I'm perished."

She got up, still keeping the blanket round her shoulders, took one of the candles, and went through into the kitchen.

She called back through the open door: "Gas is only just working, radio said one of the pipes blew up in Charing Cross Road—something about a plastic seal in a pipe. Don't seem right."

"Keep it on for a bit. Give us a bit of extra heat, won't it?"

"Got enough coins for the meter?"

"About a dozen."

She came back carrying a tray holding two cups and the candle.

"Close the door while I put this down, then."

Back in the darkened kitchen, a thin rim of foam had appeared around the sink outlet. Mutant 59 had reached up from the sewers beneath their flat, groping for its next source of food. It had writhed and pushed its way along the relatively warm underground pipes until it emerged into the freezing air of the Baileys' kitchen. As the temperature of its surroundings fell, the rate of cell division also slowed, until the individual bacterial envelopes in the small patch lay dormant, almost without internal activity. The rim of foam had begun to dry, but now the low flame of the gas stove began to warm the air.

Jack and Mary sat quietly, their hands wrapped comfortingly around the teacups. Mary was rocking to and fro in her chair. Jack was looking round at all his favourite possessions—the old pair of captured German binoculars, the inscribed brass shell-case on the mantelshelf, the pile of do-it-yourself magazines and books.

He began to muse on his next job. The shelves in the larder or the bedroom ceiling? Gradually, as the tea warmed its way into his body, his eyelids drooped and he nodded off. Mary watched him, smiling to herself. As he began to snore softly, she took the blanket from around herself and wrapped it carefully over his knees. Then she shrugged into his overcoat and settled back in the chair, picking up a thumbed paperback and turning its pages toward the candle.

In the kitchen the patch of foam was beginning to move and expand.

Mutant 59 was waking up in the warmth.

Complex bio-chemical signals began to pulse as the static protoplasm of the cells began once again to constrict and divide. By now, the mutant was an almost perfectly equipped biological entity. Defying the laws of Darwin, each generation was acquiring some of the most successful attributes of the last, learning new methods of unstitching plastic molecules to get energy and life. Learning to use the complex artifacts of man.

Gas bubbles began to form again as the cells used up the last of the food around them. One bubble popped soundlessly, spraying a few small droplets onto the draining board—newly covered in self-adhesive plastic sheeting by Jack.

Almost immediately, the droplets appeared to soak into the surface of the plastic and disappear.

In the living room, Jack woke up in the dimness and saw the blanket round his knees: "Ta. You all right?"

She nodded. "How long's this going to be?"

"Can't tell. They'll put it to rights, I expect. There's a lot of those scientists geezers working on it down St. Thomas's."

"Like the blitz, isn't it?"

" 'Ope not, went on for two bleeding years, that did."

"Don't know how we'll manage, we only got about a couple of gallons of paraffin."

"It's all right, love, I'll go down the emergency whats-it in a bit, see what's going on. They thought it all out, you know. I got the instructions here somewhere."

He pulled out a folded sheet of brownish paper printed in heavy black ink. Attached to it was a simplified, large-scale map of Central London.

"Here it is, I'll read it to you." He began slowly to pick out the words in the dim light of the candle, the ponderous phrases sounding strangely incongruous as he read.

STATE OF EMERGENCY

A proclamation of emergency has this day been made under section one of the Emergency Powers Act 1920 (a) and it is here stated that the proclamation is now in force having been signed by Her Majesty with the advice of her Privy Council.

The instructions which follow are for your protection. It is essential that you read them very carefully and carry them out with the greatest of care. They apply only to those who are inside the area shown on the attached map.

Until the emergency is over, it is the Government's intention to evacuate the region; this means that you will have to go to one of the de-contamination centres marked on the map. There are no other exits.

Do not go with any luggage or personal possessions. Put on your warmest and oldest clothes and do not wear or carry anything made from plastic. Think very carefully and decide whether you have any plastic objects on your person. If you have, discard them.

For example, if you wear dentures, these must be left behind. Shoes with plastic soles or uppers must similarly be left.

At the de-contamination station, you will be asked to remove your clothes and pass through a special shower.

While this is happening, your clothes will be subject to steam treatment and will be returned to you before leaving. In some cases, it may be necessary to retain your clothing. If so, alternative clothing will be provided at the centre. Once you have passed through de-contamination, you will be free to leave, but you will not be allowed back into the area.

Non-residents

If you are confined in the area, go to any one of the hotels listed on Paper A where you will be given food and shelter. You will also be given a numbered lapel badge indicating your place of de-contamination. Go to the nearest listed hotel and do not loiter or visit any other place on the way.

These instructions apply both to British Nationals and foreign visitors.

Residents

If you live in the area, REMAIN INDOORS.

Do not worry about food supplies, these are being brought in by the Police and the armed services and will, for the time being, be distributed free of charge.

Look carefully on the map and find your nearest emergency post. It is marked by a flashing red-striped beacon similar to the barber's post sign.

What to Do with an Outbreak

If you see any signs of invasion by the plastic-destroying agent, first of all DO NOT TOUCH anything nearby. Infected plastic objects most often show first a softening, then a melting, then the formation of bubbles accompanied by an unpleasant smell, similar to rotten eggs. The gas produced in the bubbles is explosive, so do not use any naked flame. If, for example, you see an outbreak in your kitchen, turn out all pilot lights on your gas stove. If you have any solid-fuel or gas central heating, turn it off.

Then go at once to your nearest emergency post and

report the outbreak. It will then be dealt with by skilled experts.

Remember:

Don't touch anything.
Don't try and do it yourself.
Report it at once.

Public Places

No public place may open to do business. This applies to shops, licenced premises, restaurants, theatres, cinemas, clubs, and any other establishment where the public may gather.

Vehicles

No vehicles may be driven on the roads in the area unless specifically requested by a member of the Police force, armed services, or other properly authorized person. If you are required to drive a vehicle on official business, it is not necessary to have a valid road fund licence or insurance certificate.

Public Transport

All public transport in the area is cancelled until further notice. It is most important that no person makes any attempt to go near the underground railway. This has been closed down since it is one of the principal sources of infection. It must be avoided.

Drains and Sewers

The sewers are heavily contaminated with the plastic-destroying agent and have therefore had to be closed.

Whether you are a resident or not, it is most important that you do not allow anything to go down your drains or lavatory. Fill the bath with cold water and use this only for drinking. If you wash, any water you use must remain inside your premises. It must not under any circumstances be taken outside.

Don't use your lavatory at all.

Paper sacks are being provided for refuse, so place some diluted disinfectant in your dustbin and use this as you would a chemical closet.

Be particularly careful to separate water for drinking, which should be boiled, from your toilet arrangements. Failure to do this may result in the spread of a number of dangerous infections.

Sickness

If you, or a member of your family, are taken ill, go to the nearest emergency station marked on your map, where medical staff are available. Cases of serious illness will be removed through de-contamination centre "M" at the Portland Square exit, if they cannot first be treated in University College hospital or Charing Cross hospital.

Communication

The telephone system is now almost completely out of action, so stay tuned to Radio Three, where regular bulletins of instruction are being broadcast on the hour.

Penalties

The Emergency proclamation gives the Police and other authorities wide powers. Whilst it is hoped that it will not be necessary to use these, members of the public are strongly advised to adhere to these instructions. Penalties for failing to do so are severe.

In the kitchen, mutant 59 was fully active.

The patch on the draining board had now bubbled and splashed droplets onto the vinyl surfaced wallpaper above it and onto the felt-backed plastic floor-covering below. As each single drop landed, it sank in and started to soften and bubble the surface.

As bubbles burst, more droplets sprayed out. One patch to two, two to four, and four to eight or more. Gradually the mutant consumed the Baileys' kitchen. A transparent plastic container labelled *Coffee* and containing sugar began to soften and distort.

A polythene jug sagged, buckled, and tipped over, releasing a spreading pool of custard.

The shiny covering of the kitchen table began to move—distorting the flower pattern on it into surrealist shapes.

Suddenly the black polythene waste trap under the sink ballooned weakly downwards and burst, releasing a writhing glutinous mass onto the floor. Gradually, as the rate of division increased, the foul-smelling gas residue seeped under the door into the living room.

Jack wrinkled his nose in disgust and pointed towards the kitchen door.

"What you got in there?" He looked at her for a moment, then down at the sheet of emergency instructions.

She stared back, her eyes widening. "Gawd, you don't suppose . . ." she began.

They both got up, reaching for a candle. Jack opened the kitchen door while Mary sheltered behind him, shivering.

The entire kitchen seemed to move in the dim light, almost as if the room was alive. Outlines of familiar objects were undulating, covered with mantles of softly hissing foam.

"Oh Gawd, Gawd . . ." she was plucking at his sleeve, shaking.

"Come on, out of it." He pushed her back into the living room and made her sit down.

"The gas, what about the gas? Turn it off—quick."

Bailey looked at her for a second and rushed back into the kitchen and switched off the two rings. Slamming the door behind him, he took her firmly by the shoulders. "It said we had to report it, so I'll go off . . ."

"Jack, oh my, Christ, don't leave me with that in there. Don't leave me alone. . . ."

"I got to. Now, come on, you'll be all right."

"I'm not staying if you go, I tell you." She began to get up.

"I'll be back in two minutes. There's an emergency post in Cambridge Circus." He pointed to the kitchen door. "Now don't go in there and you'll be all right. . . ."

"Jack, I'm not staying. . . ."

"You've got to—I'll be back in a tick." He pushed her firmly back into the chair.

He looked back at the door and then at the paraffin heater. "I'll have to turn this off. Said so, didn't it?" He turned the wick control right down and waited until the blue flame flickered out. "Be as quick as I can."

She looked at him from the chair, huddled herself closer in the blanket, and stared fixedly at the kitchen door.

He gave a last look round in the gloom and went out.

She waited shivering for a full twenty minutes, then Bailey came in, stamping the snow off his boots. He shut the front door behind him and leant back to regain his breath.

"What's going to happen?" Mary asked.

"They're sending a de-contamination squad. Gave 'em our address. Said they'd come as quick as they could, shouldn't be long."

For a half an hour they sat in the semi-darkness, waiting. Suddenly there was the sound of grating footsteps in the stone corridor outside and a loud, peremptory knock at the front door.

"Who is it?" Bailey said nervously.

"De-contamination. Open up, will you please?"

Bailey walked to the door, slid back the heavy iron bolt and undid the catch, and opened the door. Mary Bailey screamed.

Outside the door were three giant figures carrying heavy rescue torches. Each was dressed in a protective rubber suit complete with transparent visor and hood. On the front of each suit was a stencilled label in black: *Chemical Defense Unit Beeston.* One man had a pressure-spray canister strapped to his back, another carried a bunch of tools: a shovel, a long hatchet, and crowbars. The third was holding an electronic unit with coiled wire probes strapped to its side. For a moment they stood there like space creatures, looming in the glare of their torches.

Jack Bailey recovered himself: "Bloody hell, you gave me a turn."

The leading man replied, his voice muffled by the face piece of his suit, "Sorry, mate, didn't mean to frighten you."

The men advanced into the room, shining their torch beams into all the corners. Mary cringed back into the chair. One of the men saw her fright.

"Don't worry, sweetheart," he said, "shan't be long." Then, turning to Jack, he said, "Where is it?"

"In the kitchen, over there." Bailey nodded towards the closed door.

The leading man, who wore an armband showing sergeant's stripes, gestured to the other two. They all began unpacking gear and laying it out on the floor in the light of the torches.

" 'Ere, what you up to?" Jack said anxiously.

The sergeant eyed him carefully through the visor. "Going to make a bit of a mess, I'm afraid."

"Eh?"

"Let's have a look anyway." The sergeant opened the kitchen door carefully and shone one of the torches into the gloom. The whole room seemed to be moving and heaving in the shadow. The foul, dank smell flowed into the living room.

"Stone me, it's a bad one," the sergeant said as he began to unpack a rubberized canvas holdall. Out of the holdall, he took three pairs of large rubber overshoes. Each man put the shoes on over their boots and stepped into the kitchen. They put the holdall in the centre of the room.

Jack turned to go in after them, but the sergeant whipped round and said: "Don't come in. You mustn't walk on this floor any more; you stay in there now." Jack backed away protesting.

The men went to work with a practiced fury. One cut away the sagging sink tray with a handsaw, another swept up all the misshapen food containers, and the third began to pump the spray canister on his back with an extended hand lever. With his other hand he directed a mist of fluid from a long thin tube into the affected areas. An acrid chemical smell spread back into the living room.

Mary sat wide-eyed with fear, coughing in the fumes. Gradually, the three men reduced the kitchen to a shambles. Hacking and wrenching their way into all Jack's handiwork, they gutted the room of plastic, whether it was affected or not. Jack watched from the doorway, silent with shock as months of work were reduced to ruin.

As the men worked, each piece they cut away was put into the holdall. Vinyl wallpaper was torn down, the table-top cut away, and the floor covering ripped up.

Finally they were done. One lifted the bulging holdall next to the door, and as they went back into the living room, each took off the rubber overshoes and put them into the holdall, just before crossing the doorway. The sergeant took a small aerosol gas canister out of his suit pocket, pulled a tag on its side, and set it down on the kitchen floor. It immediately began to hiss furiously. He closed the door behind him, sealed it off with a roll of sticky tape, and turned to the shocked couple. Mary was weeping silently.

"Come on, missus," the sergeant said. "You'll get compensation—make a mint probably." He chuckled briefly behind his face mask. Turning to Jack, he said, "Better get some clothes on."

"What do you mean?" Jack asked.

"Well, you can't stay here, can you?"

"Where are we going? I don't want to go. Here, what's it all about?"

"Well, you'll have to be de-contaminated, won't you. You'd better get cracking. Charing Cross is your nearest. Only about ten minutes' walk. I'll give you a ticket so as you won't get stopped."

Mary cried out: "Why do we have to go? Oh Gawd." She wept heavily.

"Now look, dear," the sergeant said impatiently, "it's nothing to do with you. You're infected, aren't you? That means you got to get uninfected, doesn't it? Now come on, we got another ten calls, can't stay here all night."

As he reassured her, the other two were expertly

gathering their gear together. The top of the holdall was tied off and they prepared to leave. The sergeant took a card from a pocket on the outside of his suit and wrote briefly on it with a wax pencil and handed it to Jack.

"Here's your pass, then," he said. "Get moving—quick as you can." He turned to Mary: "Sorry, missus. Good-night now." The three men turned and clumped out of the flat.

The two stood there peering after them in the light of the guttering candles. Almost absently, Jack put his arm round Mary's shoulder.

14

Buchan put the phone down.

"That was the lab at St. Thomas's," he said. "They confirm our microscope findings. They have the micrographs and they're trying to identify the bug. It doesn't seem to fit any of the known species. I'm not surprised."

Betty put her head round the door, her face white and drawn: "I've been on to all the hospitals I can reach, some of them are off the phone. There's no sign of them —nothing at all. Their names don't appear on any of the casualty lists. I don't know what else I can do." She looked up to see Kramer standing at the door, his face set, immobile.

She started to speak but Kramer gestured: "O.K., Betty, I heard—you've no news." He slumped into a chair.

The phone rang again, and Betty picked it up. "Yes —yes he is—all right—yes, I'll get him at once." She handed the receiver to Kramer. "It's NASA, New York."

Kramer spoke curtly: "Yes, Kramer here. Who? Oh yes, Marker—how are you? What do you want? I see, well you must be in the picture by now, we've gotten the answer. No, it's not the Aminostyrene. How do I know? We've got the proof here. Look, Marker, you can't fix the blame on our *material,* it isn't the cause —no—of course I can prove it. It's bacteria—a bug! No, I'm not joking, it's a bug. We've got the evidence here. Look, I don't care what you say, we have first-class evidence. Well, you'll have to believe it. When?

Tomorrow, ten thirty," he looked at his watch. "That's six hours minus, I can just make it if I get a flight now. What? That's right, if they won't accept it I'll bring the Goddamn evidence myself. I told you I'll *be there!* O.K., good-bye."

He slammed the receiver down and leant back in the chair. "Don't exactly blame them."

"What?" said Betty.

"Tomorrow, ten thirty their time, the Acquisition Committee of NASA have a meeting in New York. They are going to decide whether Aminostyrene is safe or not. If they go against us we lose the contract and about a million and a half bucks in royalties. Get me a booking to Kennedy. . . ."

"You can't," Betty protested. "What about Anne? She's missing, you can't . . ."

His voice was cold: "Just get me a seat on the next plane to Kennedy while I pack." As he strode towards the door he swung round to Wright: "Get me some more specimens of those bacteria we used, pack them in a metal box—sterilize the outside and seal it in paraffin wax—right? I'll take them with me. Oh, and you'd better pack in a couple of the micrographs you took of the bug. They'll want all the proof we've got." He slammed the door as he went out.

Gerrard peered down the length of the platform lit by a sudden flare from the fire.

In the semi-darkness at the end there was a small wooden signal cabin. For a moment he thought something moved inside, then the flames died down.

He struggled painfully to his feet and went over to his clothes. They were dry and stiff. As he put them on, they felt warm and comforting.

"Be careful," said Anne.

He pulled another piece of burning timber from the fire and blew the charred end up into a flame, then held it over his head and walked along towards the signal box.

It was roughly square with a dusty glass window and a planked door hanging ajar. The door moved easily and he blew up the brand to a fiercer flame and stepped inside.

Most of the mechanism had long since been disconnected and removed but there were still heavy iron levers with attached cable clutches and, at the far end, a faded diagram of the track. Set in the wall, there was another door. The frame had been bolted to the brickwork and a large wooden door was set into it. It was heavily padlocked with planking nailed across the frame.

He felt a surge of excitement. A way out!

In one place the planking had sprung slightly, and through it he could see the actual door frame. As he put his face close to the gap, he could feel a keen whistle of cool, fresh air. He drew back and looked down at the padlock. No great problem, they could smash it off and then . . . He heard a sound behind him like a sharp intake of breath. He turned, peering into the gloom. Suddenly a thousand lights exploded in his head.

He staggered forward, dropping the brand. Then another blow crashed down and he slid forward against the wall, unconscious.

He woke up with the taste of blood in his mouth and a thudding pain in his head. As he opened his eyes he found that he couldn't focus for a moment. Gradually he saw Anne anxiously hovering over him.

He was back by the fire, lying on the tarpaulin. He started to try and raise his head but the pain increased impossibly. He put his hand up and felt matted blood in his hair.

"What happened?" he said. His words were thick and slurred.

He tried the question again. "What happened?" This time it sounded a little clearer to him, and the others understood.

"I don't know," said Anne, looking puzzled. "You must have fallen and hit your head."

Gerrard shook his head, wincing at a fresh spasm of pain. "No," he said, "I got hit."

"How do you mean?" she asked.

"You were here," said Gerrard, speaking slowly. "Didn't you see anything, anybody?"

"No, nothing," Anne said. "There's nobody here but us, is there?"

Gerrard brought his watch up near his face and tried to focus. It was seven; he had been unconscious for nearly two hours.

"I think there's a way out back there," said Gerrard. He swayed slightly on his feet and Anne put out her hand to help. He shrugged it away.

"It's O.K." He turned back to the firelight. "There's a door," he pointed along the platform. "It's a wooden one planked up, but I think we can get through it."

"We've no tools," said Slayter. "I left them back in the other tunnel."

"I think maybe we can do it another way," said Gerrard. He pointed down the track. "Just outside the box there's some old paint in drums; we should be able to burn it away."

"Won't that be risky?" aaid Anne.

"Any better suggestions?" Gerrard noted his own terseness. "We're not going to get through without any tools. The box is wood, it'll burn down in quite a short time. Besides," he said, "I've got a better reason for wanting to burn it."

The others looked curiously at him but didn't stop him as he started dragging scrap pieces of wood along the platform towards the box.

He piled the timber against the outside but didn't open the door. Then he opened an old rusty tin of paint by kicking in the lid with his heel and poured it wet and glistening over the piled wood. Finally, he took a burning stick from the fire and stood for a moment outside the hut.

"Now," he said in a loud voice. "I'm going to fire it. It's going to go up like a bomb." He raised the brand, waved it above his head until it was glowing fiercely, and then stood back ready to throw it.

Suddenly there was a cry. Bursting out from the hut came a wild, unrecognizable figure.

It was Purvis. His face blackened, his hair matted and filthy, his suit in ribbons. In one hand he held a long piece of four by two, in the other, Gerrard's torch. Anne gave a stifled scream. Slayter stepped forward.

Purvis looked at them wildly and then raised the wooden bar. "Get back," he said. "Get away from me. Go on, get away."

"Purvis!" said Slayter. "What the hell are you doing?"

Gerrard grabbed Slayter's arm and pushed him back. "Keep back," he said. "He's off his head."

Purvis slowly lowered the bar. He glared wildly, like a startled animal, his lips working. "Just—just—keep away," he said. "Just keep away from me. Don't touch me—get off—go on, get away!"

"Put that bloody thing down," said Slayter. He stepped forward and held out his hand. "Give it to me."

"Watch it!" said Gerrard. As he spoke Purvis lurched forward, grabbing Slayter by the front of his coat and pulling him down on his knees, raising the piece of wood with the other hand.

"Look out!" cried Anne.

Gerrard quickly pulled back the brand still burning in his hand and threw it at the paint-soaked timber. The planks flickered for a moment, then exploded into a ball of flame. Purvis stumbled back, lost his balance, and fell heavily backwards onto the trackway. Recovering himself and shaking his head like a wounded animal, he scrabbled around in the dust for the bar.

Gerrard shone the torch down. Purvis jerked his head up wildly in the light, and then turned and shambled off, limping down the tunnel away from them. In a few seconds he had disappeared into the blackness, but they could still hear his dragging footsteps.

Gerrard led the others away from the edge of the

platform: "Let him go. He won't get far in that state."

They turned back to look at the signal box blazing fiercely. Inside, the planks covering the door were beginning to curl away from the frame in the heat.

"How are we going to put it out?" asked Anne nervously.

"There are some old fire buckets up there," said Gerrard, pointing. "Wartime ones, I guess." He led the way up the platform. Alongside the old blocked-up exit were half a dozen red, heavily rusted buckets, long since empty of water.

"What are we going to use?" asked Slayter.

Gerrard pointed downward at the manhole in the platform: "We'll have to use that stuff."

Anne grimaced, but they tied Slayter's belt round the bucket handle and dipped it down into the foaming, viscous liquid under the platform. Soon all the buckets were full and ready for use.

It was nearly half an hour before the woodwork had burnt down sufficiently for them to approach it. All that remained was a charred black framework. The remains were still glowing, but the planks had burnt almost through. A strong draught blew sparks and ash into their faces.

Gerrard edged his way into the still-glowing signal box, poised himself, took aim, and then flung his weight against the door. The frame began to give in a shower of sparks. He raised a foot and kicked. More glowing planks fell away. Two more kicks and the hole was big enough for them to get through. The air blowing through was cool and pure after the claustrophobic fumes of the station.

Gerrard looked back. Slayter had torn off the perished end of the tarpaulin and was ripping it into strips. He had already bound the strips round two of the pieces of timber, making them into rough torches. He was soaking the ends in a tin of paint.

"Can't let you have all the ideas," he grinned at Gerrard. "These should last for a bit."

"And then?" Anne asked.

"We'll take a few more in reserve," said Slayter.

Gerrard took one of the ready-made torches and thrust it into the fire; it burst into flames and he held it up above his head. It was spluttering and throwing out flaming drops. One burnt his cheek.

Again he was struck by the incongruity of the situation. Here they were underneath an enormous city, down to their last drop of water, without food, with a half-crazed man hiding farther down the tunnel, ready to kill them out of some paranoid fantasy.

His head was now a dull throb. In the torchlight their shadows stretched across the platform. On the far side he could see long curling posters—Bovril; Craven A cigarettes, a brand he didn't even remember; an advertisement for Bournville cocoa, two children on a weighing machine with a notice: *Builds Healthy Bodies.*

"We ought to be drawing antelopes and hunting scenes on the wall," said Gerrard.

Slayter looked up, smiling wryly: "If we don't get weaving, the only thing on the walls is going to be R.I.P."

Gerrard smiled: "Doubt it." He walked off along the platform, then turned: "Keep an eye on my back," he said. "Don't want to get mugged again."

He walked up to the signal box, leaving Anne and Slayter finishing off the reserve torches. He hesitated for a moment before stepping through the charred remains of the door. There was a short brick tunnel and then he walked out into a large circular vertical shaft about fifteen feet in diameter. The air was icy. At the bottom were broken slabs of concrete and a gleam of water visible through the cracks. The sides were brick with iron ribs. About a quarter of the way up, there were two arches blocked in with a screen of iron bars; rather like old prints of Newgate Prison, he reflected.

Anne now came toward him holding another flaring torch, followed by Slayter, one torch in his hand, the others wrapped in a bundle under his arm.

The combined light of their torches lit the base of the shaft. They could just see the top. It looked to be about a hundred feet, and at the top they could just make out two round openings.

"That's where the air's coming from," said Slayter. "If we can get up, that's the way out."

"But how?" said Anne.

"We could try climbing," said Gerrard.

"I'd never make it," said Anne doubtfully.

"Nor I," Slayter said. "I've no head for heights."

Gerrard went over and inspected the wall. The rivets either side of the iron framework were at least two inches in diameter and protruded for about one and a half inches. It wouldn't be an easy climb.

"I think I can make it," he said. "What I need is a rope, then I can get you two up after me." He started climbing. He was badly out of condition and his muscles were aching and slow to respond. The flickering light of the torches seemed to enlarge, then reduce, his various hand- and foot-holds. As the shadows lengthened and then contracted, he seemed to be climbing in some sort of surrealist nightmare where nothing was solid and even the iron metalwork was subject to the ebb and flow of tidal action.

His muscles performed their actions almost mechanically. The motor-memory somewhere at the back of his brain was still working and he climbed surely and steadily towards the dark circular apertures above him.

At the top, the light from the torches diminished, but Gerrard could see two round holes at the bottom ends of two cylindrical shafts. Both were approximately five feet across.

As he'd half expected, the interior of each one was smooth with only a very thin line of rivets. There were no hand- or foot-holds. There was only one way to get up and that was the method of climbing a rock chimney, his shoulders braced against one side, his feet against the other. He had to try and inch himself up in that way.

First, there was a question of getting into the shaft. The only way he could get in was by standing on the last rim or rib and literally flinging himself out until he made contact with the outer wall of the narrow shaft. Then he would be stretched, his full six foot two, across from the inner edge of the ventilator shaft to the side wall of the big shaft. A mistake and he would join Anne and Slayter at the bottom.

He could then bring his feet, one at a time, inside the ventilator shaft, maintaining a pressure with his arms against the other sides, but, once inside, there would be no going back. The only way to go was upwards. One slip on the upward journey and he would come sliding down the shaft and fall the whole way.

What would he find at the top? Suppose it led straight up to an iron grille impossible to get through. He would be left dangling at that grille, possibly unable to attract the attention of a passer-by until his grip failed and he fell.

Suppose the shaft led up to one of the round-capped ventilator exits. There wouldn't even be a hand-hold. No way out—one way down.

His best hope lay in the possibility of a bend in the pipe enabling him to crawl along a horizontal section and possibly kick it through. The metal was rusty and not very strong. But where would it lead? And, thinking of the thickness of the metal, it could be that the part of the vertical section would have perished and give way under his weight with the stress he would put against it.

He looked down. Nausea rose in his throat.

The others, now seated, with their torches jammed in cracks in the broken concrete below, were leaning on each other, almost out with exhaustion and strain. They obviously couldn't stay there much longer. Even if they did, who would ever find them? No, there was only one way to go and that was up. Gerrard braced himself for the most dangerous climb of his life.

Three times Gerrard tensed himself and three times a surge of weakness, of irresolution and doubt, flooded him, and he felt that his legs would not manage the spring necessary to take him across.

He crouched there, huddled against the wall, shaking, feeling weak and tired, and then a sudden shame flooded his face, followed by anger.

All he knew and all he was able to relate afterwards was that his body suddenly, automatically tensed itself, prepared, and sprang backwards into space. His outstretched arms flattened against the sides of the tube, his body thudded against the far wall, and his feet swung up. For a moment he seemed almost to hang in space before his feet felt the opposite wall and he spread his legs and braced himself.

He rested for a moment. From below he heard a stifled cry, but he couldn't look down. One look and he could have fallen. Now he literally could not stop, his activity had to be continuous, wedging himself against the back wall and the front wall of the tube as he inched up like a mountaineer in a rock chimney. Turning back, he summoned his last reserves.

For the next few minutes Gerrard had no sensation of sight, hearing, or sound. The effort was intense and he was blinded with sweat. In his ears there was a continuous drumming of blood, and his mouth and throat seemed dry and hard. Like an animal struggling for light and freedom, he fought upwards, groping and scraping at the hard walls of the shaft for precious hand-holds.

Finally he stopped, his body refusing to move any more. He was breathing long shuddering gasps and he heard himself giving little sobbing sounds which echoed around him in the tube. If he relaxed for a second, then his body would fall like a sack of potatoes whistling down to the bottom. He looked down cautiously through the crook in his elbow. All he could see was a faint flickering circle of light far below. Above him everything was black, darkly shrouded.

He nerved himself for one last effort. When he did move, he slipped slightly and very nearly fell but braced himself just in time.

Suddenly, to his horror, his back started slipping; the wall no longer seemed solid and he reacted with an almost blind panic which nearly lost him his precarious perch until he realized that it meant the tunnel was sloping. He continued pressing himself upwards and round the bend until he found that he was lying flat, his feet up above him. The weight of his body was now being supported by the wall of the tunnel below him instead of by the pressure exerted by his feet, hands, and back.

The relief was intense, and he lay there for a long five minutes. The air seemed stronger and cleaner. Cautiously he turned over onto his hands and knees and began crawling. He brought out the torch. The beam was now very feeble but he could just see that ahead was another right-angled bend and then another vertical section. He crawled forward, reached the bend, and became aware of pale blue daylight filtering down from above. He switched off the torch and cautiously eased himself round and looked upwards. About ten feet above him was a grille with daylight filtering through.

His self-control gave way suddenly. For several minutes he just lay under the grille, tears streaming down his face. The last section was relatively easy; holding onto the bars of the grille for support, he listened. Where was he? There was complete silence outside. He shook his head to clear his ears but again no sound. What part of London could this be where there was sky but no sound? London was *never* silent. Fear started: What had happened? Why the silence?

From his position all he could see was a wall. He tried to shout, moistening his throat, but all that came out was a dry, bleating sound. His arms were aching with the effort of holding onto the grille. He looked to see if there was any way in which the grille could be opened. A fastening, a catch? Nothing. He shouted again and again until his body was shaking and he found himself sobbing uncontrollably. There was no one.

He clung like a monkey to the grille and found himself yelling obscenities and screaming, but still nobody came, still there was no reply. Then, finally, in a fit of impotent fury he swung his feet crashing against the side of the shaft in total frustration. Suddenly he felt his feet give. With a sudden panic he gripped the grille tighter, dangling in space. Then he put his feet up and gingerly felt the side of the tube. With one hand, as he hung precariously, he felt for the torch in his pocket.

He had kicked a panel partly away. There was something beyond, another space. He shone the dim beam of the torch through the space. He could just make out a wall and below it some steps. Quickly he put the torch away, swung his other foot up, and then, getting as much leverage as possible, he swung like a pendulum smashing his feet against the loosened panel.

Once, twice, three times, and on the third kick it broke away. He swung himself onto the rough edge of the opening, and with one movement forward, fell heavily down on to some steps. The steps ended in a wooden door. His strength was now almost gone, he could hardly move up the steps. He climbed one at a time, slowly, like an old man.

The door seemed to waver before him as he put his hand out and felt for the lock. If this was locked he was sure he would never have the strength to break it down. He turned the handle. Nothing happened. He turned it again and pulled it towards him. Suddenly the door swung open and a great gust of icy winter air blew dust into his face.

He staggered out into the daylight.

15

The small courtyard was about three inches deep in snow. During the climb Gerrard had been drenched in sweat, but now his clothes were rapidly stiffening in the freezing air.

It was completely silent. There was no traffic noise outside the small, walled-in rectangle; no footsteps in the snow.

He walked across to a wooden door set in the far wall. It was locked. He cursed for a moment and then smiled. After the climb, the door seemed a very small obstacle. He looked around. Against the opposite wall, partly hidden in the snow, was a ladder. He dragged it over, set it against the wall, climbed, and swung himself over, painfully dropping to the ground on the far side. He picked himself up among dark evergreen bushes. Some sort of park, where?

He staggered through the bushes and came out by some iron railings facing a road. Gerrard stared uncomprehendingly for a moment. It was familiar. A wide road, separated in the middle by a strip of parking meters and bays. Punctuated by statues. To both sides of where he stood the road divided around the small crescent of park.

Suddenly the scene clicked into position in his memory: Portland Place. Farther down the street was the British Broadcasting Corporation; behind him, Regent's Park. There was something badly wrong. He glanced at his watch: five o'clock.

Five o'clock, seventeen hundred hours, five p.m.

Where was all the traffic? It couldn't be five a.m. No, it would be dark. It must be afternoon and yet . . . there were no cars parked in the bays. No traffic, no sound of traffic, only a distant rumble coming from a long way off. No lights in the offices and houses. As far as he could see down to where the road curved into Upper Regent Street—no people!

He levered himself over the railings and dropped down. The snow on the pavement was almost completely unmarked, not a sign of a footprint and only two or three heavily ribbed tire tracks in the wide road.

He started off down Portland Place, keeping to the middle between the two rows of parking meters, instinctively avoiding the empty roads. As he went, hugging himself with his arms to keep warm, jog-trotting towards Oxford Circus, he scanned the empty faces of the buildings. There was no glimmer of light. The entire street was dead, closed as if after a nuclear holocaust. As he ran, the icy air bit through his clothes and he felt the limp weakness of complete exhaustion soaking into his limbs.

As he shuffled into Upper Regent Street, barely able to move one leg in front of the other, it was like moving through a ghost city. Windows were shuttered, doors closed and barred.

He passed a music shop, a cinema with posters still prophetically featuring a film entitled *Panic in the Streets,* and a restaurant. He stopped and looked in hopefully, but the food under the glass cases had all been cleared. Gone were the Danish pastries, rum babas, and thick slices of chocolate cake. The stainless-steel shelves gleamed bare and empty. There was a stench of corruption in the air.

Suddenly his exhausted senses registered a movement behind him reflected in the plate-glass window. He turned quickly. Opposite, a little farther down the road, was an open door and a man standing beside it silently, intent. He broke into a stiff-legged run towards him.

Because of the carpet of snow, Ackerman failed to

hear Gerrard until he was almost on him. He turned, automatically assuming a defensive crouch, his hand on the pistol in his pocket.

Menzelos and Alford came out of the open door behind Ackerman just as Gerrard reached them.

Gerrard was gasping for breath, his strength almost gone. He grabbed at Ackerman's arm for support, not noticing the lack of response; the curious immobility of the three men as they carefully studied his face.

"I've . . . been trapped . . . got to get them out . . . they're still down there."

An overwhelming wave of nausea swept through his body; his knees buckled. Alford caught him and propped him against the wall as he fell.

"He's seen us leave," Ackerman nodded towards the jeweller's shop behind him.

"Poor bastard's nearly gone anyway," said Alford. "If we just leave him, he'll snuff it anyway."

"No," Menzelos came to a decision. "We take him back to my place."

"You—what?"

"You heard. We can use him. Let's carry him back."

Later, in Menzelos's flat, Gerrard sat hunched in a chair, holding a large glass of brandy. The three men sat watching him without expression. Menzelos held a map on his knee as he gestured to the array of drinks on the corner bar.

"Take another if you want it."

Gerrard nodded and walked over to the bar. He felt warm, but unbelievably tired; the drink was going to his head, making him stagger slightly as he sat down. Dully and almost without caring, he noticed the butt of a gun sticking out of Ackerman's pocket. Menzelos followed his gaze. He put the drink down and got up unsteadily.

"I've got to get moving, got to get these samples to St. Thomas's." He moved towards the door and without any real surprise saw Alford quickly step in front of him, hand in pocket.

"No, Doctor!"

"Doctor? How do you know I'm a doctor?"

"We had a little shufti in your pockets while you were charping."

"Look! You've gotta let me go. There are people trapped down there. I've got to get . . ."

"Dr. Gerrard," Menzelos spoke quietly. "Solly here thinks you ought to be killed."

"I thought you just saved my life."

"I don't like to kill people, it's very risky, but you are going to help us."

"And if I don't?"

Ackerman leant forward in his chair; Menzelos continued: "You want to get your samples to the hospital, you want to get help for your friends. We want to get out too, so we'll help each other. Let me see your samples please, Doctor," he held out his hand.

Gerrard slowly took a small metal case out of his pocket. It contained the specimens he had collected under the tube station platform.

Menzelos took the case out of his hand. Gerrard started to protest.

"You'll get them back, Doc." He opened the lid of the case. "Solly?"

Ackerman took the velvet bags of diamonds out of his pocket.

"They'll go in all right, wrap them up in something else, make them look more medical like." Ackerman began to wedge the bags in between Gerrard's specimen bottles.

Menzelos was unfolding the map on the floor. He looked up at Gerrard.

"Now listen . . ." he began.

The four men walked quickly through the deserted streets across Piccadilly, then down towards a ghostly, deserted Trafalgar Square. The light was fading. At the lower end of the Square, by the entrance to Whitehall, they stopped, looking ahead carefully. The only sound was the twittering of starlings. At the far end of Whitehall, just past the Cenotaph, starkly visible against the carpet of snow, a barbed-wire barricade was stretched across the broad street. Behind it were three vehicles, a large military lorry and, incongruous in the setting, an armoured car and a long, olive-green caravan. They paused.

"Do you reckon . . . ?" began Ackerman. He didn't finish the sentence.

"We've no option," said Menzelos. Ackerman took the gun from his pocket and jabbed it into Gerrard's back.

Gerrard stood absolutely still. Menzelos shook his head, leant over, and took the gun from Ackerman. Taking a handkerchief out of his pocket, he wiped the surface of the gun carefully, bent down, and dropped it through the grille of a drain.

"Hey," began Alford. "What the hell . . .?"

"No use," said Menzelos. "We don't want that, they're going to strip us. Use your loaf, eh."

"What about him?" Ackerman nodded towards Gerrard. "The bastard can shop us while we're going through, can't he?"

Menzelos walked slowly up to Gerrard: "Solly's right, isn't he? Nothing to stop you when you're in there," he pointed down Whitehall. "Once you're there you can shop us, can't you? What you going to do about that, eh?"

Ackerman loomed behind Menzelos: "You do anything clever like that, mate, and I'll hurt you rotten."

"I don't know what's in those bags," Gerrard began, "and I've told you I don't care. I just want to get across the river to St. Thomas's. I give you my word . . ."

"Guide's bleeding honour," Alford sneered.

Menzelos was looking straight at Gerrard; he was studying his face silently. Suddenly he reached out and deftly lifted the specimen case out of Gerrard's pocket.

"Now your papers, Doctor."

"What do you mean?"

"The papers, in your pocket, we looked, remember?"

Slowly Gerrard fumbled in his inside jacket pocket and pulled out his wallet. Menzelos took it.

"I don't want to know what you've done, I told you. I'll . . ."

"Doc," said Menzelos, "you must think I'm a very trusting person. Now listen. I've got your samples and I got your papers. I'm Dr. Gerrard and you're nobody. Now down there," he jerked his thumb towards Whitehall, "they're getting people out as quick as they can. You want to get these"—he gestured with the metal case—"to the hospital and you want to rescue your friends down the tube. Now we don't need you any more, but you need us. So, we'll all go through nice and quiet, and when we're out the other side, you have your samples, we have ours. All right?"

"How do I know you'll give them back?"

"You don't."

"Why don't we chop him here . . . ?" Alford began.

"No need." Menzelos continued: "Now, Doctor, don't you say a word—you're just an ordinary person. They're not stopping anyone. They want everyone out anyway."

"I've got to tell them where my friends are trapped . . ." Gerrard almost shouted.

"You don't have to be a doctor to tell them, do you?" He turned and began to walk across the empty street towards Whitehall. He spoke over his shoulder: "Come on, we're wasting time."

As they reached the barbed-wire barrier, two soldiers sprang forward holding automatic rifles. They were dressed in full protective clothing: helmets with transparent face visors, rubber suits, and heavy gloves and boots. One of them pointed towards a short queue of people leading up a short flight of steps into the long caravan.

After a short wait in the freezing air, the four men walked up the steps into the warm, humid air of the de-contamination caravan. Menzelos, using Gerrard's papers, explained to a tired R.A.M.C. sergeant sitting at the entrance to the shower cubicles that the sample case should not be sterilized. After a number of suspicious queries, the sergeant made him open the case. Seeing the array of bottles inside, he was grudgingly satisfied and took the case away with large forceps, to be wiped down externally with disinfectant.

For the next thirty minutes, the four men went through the full de-contamination routine: stripping down, handing their clothes to another soldier who packed them into wire cage boxes, then showering in hot water reeking of chemical disinfectant. Finally, drying off with harsh, brown Army-issue towels, collecting their clothes in the cage boxes from the sterilizer outlet, and then stepping down from the far end of the caravan. The air seemed twice as cold after the Turkish-bath atmosphere inside. Menzelos was carrying the sample case as they walked towards Parliament Square.

On the pavement were small knots of people silently watching. Near the entrance to the House of Commons, two outside-broadcast television vans were parked. Technicians were paying out cables and setting up arc lights and cameras. A commentator was talking into a hand microphone. Police cars were parked on the pavement, rotating blue lights flashing silently, and an ambulance moved slowly away over Westminster Bridge, its exhaust steaming in the cold.

Overhead, a helicopter was wheeling slowly west along the river, its rotors blattering in the clear air.

Menzelos turned to Gerrard, opening the sample case: "Now our specimens, eh?" He took out the velvet bags wrapped in aluminium foil by Ackerman. He closed it and handed it to Gerrard together with his wallet.

"Matter of interest," said Gerrard. "What's in those?"

Ackerman looked at him unsmiling: "Marbles, mate!"

It took Gerrard all his remaining strength to walk over Westminster Bridge and along the embankment to St. Thomas's Hospital.

Hours later, he came to in a bed in a small cubicle. Slowly, as his exhausted mind cleared, he remembered people gathering round him in the hospital entrance—Buchan's face. Suddenly, panic struck him. Had he told them about Anne and Slayter?

Gradually, as he took in more and more of his

surroundings, he remembered. There was a large police inspector—yes, that was it. The policeman was talking about ropes, rescue gear, Regent's Park—it must be all right. With a tremendous effort he managed to raise his head off the pillow to look at his watch. Slowly he worked it out; he must have slept for nearly eight hours. Flopping his head back, he tried once more to resist a feeling of almost euphoric fatigue. They must have given him something.

As sleep overtook him, his last thoughts were of Anne.

16

At London Airport, the great, untidy complex of buildings and walkways was gradually closing down. One by one, the terminals emptied and the usual smell of coffee, kerosene, and expensive scent was replaced by dank-ammoniacal smell of mutant 59.

Finally, only one building was active. A de-contamination station had been set up in one of the transfer lounges and only passengers with special-priority passes were allowed through to the few remaining planes that had permission to take off.

Flight 1224 to New York was boarding. Passengers still wrinkling their noses from the acrid smell of the showers in the de-contamination centre were showing their papers to police and immigration officials who sat behind a glass panel. No one spoke; the stench of the mutant reminding each person of the dying city they were leaving behind.

Men in protective suits and face-masks were spraying the outer surface of the great jet with fine aerosol mists of disinfectant as Army patrol jeeps circled round the boarding gate.

In the rush to pack, Kramer had flung his gold-plated pen into the depths of his leather briefcase just before leaving for the New York flight.

Now, as he tightened his seat belt, he half-listened to the neutral sweetness of the air hostess's voice: ". . . extinguish your cigarettes. We shall be departing in a few minutes non-stop to Kennedy Airport via Shannon and Gander. On behalf of Metro Airlines, Captain Howard and his crew welcome you aboard. Thank you."

As de-humanized tape music trickled through the passenger compartment, on the flight deck Captain Howard began his pre-flight checks with P2 and P3, his two co-pilots, and the flight engineer.

In the galley to the rear of the passenger compartment, the chief steward and three stewardesses began to sort prefabricated packages of food into neat piles and then arrange stacks of pressed plastic trays—carefully fitting a neatly wrapped cheese portion in one hole, cellophane-covered trifle in another, until each tray resembled a miniature shelf from a supermarket.

Kramer settled down into his seat, had a careful look to make sure the specimens were properly sealed, and immediately took the report for NASA and his pen out of his briefcase and began to make notes from the report.

By no stretch of the imagination could he have felt what his fingers touched on the metal barrel of his pen. No human eye could have perceived a minute, drying patch of gelatinous material only one-tenth of a millimetre in diameter.

Chemical analysis would have revealed a few microgrammes of protein, water, some salts of phosphorus and magnesium. A more sophisticated examination might just have shown traces of D.N.A., the complex molecule essential to some forms of microscopic life. D.N.A. and its stablemate compound, R.N.A., have the ability to act as a code store. Memorized indelibly on the spiral molecules is the blueprint for the structure of a whole organism. A sub-microscopic plan of behaviour.

The D.N.A. on Kramer's pen did not exist free as a chemical, but was inside the spores and covering membranes of the fifty-ninth mutant embedded in the patch. Each organism was only seven-thousandths of a millimetre in length.

Each was blind and senseless but nevertheless possessed in its own frail envelope a complete behaviour pattern to carry it through the brief time interval between birth and death. From the division of one parent cell into two, and the two progressing to four, the four into eight, and onwards in a beautiful but totally unappreciated mathematical precision.

Normally, bacteria do not divide at an even rate, because events in their own microcosm decree that first they divide rapidly, then they enter a stationary phase which leads finally to a decline and death.

If it were not for three factors preventing the totally disciplined mathematical extension from two to four to eight and so on, it has been calculated that one pair of bacteria dividing every second would cover the surface of the earth in twenty-two hours.

Two main factors enable bacteria to escape these growth restrictions. First, if new food is provided at regular intervals and, second, if they are mutating to survive better in their own surroundings, then division of each cell will accelerate. The rate of acceleration is often dependent on the suitability of the surroundings but quite independent of the normal process of evolution. In the early phases of division, each generation may last only minutes, and in special circumstances may last a few seconds.

The late and unlamented Dr. Ainslie had taken advantage of these special properties. The fifty-ninth mutant had no stationary, or decline phase.

The circumstances surrounding the bacteria on Kramer's metal pen were special. They had almost dried out, and had he not touched it, they would have perished. As his fingertip, damp with sweat, touched the dying life forms, each cell envelope sucked in traces of water. Almost inconceivably small amounts, but just enough to flood the partly dehydrated mechanisms of each cell.

A tumult of tiny signals sped throughout the cells as they swelled. Once again they prepared for their only task: to live, to feed, and to divide.

Kramer leant forward and pulled down the folding table from the back of the seat in front of him, his fingers lightly touching the plastic arm surrounding the melamine surface.

On the flight deck, Captain Howard received the

"engine start" signal from the control tower. The flight engineer made his final pre-start check, noting carefully that the doors were secure.

He double checked with the ear-muffed ground engineer on the tarmac and received the thumbs-up sign showing that the external locks were also closed.

He switched the four banks of fuel pump controls to the "feed" position.

Kerosene began to flood out of the complex of wing and fuselage tanks into the four great turbofan units hanging in their pods like bombs, below the wings.

Captain Howard activated the start controls beginning with number four engine on the starboard wing. Slowly, like a reluctant banshee, the low moaning of the turbine filled the aircraft, rising to a shriek. Number three engine followed as if to add to the baying of the great machine, then number two and number one, until the whole fuselage was thrown into a low-pitched oscillation.

The flight engineer logged fuel pressures and turbine temperatures, and P_3, the reserve co-pilot, began "push-out" check as the ground tractor backed the aircraft away from the loading gate, engines singing with anticipation.

The tractor driver, huddled in a hooded Anorak and ear muffs, gave the second thumbs-up signal, disconnected the bar between the nose wheel of the aircraft and the tractor, and drove away.

Slowly, with a tiny six-inch steering wheel on a bulkhead to his left, Captain Howard guided the clumsy bulk of the jet down the taxi lanes picked out for him in deep-blue lights, the steering wheel effortlessly turning the great nosewheel under his feet. The flight engineer called out the items of the taxi check intently reading off the state of the giant machine as it lumbered unevenly over the concrete towards the main runway.

Then came the "pre-runway check" intoned almost as a ritual, the second pilot ticking off items on a pre-flight log.

In his seat Kramer paused for a moment and stared out of the window at the wheeling panorama of the airport lights, wondering whether they would still be on when he returned.

In the pantry the cabin crew left the stacks of trays and strapped themselves into their seats, each one dully aware of the danger of their job, each blotchy and pale beneath carefully applied make-up.

Finally, cleared for take-off, the aircraft wheeled round, pointing down over the multitude of black tire marks on the runway surface.

Captain Howard moved the throttle quadrants forward and the almost relaxed singing of the engines grew to a deep-throated thunder. Panels shook and vibrated, and the entire machine began to lurch as the roaring thrust of the engines battled with the brakes. Then, as Captain Howard released the brake pedal, the aircraft propelled itself down the centre marks of the runway. With an acceleration greater than any racing car, it gathered speed, bumping and cracking over the joins in the concrete beneath it. Swinging from side to side, it bit through the icy air, searching for its own elements.

As its speed increased, the controls began to respond to the shrieking airstream and it changed from its earthbound clumsiness into a smooth airborne rush. The nose swung up and it leaped on black, jutting streams of smoke from its engines, in one last bound away from the hammering concrete of the runway.

The flight engineer called out the cryptic comment which reduces the pulse rate of all airline pilots—"V_2" —the second critical velocity, which a commercial jet must achieve to get safely away from the ground.

Kramer looked up through the window and saw the cloud base billowing nearer and nearer; then, after a last look at the yellow-lit spiderwebs of London streets, he sank back in his seat as vision was blotted out by the clouds.

At the rear of the plane the cabin crew unstrapped and went back to arranging their first prefabricated meal.

On the flight deck, the tension and anxiety of take-off was diminishing as Captain Howard dialled up the first beacon station at Falmouth for time-checks and directional readings.

In the passenger compartment seat belts were released and cigarette smoke sucked gratefully down. The cabin crew moved up the sloping aisle as the aircraft climbed.

Kramer bent in concentration over his report, rapidly making notes. For several seconds he was unaware of the stewardess leaning over the empty gangway seat towards him, handing him a tray.

"Coffee or tea, sir?"

"Mm? What? Coffee, thank you."

The stewardess fitted an empty plastic cup into an empty depression on his tray. "It'll be along in a moment."

As he turned back to the note pad, the stewardess tested the table in front of him to make sure it was fixed, her hand gripping its edge. She moved away to the next bank of seats, carrying a separate tray of empty cups.

On the flight deck, the crew were relaxing into the six hours of relative quiet which lay ahead of them over the Atlantic. The cabin door behind them opened and a stewardess said: "First orders, gentlemen?"

"Coffee, but not Metromud. Make us a proper cup."

"Can I help you wash up?"

The remarks came as an easy joke-habit. The stewardess smiled, noted down what they wanted, and went out.

Kramer was writing furiously on the table in front of him, unaware of the microscopic nucleus of feral activity on one edge.

The stewardess, seeing a call light on one seat back, leant over a young dolly girl who had rung and envied the latest trendy plastic mac she was wearing.

In the galley the other stewards were beginning to distribute the trays of food, one walking ahead of the others, pushing a drinking trolley. He handed out small fake cut-glass plastic tumblers and miniature bottles of liquor.

As the Isle of Wight slid past thirty thousand feet

below it was as if all the passengers and crew had made some sort of peace with the great jet—a deal which enabled all the complex systems of the aircraft and the people on board to fuse together in a common task.

The second co-pilot went through into the passenger compartment and jealously noted for the hundredth time that the engine-noise level dropped as he entered. Half-way through the first-class section he viewed one of the passengers slumped back asleep, mouth slackly open in a face veined and coarsened by years of excess.

Ahead, the last light of the sun picked out the edges of the wings in deep-orange highlights. Gradually, as the plane bore on westward over the cold, grey sea, the sunlight faded, giving way first to a deep violet-blue and then finally to total blackness and the ice-blue points of the stars.

Outside, the air temperature was ten below zero; inside the warmly lit cocoon of the plane, there was no awareness of all of the deadly hostility of the air honing the alloy panels of the outer skin. The cabin air, pumped under pressure from twin compressors in the nose of the plane, had a friendly social smell of cigarettes and whisky.

Animated conversation flowed and passengers looked out at the darkness, secure and protected from the raging gale outside by the sealed plastic panels on each window.

On the flight deck, the crew had finished their coffee; the cups were stacked on a side shelf ready for collection.

Kramer paused for a moment to steady the table in front of him as the aircraft gave a slight lurch. His hand touched the edge of the table. Finally he got up and walked forward up the centre aisle to the lavatory.

In the galley a stewardess was separating out the disposable plastic cups. She picked one off its tray and noted with slight distaste that its outside surface was sticky. She looked at her fingers, they were covered with a thin, grey-white film. She sniffed her fingers, grimaced, and put the cup back on the table.

On the flight deck, the engineer saw a main current indicator dip suddenly and then recover. He reached up, undid two handscrews, and slid out an electronic unit labelled *Voltage Stabilizer Chokes*. He attached test wires from another unit labelled *Check Prods*. He made notes on his log sheet.

Captain Howard set the on-board weather radar sweep going and studied the orange screen as the light bar swept to and fro marking out concentrations of high-density air ahead. Then he turned and dialled up Shannon beacon station and waited until the Morse identification sign bleeped on the overhead loudspeaker. Finally, he stretched back in his seat, putting his hands behind his neck.

P_2, the second pilot, moved the control column wheel and set course on the Shannon readings, then set the controls to autopilot. As he took his hands away from the control column, he paused for a moment, then looked down in silent amazement.

On the palm of one hand was a black sticky patch. On the control column where his hand had been, the black cylindrical cover of the wheel was wet and shiny. There were depressions where his fingers had been.

"What the hell's going on?"

The captain looked over: "I'll be damned . . ."

"On the column, look." He pointed.

"Some guy probably spilt some thinners. Wrap it with some paper or something."

"Thinners, hell, get a load of that," he pushed his hand across towards the captain, who wrinkled his face and sniffed.

"Smells like crap. Benny, make a note about this, will you?"

The flight engineer grinned: "Like what do I say—we're driving a shit-bucket?"

"There's another smell as well. What is it? Yeah. Ammonia." The co-pilot was sniffing.

"Leave it, eh?" The captain was firm. "Just bind up the column and get the stuff off your fingers."

Kramer finished his notes, packed away his report, pocketed his pen, and settled down to sleep.

Outside, the clouds flickered with blue light from an electrical storm far below.

In the galley the stewardess wiped the stickiness off her fingers and looked down at the table, her eyes widening with disbelief.

The cup was very slowly beginning to alter in shape. A small patch on one side was buckling and flowing down onto the table. Then, almost as if it were in a hot oven, the remainder followed suit and began to collapse in a viscid pool. She stared at it for a few seconds and then went out into the corridor and silently beckoned the chief steward, who was still serving drinks from the trolley. He looked up, then seeing her expression, went quickly down to the galley.

"It just went," she said nervously. "I watched it, I didn't do anything. Look!"

The chief steward thought for a moment, looking at the sticky pool on the table. "You haven't been using nail varnish remover—anything like that?"

"No. I told you, it just happened, it just melted."

The chief steward touched the pool on the table: "Any more gone like it?"

"No, I don't think so. . . ."

"Well, chuck it, anyway. Forget it."

On the flight deck, the engineer replaced the stabilizer and finished writing out the log entry describing the fault. Inside the unit, mutant 59 found food.

A woman returned to her seat from the lavatory and reached down for her handbag, feeling for the handle. As she tried to pull it out from under the seat, the handle gradually stretched like a sluggish elastic band, snapped, and came away in her hand.

She swore briefly and reached down again for the bag and rang for the steward. He leant over to her: "Yes, madam?"

"Have you some sort of heater under here?" She showed him the broken handle.

"Pardon, madam?"

"Look, see for yourself." She gave him the broken handle. "I put my bag under the seat and now look at it, it's all burned up."

"Sorry, madam, but there aren't any heaters in the cabin. It must have been old; plastic isn't so good as leather."

"It was not old, my daughter gave me this bag just a few weeks back!"

"Tell you what I'll do, madam, I'll arrange for the airline to present you with one of their own bags when we reach Kennedy." He smiled professionally.

Mollified, the woman settled back in her seat.

Taking the handle, the steward said: "I'll get rid of it for you, madam," and went thoughtfully back to the galley.

On the flight deck, the engineer was watching two dial indicators labelled *Input Power Distribution*. Reading off the levels, he sat back and picked up a thumbed paperback. Above his head, the mutant was already feeding in the maze of coloured wires in the stabilizer, gathering strength, dividing.

A wire was bared to the core, current flashed, one hundred amps drove through wires designed for two. There was a sudden explosion and a flood of acrid smoke. The engineer jerked up off his seat and cannoned into the back of the co-pilot, who lurched forward over the control column.

Immediately, the aircraft began to dive, the passengers all reacting to the nauseating sensation of the floor dropping down away from them.

The co-pilot, recovering quickly, pulled the column back and the nose of the aircraft thrust upwards against their feet. The captain reached for a small hatch labelled *Smoke Goggles* and took out the transparent eye protectors. Smoke was pouring from the damaged unit, and the co-pilot opened the cabin air exhaust to full to clear the choking air.

Howard pulled down the passenger compartment tannoy mike and spoke, carefully pitching his voice level: "This is Captain Howard speaking, we're now flying at a height of thirty-one thousand feet and running into headwinds which will delay our arrival by about thirty-five minutes. There is also a little turbulence ahead, so will you please fasten your seat belts and remain seated.

Thank you." His voice clicked off and the red seat-belt sign glowed.

Kramer, woken by the sudden dive, moved around in his seat to find a comfortable position, his knees jamming the table hanging down from the seat in front of him. As he leant forward to fold it away, he saw the edge of the table. The rim had softened and melted in a wet, sticky stream dripping down onto his trouser leg, leaving an opalescent grey patch just above his knee. Looking carefully to see whether the passenger beside him was watching, he bent forward and sniffed. Very slowly he moved back in his seat and reached up with his right hand for the push button to call the steward. He then withdrew his hand and put it on the arm of the seat, palm uppermost. He searched carefully around, and then, with his left hand, picked up a pencil and used it to press the overhead button. He sat back waiting, absolutely motionless.

The steward bent down, carefully studying Kramer's awkward position: "Yes, sir, can I get you something?"

"I want to speak to the captain."

"Can you tell me what about, sir?"

"Not right now, no. There's a . . ." Kramer checked that the passenger beside him was still asleep. He kept his voice low. ". . . something's happened which may be of some danger to this aircraft. I wish to talk to the captain. Will you please get him—now!"

The steward, warily studying Kramer, wondered whether he was crazy or drunk.

"Would you like to come forward into the first-class section, sir?" he asked. "I'll get a member of the flight crew to . . ."

"Listen, and listen very carefully. You're not going to find this very easy to understand, but I can't leave my seat. I must stay exactly where I am!"

Oh God, thought the steward, we've got a nutter, probably a bomber. He spoke reassuringly: "All right, sir, yes I understand, now you stay right where you are and I'll go up front and talk to the captain."

He walked off, Kramer glaring after him at the condescension in his voice.

As the steward walked through the forward bulkhead he had to make his way past a queue of passengers waiting for the lavatory.

On the flight deck he spoke quietly to Captain Howard: ". . . he looks odd—sits there all cramped up; it's almost like he doesn't want to touch anything."

"Think he's going to do anything?" Captain Howard asked.

"Can't tell. No threats, not yet anyway."

"I'll come back and have a look."

Kramer waited impatiently.

The captain spoke smoothly: "Good evening, sir, the steward tells me you've got a problem."

Kramer pointed to the sleeping passenger beside him: "Get him out . . ." he stopped, collected himself. "Right. Now, first of all, I'm not mad, I'm not going to hijack you, and you're going to find what I'm going to say extremely hard to believe."

"Yes?"

"My name is Kramer, *Doctor* Kramer, and I'm a scientist." The captain and the steward listened, motionless. "In some way I don't exactly understand, I've brought an organism with me on board this aircraft and it's dangerous."

"Organism, what do you mean?"

"Captain, you know about the events in Central London."

"Yes."

"Well, I am part of a Government group investigating its cause and I'm on my way to New York with an urgent report for NASA concerning its nature."

"Can you give me some sort of identification, sir?"

"What! Oh yes, I can." Kramer reached for his bag, hesitated for a moment, and then said: "Captain, I'll produce the papers and show them to you, but I must ask you just to read them as I hold them up—don't actually touch them."

The steward and the captain exchanged glances as Kramer took the NASA report and letters of identification out of his bag and held them forward. The sleeping passenger stirred and turned in his seat. They peered at the documents and nodded.

Kramer went on: "Captain, we now have good evidence to show that the breakdown in London is caused by a unique micro-organism—a germ."

Captain Howard remembered his training; he remembered the psychiatrist who had lectured on the early symptoms of paranoid schizophrenia so that potentially dangerous passengers could be spotted.

"This germ, Mr. Kramer," he asked, "what do you say it does?"

Kramer stared at them both, then said flatly, "It eats plastic."

The captain's manner hardened. "Mr. Kramer, everything said to me about possible dangers to the aircraft I'm obviously bound to take seriously, but I think you're wasting my time. I must ask you please not to cause any more disturbances and . . ."

"What about this!" Kramer pointed at the rim of the table and the patch on his knee. The captain bent down to examine the table.

"Don't touch it! Smell it—do you smell anything?"

"Mr. Kramer, you could have done that with almost anything. You could have poured a solvent on it, you could have heated it with a lighter. . . ."

"No charring. Anyway, will you accept a visual proof?"

"Captain Howard, sir," the steward spoke nervously. "Can I have a word with you. I'd like to show you something." He beckoned the captain down the aisle towards the galley.

The sticky patch where the cup had been was now foaming into a small localized hemisphere of undulating bubbles.

"Then there was this woman's bag. Look, I've got the handle here." He reached down for the trash shute. As he opened the hatch, they both stood transfixed. From the open hatch pouted a greyish mass of glutinous foam, bulging out of the square aperture and dropping silently down onto the floor. Where it touched the vinyl floor covering it seemed to creep almost immediately into the shining blue surface like oil creeping into the surface of rust.

"Right! The passenger next to that man, what's his name? Kramer." Howard's voice was firm: "Get him to another seat."

On the flight deck, Howard sniffed the taped-up column handle. He turned to the engineer: "Done anything about the voltage stabilizer?"

"Yeah, I strapped out the lines; we're running without it."

"Did you have it out to see where the fault was?"

"No point, can't do anything about it up here. They'll change it when we hit Kennedy. It's kaput."

"Benny, I'd like you to have a look."

"It's a stabilizer! We can run without it. O.K., there's a small risk of a voltage surge from the generators but . . ."

"Take it out, Benny."

Seeing the gravity of his expression, the engineer reached silently and unscrewed the stabilizer panel. He pulled it out on slides and stared, motionless. "Jesus Christ, what the hell's going on?"

From the under-surface of the unit, there was hanging a multi-coloured blob of slowly moving sludge. As they sat transfixed, the blob stretched, thinned out, and dropped wetly to the floor. The engineer moved to touch the sticky material.

"Don't touch it!" Howard cried out.

"Why not, what's the matter?"

"Put it back, just don't touch it."

The steward put his head round the door. "O.K., he's moved."

"Good, now will you ask Dr. Kramer to come forward here, please?"

"Yes, sir."

"And then go back to the galley. Tell the girls as little as necessary—and don't leave, right?"

"Yes."

Both co-pilots and the engineer began talking at once: "Now look, what is this, skipper?"

"Would somebody mind . . .?"

"Who's Kramer?"

Howard looked hard at each one of them before he replied: "I want you to hear this man's story for yourselves."

Kramer came in.

"Take a seat." Howard pointed towards the empty trainee's seat behind him. "Could you tell these gentlemen what you told me back in there?" He pointed towards the passenger compartment.

Kramer was sitting awkwardly, still trying not to touch anything with his hands. The patch on his trouser leg had soaked into the cloth leaving a dark patch.

He began rapidly: "A little earlier on I told the captain that I am part of a British Government inquiry group working on the Central London disaster. . . ."

Quickly and concisely he outlined the story.

The internal surface of a jetliner's passenger compartment is designed with just three major requirements. First, lightness; second, easy maintenance; and third, resistance to ageing or corrosion. In practice this has produced a design that is almost 80-per-cent plastic. The ceiling, wall, and seat trim is vinyl cloth. The overhead shelves are extruded polystyrene. The service binnacles over each seat are vacuum-formed polypropylene, and the edge seals for the windows are a special, high-grade plastic sheeting. Food for a million generations of mutant 59.

Gradually, almost unseen in many places, the mutant was taking hold of the ship. In the lavatory a notice labelled *Used Towels Only* was beginning to soften, the letters elongating as the backing sagged.

Next to a passenger who had visited the lavatory, a window seal began to expand and distort. The plastic sole of a man's shoe flattened slightly under the weight of his leg.

On the flight deck, Kramer had finished his account. The crew sat in silence; only the first co-pilot appeared uninterested as he flew the plane and monitored the maze of instruments in front of him.

Howard tapped the back of his thumb against his teeth: "If I keep everyone where they are—nobody moves—we can put down at Kennedy. . . ."

"Not Kennedy," Kramer frowned. "We can't put down there. Don't you see, we're like an infected community. . . ."

"We've got to be isolated?" the co-pilot spoke with the tremor of scarcely concealed fright.

"That's it. We'll have to go through a complete decontamination. . . ."

Howard cut in: "We can maybe use Taor Creek."

"What's that?"

"It's an emergency strip about forty miles south of Boston, on the coast."

"We'll need the complete treatment." Kramer was ticking off the items in his hand. "Each passenger will have to strip, shower, and hand in his clothes for sterilization. The plane will have to be cordoned off . . ."

"Who the hell do we get to do all this?" Howard was thinking aloud. "The airport medical authorities don't carry that kind of gear."

"You've got Dugway."

"What's that?"

"Dugway proving ground. A germ-warfare test place. They can put some people down at Taor Creek by chopper—protective suits, the lot." He smiled grimly: "Give them something positive to do!"

The window seal next to the woman dripped away down onto the surrounding trim panel, but there was no explosion, no sound.

The windows on a jet are a concession to passengers by designers who would very much rather do without them altogether, since they raise the cost and weaken the structure of the hull. Each one has either three or four layers of transparent plastic, each one separately sealed into the surrounding structure of the hull. Between the inner layers, air is kept circulating by the two cabin compressors situated under the flight deck. This is to avoid condensation and the air is pumped at the same pressure as the interior of the plane. Between the outer two layers, air is circulated at the same pressure and temperature as the outside air.

A thin layer of the fifty-ninth mutant soaked in mindless determination across the one-inch gap between the innermost layer and the next. Cells released enzymes which dissolved the intricacies of man-made molecules.

The girl in the plastic coat lay back fast asleep, and as a passenger passed in the aisle, he touched her shoulder. She woke up and tried to move her head. As if in some waking nightmare she pulled the side of her face away from the seat back.

Slowly, like an old piece of candy in its wrapper, her head moved away. Between the side of her face, the collar of her coat, and the seat, there was a soft dripping patch pulling out into long wet strips as she moved. She turned in panic and saw the shoulder of her coat collapsed like a Scuba suit around the contours of her shoulder. For a long moment she stayed absolutely still, her face immobile. She screamed. A stewardess came running.

In the first-class compartment the large, florid man still snored the flight away. Oblivious to everything around him and breathing brandy fumes, he failed entirely to see the shape of his spectacles begin to alter.

First, the brown plastic bridge across his nose softened, allowing the weight of the lenses to pull the shape down over his face like a caricature. Then one glass popped out of its sagging frame and rolled down into his lap. Like a stream of chocolate, a brown rivulet began to make its way down the lines of his face towards his open mouth. His face twitched unconsciously as it moved.

The girl in the plastic coat was calming down and the stewardess was trying to prevent her getting up to go and wash.

The captain's voice came over the tannoy: "This is Captain Howard speaking. Because of a small electrical fault, we shall not be landing at Kennedy Airport, New York. Instead we shall make our way to an airfield just south of Boston. Because of the—fault—I must ask you please to remain in your seats with seat belts fastened.

I am sorry for this inconvenience. The cabin crew will make you as comfortable as possible, but I must ask you all not to smoke please."

On the flight deck, Howard switched the microphone off.

"Surely you must tell them before we land," Kramer said.

"Of course," Howard replied, "but if I give it to them all at once we'll get panic; I'll do it bit by bit." He turned to the second pilot: "Any luck?"

"Yes, they're raising Taor now."

"Right." He turned to Kramer. "Now, Doctor . . ."

Behind them the door suddenly opened and then shut again. There were sounds of a scuffle. It opened again, revealing the brown-steaked face of the man from the first-class lounge. His eyes were blazing.

"You the Captain?" he shouted. "What do you think you're goddamn well doing?" He lunged forward.

Benny, the flight engineer, whipped round in his seat and grabbed him just before he could get his hands on Howard. "Get back to your seat."

"Look I got shares in your lousy airline. I know your directors. I'm going to make good and sure . . ."

The flight engineer leapt to his feet and slammed the man against the door. He towered over him. All his anxiety reacted in violence.

"Now listen and shut up!" he shouted. "This aircraft is in danger, and by coming in here you've added to that danger. You heard the captain's instructions, now get back in there, sit down, strap in, and shut up! If I get one more peep out of you, I'll come in there and kick your head in, you got that?"

The man glared silently, his face working in a mixture of fear and anger.

"Go on, get out!"

Slowly his anger gave way to shaking, then to complete collapse. He leant back against the door, his mouth slack with fear.

"What are you doing?" He wiped his face, smearing the brown stains on his cheeks: "Wha—what's going on? I wanna know—we going to crash?"

The engineer reached silently round behind him and opened the door. He guided the man back to his seat and strapped him in.

The bacteria now had the aircraft almost completely in their grip. At hundreds of different points, plastic trim cloth, overhead shelves, and the floor covering silently began to change in shape, first buckling, then turning wet and glistening, finally giving rise to small bubbles of foul-smelling foam. Over one passenger the air-conditioning binnacle began to sag slowly down towards the top of his head, almost as if the bacteria inside it were turning it into a limb.

The captain's voice on the cabin tannoy had changed. The usual polite concern and confident trivialities had disappeared and he was giving sharp orders:

"You must understand that what is happening is of no danger to life—it is only in the plastic parts of the aircraft. As I've said, we shall land at an airstrip near Boston, and until we do you are all to remain seated. It is very important that you do not move about the aircraft, because if you do you will cause more plastic parts to be affected and endanger our flight."

The chief steward was trying to restrain a panic-stricken man in the corridor. They slipped and fell on the wet, glistening floor, the floor colour staining their clothes.

The woman with the handbag sat transfixed with horror as a writhing bubble of black foam rose obscenely up between her legs.

The stewardesses were backing slowly out of the galley, staring with silent horror at the shambles inside. The stacks of trays were collapsing, the cups lay in pools of foaming slime, and the neat packets of knives and spoons had coalesced and bent into mad surrealist shapes.

There was now an evil-smelling foam running out into the main corridor from dozens of points. The girl in the plastic coat was struggling weakly in an almost spherical covering still retaining an imprint of the patterns in her coat.

Most of the passengers were completely silent, some

praying and others weeping. Every few minutes a steward tried vainly to prevent people from getting up. The air grew fouler as the gas level built up.

On the flight deck no one spoke. Kramer sat hunched in his seat. Howard was flying the plane, and the two co-pilots and the engineer were studying the banks of instruments with total absorption.

The end came swiftly. Overhead in a roof panel two bared wires touched and the mixture of gases generated by the fifty-ninth mutant flashed and ignited.

Far down below in the icy seas to the east of Nantucket, the skipper of a small diesel fishing boat heard the boom and crack of the explosion high overhead. As he looked up, he could just make out small points of fire trailing down through the night sky.

He reached for his shore-radio.

17

Anne woke to find herself in a hospital bed in a private ward at St. Thomas's Hospital. Sitting patiently beside her was Buchan, sturdily resisting the demands of nurses and doctors to move.

They had just heard of Kramer's death, and Buchan wanted to be the first to tell her before she heard it on the radio. Gerrard was still asleep in another wing of the hospital, unaware of the news.

Anne turned to Buchan and held out her hand. There was something massively reassuring about the angular Scot with his tightly buttoned tweed coat and shock of grey hair.

Gradually, with his help, she reconstructed the events of the last few hours. An Army team had gone down the Portland Place shaft with rescue gear and cut their way through to Slayter and Anne at the base of the old shaft. The whole operation had taken no more than half an hour with the help of experts from British Transport. They had also brought up the stationmaster, who had been taken to hospital. Purvis was found dead in the disused tunnel.

She asked about the disaster situation, and Buchan gave her the latest information.

Anne began to worry about Kramer. She'd expected him to be there. Why wasn't he?

Buchan paused before replying: "There's been an accident," he said.

"Accident?"

"To his plane," Buchan continued. "He took off yesterday for the States and it's been reported missing. I'm sorry."

Anne sat up in bed: "I don't understand."

Buchan explained slowly. He told her of Kramer's determination to face the NASA committee in person.

Anne's face altered slightly and she turned away, fighting to keep control. "Didn't he know that I was . . . ?" She didn't finish the question.

"He felt there was little he could do," said Buchan. "He hoped to be back by the time you got out."

"But how could he know that I was going to get out? How could he know I wasn't dead down there?" She spoke wildly, and when Buchan tried to hold her hand she pulled it away furiously. Buchan didn't answer.

Anne thought for a moment: "Surely it wasn't that important to go to NASA in person!"

"He thought it was," said Buchan. "You know him, once he's made up his mind . . ."

"But he knew I was missing," she went on.

"He not only went to defend the consultancy," said Buchan, "but he also quite genuinely felt that if these bugs ever got into space—to another planet—then they might be a . . . what would you call it? A time-bomb for future astronauts."

Anne leant back against the head of the bed. The tears were there but they refused to come. Suddenly the overwhelming fact of his death hit her. She collapsed weeping.

Anne slowly cried herself out. She felt drained. There were too many conflicting emotions; she wanted peace, a refuge. She turned to Buchan and held both his hands. "Buck," she said, "I'm very grateful. Thank you."

"I've not done anything, lassie."

"Now I want to go home," said Anne.

"I'm not sure you should be leaving just yet."

"I'm all right," said Anne. "Really, I need to go home."

"I'll get the ward sister," said Buchan doubtfully. "Then, if they say you can, I'll drive you back."

"No," said Anne. "Please don't, you've done enough.

I'm sure you're wanted with the others in the lab. Leave me—really, I'd much rather. Thank you."

Buchan left the room and it was only when she had finished dressing and was preparing to face the ward sister that she remembered the letter.

Had this contributed to Kramer's decision? After seven years of marriage, she knew him less than she had ever done. He was entirely unpredictable. Did he read the letter before he went?

She rejected the thought. Of course not. How could he have known the flight would crash? That was not in his make-up. But, to wash his hands of somebody, that was entirely in character. She remembered with a sudden chill that the letter left no room for compromise. It must have seemed entirely final to him and was obviously why he had abandoned such a cold, unfeeling wife in her dangerous situation.

How could she blame him? There were many ways of approaching their central problem and, the thought suddenly struck her, suppose it was entirely in her mind?

Suppose the trip to Cambridge had been totally unconnected with this woman? Suppose she had built the entire thing up in her imagination?

No, the letter was proof they had been lovers. But so what? Perhaps it was just a physical thing. Perhaps the woman had built a great deal more into it than Kramer had felt. She had never seen one of his letters to her. And on this flimsy evidence she had wrecked her life and probably sent her husband to his death.

The house doctor was reluctant to let her go and made her sign the voluntary discharge form. They were in fact glad to get a vacant bed for more urgent cases. After advising her to rest and see her doctor on the following day, they called a taxi for her and she went home.

In the flat Anne collapsed on to one of the over-size armchairs. The familiar smells and the atmosphere soothed her. There was more of her in the flat now than of Kramer. It had been her refuge, almost a place of hermitage for her. There was little, in fact, to remind her of him at all.

With a shock she realized that there never had been any imprint of his character in the flat. It was as if he had used it as a hotel room—in transit. Always in transit—a fleeting kiss—sorry, honey, I've got to be in Geneva this evening— sorry, honey, can't make dinner tonight—sorry, honey—sorry, honey.

The words reverberated and she dozed lightly in the chair, then slowly opened her eyes. She longed for a friend, someone to hold her, look after her. Both her parents were dead, and despite her many business acquaintances, she had few friends. She looked across the room and then something caught her eye. She rose to her feet.

It was quite unmistakable—there on the mantelpiece, the letter. She ran over, picked it up. It had not been opened.

Menzelos's thirty-foot ocean-going cruiser lay at anchor riding a slight swell in Chichester harbour; its sleek white and gold lines reflected brightly in the dark water.

On board, Menzelos was at work in the engine bay, making the twin-Volvo engines ready for the long haul over to Bordeaux. Ackerman sat morosely watching him, whisky bottle in hand, while Carole Menzelos stocked the galley cupboards with tins of food from a holdall.

They had had no trouble on the way down to the coast. Alford had dropped off to lie low with friends in the town and the Customs official quite understood that their time in London had been a great strain and now they were off to France for a few days' break. Menzelos had, in fact, wanted to go over with his wife, but Ackerman, in a fury of paranoid mistrust, had insisted on going with them.

Ackerman checked the jewels. They were hung in polythene bags suspended from a nylon cord inside the main gasoline tank. Even a zealous Customs official would never have seen them, since the hook from which they were suspended was well round the corner of the tank, away from the neck of the filler opening.

As he screwed back the filler cap, he checked the plastic fuel-feed pipes to the twin engines, pulling them with his fingers to test the brass unions at each end.

Mutant 59 began to feed.

Nine hours later, with Cap Rochelle six miles away on the port side, the sleek fibreglass hull forged on through the growing seas of the bay. All three were now drowsy with the hypnotic roar of the engines.

The fuel pipe to the starboard engine began to sag.

In the main cabin, Ackerman was surly drunk. Carole Menzelos tried to concentrate on a paperback, and Menzelos stood in the cockpit vainly trying to see ahead through the wash.

The rate of division of mutant 59 accelerated until it had gorged its way through the fuel pipe. Finally, the pipe burst, releasing a gushing flood of high-octane fuel into the closed-off engine bay. Float levels in the twin-Weber carburettors fell, and the engine coughed once and then died.

Menzelos looked at the dials in front of him and pressed the red starter-button irritably.

As the motor whirred protestingly against the dead weight of the fuel-starved engine, its armature emitted a small corona of sparks.

The fuel vapour in the engine bay abruptly flashed into flame. The main tank fractured and with a terrible roar exploded in a great orange ball of flame, engulfing Menzelos and blasting through the companionway into the main cabin.

The impact of the blast tore the bottom away from the engine bay, and water fountained upwards into the cockpit, engulfing the charred remains of Menzelos's body.

Ackerman, his face blackened and fixed in a mask of pain, struggled through the cabin door against the racing, icy water. Abruptly, the hull of the cruiser tilted around him and began to plunge downwards.

As the water level rose, forcing him against the roof

of the cabin, his last action was to reach out ineffectually for one of the jewel bags tumbling past in the roaring water.

The bacteriological laboratories were in a fury of activity.

On one bench, technicians were busy plating out samples of the fifty-ninth mutant onto flat dishes containing a thin layer of gelled culture medium. They were working through armholes in sealed cabinets, awkwardly trying to manoeuvre the dishes and the samples through rubber gloves sealed into the armholes. Inside, the cabinets were lit by a harsh ultra-violet light. As each dish was inoculated, it was stacked on a pile. Every few minutes, another technician opened a side door in a cabinet, took out a pile of dishes, and transferred them to an incubator with a glass door, making a note on a clip pad hanging beside the incubator.

On another bench, a row of haggard and unshaven scientists were gazing with fixed concentration down binocular microscopes. As they completed each slide examination, a note was made and the slide discarded into a large vessel of disinfectant.

A third group were examining antibiotic-sensitivity test dishes. These were similar to ordinary culture dishes, but on top of an even layer of incubated bacilli there had been arranged a ring of small filter-paper discs. On each disc a drop of a particular antibiotic had been released, so that any restriction of growth caused by the antibiotic would be seen as a clear area surrounding the disc.

In the immunology section, three gowned women seated in front of an improvised Perspex shield covering a fume cupboard were pipetting carefully measured drops of clear serum into hundreds of small glass tubes stacked in rows in copper racks. As each rack was inoculated, they were taken to a near-by water bath for slow warming at blood heat.

Over the continuous activity hung the stale-soup smell of culture medium. The air was humid with the water from the steam-sterilizing ovens in a near-by laboratory. Moisture ran down the insides of the windows.

At one end of the main lab was a closed-off, glass-walled room. Inside, the atmosphere was dry and cool, away from the tropical fetor of the lab. Professor Kendall sat at his desk. A thin, bird-like man with a shock of soft white hair, he sat surveying the others as they talked animatedly.

Wright was sitting on the edge of the desk, and Gerrard was slumped wearily in an easy chair. Scanlon came in and sat on an office chair next to Kendall.

Kendall spoke with a meticulous use of consonants: "If we're really quite honest about it, we're drawing an almost total blank. Consider: We've now run through all known antibiotic agents. Only one showed any sensitivity—Neomycin D. . . ."

"Why don't we use it?" Wright broke in.

"Because, my dear Dr. Wright, there isn't enough 'D' in the world to sterilize more than a few square yards. We have to be considerably more ingenious than that, I'm afraid. No, we've drawn a blank. We might just as well admit it and that's that."

"I'm sure the growth of the mutant is related to the polymer used for the bio-degradable bottle," Gerrard said. "Down in the disused tube station, every time we saw a piece of bottle, there was an increased activity of the bacteria around it. I brought the bits up, you saw them."

"How does that help us?" Wright said defensively. "Just because it likes our bottle material doesn't mean to say it's the prime cause."

"I didn't say it was," Gerrard replied. "I just said there is a connection."

"What are you suggesting?" Kendall asked mildly.

"I'm not clear yet," Gerrard said absently. "Something I'm trying to get out of my head, just a vague notion, that's all." He thought for a moment: "Why don't ordinary disinfectants work?"

"They do, after a fashion," replied Kendall. "In fact that's what the de-contamination squads are having to rely on at present. Trouble is, they only really act on surfaces. What we need is a much more deeply seated attack. Something which will get at the roots of the problem. To make disinfectants successful, we'd have to literally flood the whole of Central London with Lysol or something. It's just not practical. No, we must find a more specific method—something related to the mutant itself."

"Supposing I'm right," Gerrard went on. "Supposing that there is something about the plastic our group used to make the bottle." He turned to Wright: "When you first designed the plastic molecule, what was your reasoning? How did you arrive at its shape?"

"The main requirement," Wright said, "was to make a long polymer chain with unstable reactive cross-links. To use photo-sensitive links in a way which would ensure that the action of light released bonds and fixed oxygen onto the remaining valencies."

Kendall interrupted: "Sorry, I'm a bit lost."

Gerrard explained: "Long plastic molecule chains which will break apart under the action of light and oxygen."

"How very ingenious," Kendall murmured.

Gerrard turned to Wright: "Can you draw the shape of the molecule?"

"Yes," Wright replied. He picked up a felt pen and began to draw expertly on a large sheet of paper.

"The main chain looks like this," he explained, "and these are amino-groups here"—the drawing of lines, dots, and symbols grew—"the oxy-phenyls here and the quinol ring here. These, as you can see, are unstable bonds which will result in the fulfillment of electron density if this part of the chain unfolds. Only a few quanta of light are enough."

"Then what?" Gerrard asked.

Wright looked surprised: "Well, surely you know! Then the molecule breaks into these four components here." He pointed to the drawing. "It is then available for destruction by ordinary bacterial action."

"But, why?" Gerrard persisted. "*How* is it available?"

Wright was growing impatient: "Look, I've been over this hundreds of times with you. . . ."

"Great! Now once more, please. There's something I'm trying to get clear. Tell me again what it is about the molecules which ordinary bacteria can break down."

Kendall interrupted: "This is no ordinary bacterium, there's nothing like it on earth anywhere. It's a totally new mutant."

Wright continued: "Well, once we had a molecule which would disrupt into smaller units under the influence of light, we tried to design the units to be as similar as possible to polypeptides. . . ."

"Polypeptides? Sorry, I don't really see . . ." Kendall began.

Gerrard broke in: "Polypeptides are middle-size molecules that go to make up protein."

"I see!" replied Kendall. "You tried to make a plastic residue which would resemble protein."

"Exactly," said Wright. "To aim at a sort of middle-of-the-road structure, so that before, it would be a perfectly good container material, and after light exposure through the strip, a perfectly disposable material which would be consumed in the normal way—something people could put on the compost heap."

"It's a really clever idea," said Kendall. "But you didn't reckon with the mutant, did you?"

"How could we?" said Wright. "It doesn't exist. According to the books, there's no such damned species."

"How do we know our bottle material didn't help it to evolve?" asked Gerrard.

"What evidence?" exclaimed Wright.

"We can't exclude the possibility, can we?" Gerrard continued.

"Oh, for God's sake," complained Wright. "We can't exclude the possibility that it came from the moon either, can we?" He looked derisively at Gerrard: "Let's stick to what we do know."

Gerrard persisted: "I'm sure it's related to our plastic. As I said, each time I recognized a bit of one of our bottles, the growth rate near-by was higher than anywhere else."

Wright was now openly hostile: "That proves nothing at all!"

Gerrard glared at him: "You don't really *want* us to be involved, do you? What you really want is to exonerate our bottle—so we don't take any rap."

"Even if what you say has some basis—which I very much doubt—that still doesn't make us responsible. That mutant is the problem, not the bloody plastic."

"Not at all. If our product is even slightly responsible for all this disaster, then we're going to have to assume some blame."

Wright laughed harshly: "I simply don't follow your line of argument. Supposing we made petrol. Supposing we sell petrol and somebody blows himself up with it. Does that make us responsible for his death—simply because we made it?"

"This is completely different," said Gerrard. "We knew in the first place that we were making a substance which would degrade under the action of bacteria, that we were mimicking a natural process. We knew . . ."

"For God's sake . . ." expostulated Wright. "We *didn't* know about this mutant organism. How could we possibly have said to ourselves: no, we mustn't go on with this process because a new germ might appear which would mutate. It's a completely speculative idea in the first place—you haven't got any evidence whatever and yet you expect us to go cap in hand to everyone and say *mea culpa!* You know I think you *want* to get the blame. You're a *victim* looking for a cause."

Kendall was embarrassed at the outbreak: "Gentlemen. I think we might . . ."

Gerrard gestured him to silence: "All right, so I'm swimming in guilt, so what? You don't want to lift a finger . . ."

"Prove to me what to do and I'll do it," Wright retorted.

"Right. First, we have an organism which eats plastic, then we have a plastic which degrades to a protein-like structure following exposure to light and air. Never mind for a moment where the bugs came from, but we know they interact. . . ."

"*We* don't know," Wright replied. "You're guessing—there's no evidence."

"Never mind," Gerrard went on, "if they do interact, then why don't we exploit that?"

"I don't follow," Kendall began.

Gerrard was gaining confidence. "Yes, that's it, why not?" He turned to Wright. "How easy is it to alter the structure of the plastic molecule?"

"Depends what you want to do with it," Wright said suspiciously.

"Nothing radical," Gerrard replied. "How easy would it be to replace—say—one of the amino groups?"

"Easiest of them all actually," said Wright. "Just a matter of hydrolysis and then . . ."

"Never mind how," said Gerrard excitedly. "As long as you can do it quickly."

"Yes, I said so," Wright replied irritably. "But I don't see . . ."

"Would an azide or cyanide molecule go in easily?"

"Yes, it would actually. I tried it in one of the earlier experiments. No good obviously—poisonous as hell."

"Precisely!" shouted Gerrard. "Poisonous!"

Kendall jumped up. "I see! Alter the construction of the plastic so that . . ."

". . . it's *poisonous.*" Gerrard was shaking with excitement. "Then put it down—like rat poison—and the bacteria will feed on it and die."

"Good God!" Kendall exploded. "A good idea. Yes, I like it. But what would . . . ?"

"You've nothing really to go on. Just a waste of time," said Wright.

Gerrard ignored him: "Have you still got the pilot apparatus at the lab?"

Wright started to protest again.

"Have you got it?" Gerrard was standing over Wright almost menacingly.

Wright looked up; the Canadian towered over him. "Yes, it's there, it's set up actually. Scanlon was working on it last week, as a matter of fact. Trying to . . ."

"Will you get it working?"

"Well, I can, but it's a complete waste of time. Besides, I don't . . ."

"Will you do it?" Gerrard was almost shouting.

Wright stared at him, openly hostile. Suddenly, he looked down, away from Gerrard. "Yes," he said flatly. "Yes, I'll do it."

Outside in the freezing winter air, the stench of Ainslie's bacillus lay over the deserted streets. Snow was falling heavily, and the only sounds were from small squads of soldiers in full protective clothing, marching through the deserted streets like spacemen exploring a new planet. Their heavy boots scrunched in the snow.

Outside the sealed perimeter, broadcast television vans were crowded around the exit points and the decontamination station. With arc lights glaring, interviewers tried to talk to bemused people who staggered out of the area either dressed in overall smocks or ill-fitting clothing.

Anxious relatives gathered at the exit gates for news.

An ambulance, its blue light flashing, skidded around a deserted Trafalgar Square and tore off up the Charing Cross Road, the untrodden snow billowing up behind it in a fine, white cloud.

Overhead a helicopter hovered. A cameraman hung dangerously out of its open door, recording the story of a lifetime.

Ainslie's fifty-ninth mutant probed into new areas, searching for food. Some growths died on metal or stone surfaces. Others found new continuities of growth in plastic cables and wires underground. Slowly and efficiently, the bacillus ate the heart out of the city.

At the Kramer laboratories Gerrard, his face grey with fatigue, was standing by the blackboard writing complex mathematical expressions and checking them on a desk calculator which whirred and clicked its answers as he punched in information. It was three a.m. On a bench in the main lab, Wright, Scanlon, and Buchan were tending a mass of inter-woven glass apparatus mounted on a makeshift metal scaffold. Inside the apparatus, coloured fluids travelled through joint glass tubing, and at one end, a viscous brown fluid dripped slowly into a conical flask. There was about an inch of fluid in the flask. Wright turned off a glass tap above the flask, picked it up, carried it to the desk next to Gerrard, and sat down wearily. He spoke in a flat, off-hand tone: "That should be it—poly-Aminostyrene with fangs."

Gerrard turned off the calculator: "You absolutely sure?"

"Of course, but we'll check it on the chromatograph. We should have inserted a cyanide radical in place of the nitrosamine group on side chain four."

"Will it be active? You might have shielded all its valency."

"Our chemistry is excellent, thank you," Wright replied edgily. "It's you who wants to test it."

Gerrard eyed him carefully for a minute, then replied: "I put four sub-cultures of the mutant in the incubator when we got here, they should be going like a bomb now; I'll get them." He walked over to the incubator and took out three large, open-topped beakers.

In the bottom of each one, there was a flat, lidded Petri dish. He carried them gingerly through into the main lab. Wright followed, bringing the conical flask containing the poisoned plastic. Gerrard then wiped a flat, square porcelain dish until it was quite dry, put it down on the bench, and poured a little of the sticky brown fluid from the flask into one end of the dish. He then tipped the dish to and fro until the fluid spread out in a thin layer over one-half of its surface. Then from one of the beakers he took out a Petri dish and held it to the light carefully, not tipping it out of the horizontal.

In the light they could all plainly see that the inside of the dish was a semi-liquid, bubbling mass. Taking the lid off the dish he slowly poured the foaming contents into the other end of the dish, away from the cyanide-containing plastic; then he tipped the dish so that the edge of the foaming bacterial culture was about an inch away from the edge of the spread-out layer of plastic. All three men were unpleasantly aware of the dank ammoniacal odour. Finally, Gerrard put a glass plate over the dish, started a stop-watch going, adjusted a bench light over the glass cover, and sat down to watch.

As the minutes ticked by, the three men sat completely immobile, their gaze fixed on the slowly writhing line of bubbles as they approached the edge of the plastic.

After what seemed like an age, the edge of the foaming bubbles touched the brown layer. Gerrard leaned forward, every muscle in his body taut. The bubbling showed no sign of reduction as the growing mutant spread out over the plastic.

Wright glanced up at Gerrard, the suspicion of a smile hovering on his thin lips. Scanlon sat silent, his lips pursed with concentration. Buchan, inscrutable as ever, puffed away at his pipe.

The foaming continued and even seemed to increase in rate. Gerrard was swearing under his breath. Each one of them was fully aware that the fate of an entire city, perhaps of the whole civilized world, was being played out under the glass in front of them. As the three craned forward over the glass, the reflections from the light underlit their faces in the semi-darkened laboratory, making them look like ancient sorcerers.

Suddenly Gerrard gave a cry: "It's slowing—I'm sure—yes, look, it's slowing down."

The others peered into the dish. The line of bubbles on the edge of the advancing bacteria was smaller, the movement of the edge slower. As they watched, fascinated, the groping movement of the culture stopped. As each bubble broke, it was not replaced.

Finally, the mutant bacilli in the dish gorged itself to death. As it advanced, mindlessly searching for more food, it absorbed molecules of poly-Aminostyrene through its individual cell walls. But with a difference. As the molecules became part of each cell's internal structure, the cyanide went to work, poisoning essential enzyme systems until the bio-chemical perfection of the mutant—hand-tailored by Ainslie—lay wrecked and useless.

"We've only made ten grams," Wright said. "There's a whole city out there—they'll need tons of the stuff."

Gerrard was beside himself with relief: "I know. We'll get Polytad to mass-produce. They've got all the large equipment. Then we put it down all over the area. In the tunnels, in the sewers—it'll be like rat poison." He flopped back in the chair, allowing total exhaustion to soak up through his body.

Scanlon looked at him carefully: "We'll have to do a field test. We'll have to go where there's been a recent outbreak and see whether it works there."

"All right," Gerrard agreed. "Let's do that." He turned to Wright. "How much more can you make in, say, the next six hours?"

Wright thought for a moment, then replied, "Using that gear in there, about another three hundred grams."

"Not enough to do anything," Scanlon said.

"It is if we can dilute it with a volatile agent, then spray it," Gerrard replied. "Then the volatile will evaporate, and the stuff will be available for the mutant." He turned to Scanlon. "Get on to Polytad, get them to set up their gear for a major production effort."

He turned to Wright: "We'll need every gram you can make. I'll get on to the control centre and tell them we've busted it. Then we'd better look and see whether we've got enough volatile—toluene should do it—enough to make a suspension for spraying."

He broke off for a moment and looked at the inside of the dish again as if to reassure himself. The last of the bubbles had gone. "Goddamn it . . . it really worked!"

Buchan spoke for the first time: "What do you want —a Nobel Prize?"

18

The air in the great underground control complex was humid and stale. Three out of the four giant fans feeding its tunnels and concrete chambers had been turned off as they were drawing in air from the affected zone and were liable to spread an aerosol of infection throughout the system. The fourth fan, working at full blast behind a grille beyond the danger zone, was able to provide just enough fresh air for safety, but not enough to dispel the stench of the fifty-ninth mutant which had already been pumped in.

The smell—a mixture of ammonia and rotting meat—had nauseated everyone to a point where the prefabricated food constantly available in the canteens was left almost untouched. It clung tenaciously to clothing and soft furnishings.

Above, on the surface, the smell lay in the still, cold air like a pall of death.

Slayter was sitting at one of the coffee-stained tables, trying to appear interested in the conversation of the man sitting opposite him who was talking about the anatomy of the water mains in the area and how they were controlled. As he half-listened, his imagination was away back down in the tube tunnels.

Suddenly he heard the tone of the man's voice coming to a conclusion and realized that he hadn't taken anything in at all.

He took a risk: "Really, that's most extraordinary," he said, hoping the comment would fit. To his relief he saw no surprise on the man's face.

"Yes it is," his companion went on, "and do you know there's no complete map of the area showing all the services, really it's quite . . ."

Slayter suddenly looked up as Buchan rushed into the room. "Dr. Buchan! How did you get here?"

"Never mind. I must talk to you." The great angular Scott could hardly contain himself: "I've got it, man!"

"What?"

"The link, the common factor—the nucleus!"

"Steady." Slayter waved to a chair. "Sit down. This is Mr. Parkin by the way—from the Water Board research labs. Mr. Parkin, Dr. Buchan from the Kramer laboratories." The two men nodded briefly to each other.

"What's it all about?" Slayter asked.

"Now," Buchan said, "you remember you found a faulty component in the computer in your roads system and there was a faulty pump monitor in the Heathrow smash?"

"Yes."

"The playback showed insulation failure, is that not so?"

"Yes, I remember perfectly well. We'd got further than that, in fact, we found the same thing in the Heathrow crash, and the Navy think it was probably the cause of the sub—the *Triton*—going down."

"Exactly," Buchan continued. "Three events, one common cause!"

"Not at all." Slayter shook his head. "That doesn't make a case. Very well, I admit insulation failure is a common factor but . . ."

Buchan broke in: "I agree, but a case can be made if it's the *same* insulation failure."

"How do you mean?"

"If it's the same *component* that lost insulation."

"I'd be more impressed, yes."

"Well, for the last three days, I've more or less been living on the telephone. I've done more checking and . . ."

"Go on."

"Well," Buchan was gesticulating, "it *is* the same

component. It is! In the fuel pump monitor in the plane there was a small integrated circuit element—a logic gate. In your computer the same circuit element also forms a vital part of the adaptive network and—I've checked this with Naval Research at Portsmouth—the same component was built into the missile range computers on H.M.S. *Triton.*"

"All right, so you've got a common component, but it's *not* a case. You might as well say they've all got nuts and bolts made by the same people; it doesn't prove anything."

"I agree. *Post hoc* rationalization and all that," Buchan was in full flight, "but there's more. The Apollo Nineteen disaster—you read about it?"

"Yes."

"It was in the command module! I've checked with NASA."

"Dr. Buchan, I'm sorry to be so persistent, but it really doesn't matter how many places you find it, you still . . ."

"You admit a strong circumstantial link anyway?"

"Not strong, but it's odd, I agree."

Buchan was unpacking a briefcase. "Now for proof," he said, extracting a small metal box from the case. From it he took out a sealed polythene envelope containing a small plastic cube with ten short wires protruding from it. He put it down on the table.

"Logic gate M.13," he said, "that is to say, before use —just as it comes off the shelf."

"What do you mean, before use?"

Buchan swept on, pointing to the small electronic cube: "When I found this thing was built in to all the three disasters I rang up the makers and asked them to send me a few to look at. I took one apart in fact and shipped it off to Baron."

"Baron?"

"Public Health laddie at Colindale."

"I don't see . . ."

"He examined it for the bug!"

Slayter looked up in amazement.

"The inside contained several spores!"

Slayter sat back slowly, staring straight at Buchan: "Now you have a case."

"Exactly so. The spores belong to the plastic-eating organism."

"You've nothing like proved it," Slayter exclaimed. "You see, what you've said is this: one electronic component common to three disasters and in some examples of the component you've found the spores of the plastic-eating bacteria—it's no good at all. Spores are like seeds; they have to *germinate*. How do you get round that?"

Buchan was grinning, enjoying Slater's attempts to unseat his case: "What do bugs need to grow?"

"Well," Slayter began, "I'm no bacteriologist, but—let's think—food and warmth and . . ."

"Excellent!" Buchan almost shouted. "*Warmth.* What happens to most circuit units when they start to work?"

"My God," Slayter was sitting bolt upright. "My God, yes!"

"You see," Buchan was triumphant, "once the unit started to work, whatever computer or system it was built into—once it started to work, it warmed up—the spores germinated and started to eat . . ."

". . . the plastic inside the unit," Slayter finished.

"Yes, but that's not all. I checked this with Baron and with the makers of the unit. Baron says that the germinating spores would need water very quickly. Now I'm not absolutely certain, but when the unit starts to work it gets warm, and we think now that there must have been just enough condensation on this cadmium plate here," he pointed, "to provide a few droplets of water. Just enough to give the spores enough water to start dividing. Once they had started to live and divide again, they made their way along the insulation of the wires leading out of the unit here," he pointed to the short wires protruding from the unit, "and from there, along the wires to whatever other wires the unit was connected to."

Slayter sat very still. "So once it started operation, the bugs spread out into any system the unit was connected with."

"That's it," Buchan eased his bulk back into the chair.

"How can you prove all this?" Slayter asked.

Buchan silently took a second metal box from his briefcase and put it carefully down on the table. Out of it, he took a sealed glass jar and put it down gingerly beside the box.

"This is another unit," he explained. "We gave it five hours continuous operation." He pushed the jar towards Slayter.

Inside, the small, cubical circuit element was distorted and misshapen. The yellow insulation on one of the wires leading out of it was slowly falling away from the gleaming copper core.

"A biological time bomb," Slayter said softly. "Once it starts work, it starts infecting."

"One thing that worried me," Buchan went on, "is that nobody apparently saw any evidence of softening in the earlier investigations; they only found bare wires. I checked this with Baron and he reckons that when this bug—wherever it came from—started to eat plastic, it probably did so very slowly, and as each generation came along it began to consume more rapidly."

"So the earlier outbreaks were relatively mild," said Slayter.

"Yes," said Buchan. "It gradually adapted and increased its efficiency until it got completely out of control. Now we have the centre of London dying."

"One little component," Slayter mused. "It's unbelievable."

"So far we've managed to do quite a lot. The firm—quite a small one near King's Cross—have managed to trace most of their sales, it'll take a few days yet, but it all fits. They made large sales to the aircraft makers, to your road-computer makers, and to NASA. There's only one they can't do anything about, though."

"Why's that?"

"They exported it to the California Rocket Corporation. You know, the people who are building Argonaut One, the unmanned Mars probe."

"I don't understand. Why can't they do anything about it?"

Buchan spoke evenly: "Because it took off six weeks ago."

Gerrard was feeling awkward and uncomfortable inside the Beeston protective suit. His body still ached from the climb out of the underground.

Behind the transparent face visor there was a strong smell of rubber and disinfectant. And as he walked stiffly along the street with the other three men, the folds of the hard fabric caught in his armpits and behind his knees. The sound of his breath was harsh and exaggerated in the steamy envelope of the suit.

Their footsteps squeaked drily in the snow as they walked. A soldier trudged along beside him, carrying the portable spray unit filled with the poisoned plastic. Two other uniformed men were consulting a map, one of them bore lieutenant's pips on a shoulder tag.

He turned to Gerrard: "It's just down here off Gerard Street."

He pointed on the map and looked up, then turned and walked over to a corner shop with a sign in Roman Purple letters: *Gear Trend.* In the window was a display of brilliantly coloured shirts, mock-leather jackets, and posters. Behind the shirts, pinned on the backboard of the window, were "wet-look" plastic coats and boots, unisex outfits, and an array of record labels. Above were two rows of picture windows. At one, a face appeared briefly from behind a curtain, looked down at the suited figures approaching, and disappeared. The lieutenant walked firmly up to the glass door and thumped hard on it with his gloved fist.

As he waited, his hard brown eyes wandered over the garish window display with some distaste. Then there was the sound of bolts being drawn. The door opened. The lieutenant's look of disapproval deepened.

The man was about thirty-five with a mop of carefully coiffed grey hair. He was wearing a pale-pink cashmere sweater and white velvet bell-bottomed trousers with boots. His face was good-looking in a smooth, rounded-off way, and he spoke with a rhythmic emphasis on first syllables: "Oh my God, thank goodness you've come. It's an absolute shambles—you've no idea. All my stock, it's absolutely ruined. I don't know . . ."

The lieutenant cut in brusquely: "Where's the outbreak?"

"In the back here," the man simpered at him. "I'm sure you'll cope."

The lieutenant brushed past, the others following into the shop. They all stopped in complete disbelief.

Rows of shoes were slowly undulating on the surface of a mass of foam as if they were dancing without music. The multi-coloured plastic décor had ballooned obscenely off the walls and lay on the floor bubbling with the bright fluorescent colours of the original designs. A row of plastic coats dripped off hangers on a chromium rail. One still remained, writhing in the foam almost as if animated by an occupant. The whole shop was crawling in a slow, nightmarish dance. The air was thick with the stench of Ainslie's bacillus.

The owner was wringing his hands and complaining. "It's really quite dreadful. All my lovely designs, I'll never be able to repeat them."

The lieutenant whipped round: "Do me a favour, old fruit—shut up." The man sulked as the lieutenant gestured nervously to the soldier with the spray unit: "O.K., let it go."

The man stepped hesitantly into the shop and started pumping the lever on the spray pack, spreading a brown mist of poisoned plastic ahead of him. The lieutenant watched the anguished expression of the owner with a barely concealed pleasure as the spray settled down on the surface of the foam. The air was filled with the petrol smell of toluene as it evaporated, leaving behind a thin, sticky, brown layer which covered the bubbling, active masses.

They settled down to wait, Gerrard pulling back the cuff of his glove to mark the time. For some minutes, nothing happened, and the contents of the shop continued to suck and hiss as the mutant fed.

Then, very gradually, the rate of movement started to slow; bubbles started to collapse and the sibilant noise of the foam diminished. Finally, after about seven minutes, activity had almost ceased. Occasional pockets of activity not reached by the spray still remained, but it was clear that the plastic containing the cyanide molecule had done its work. The fifty-ninth mutant of Ainslie had eaten itself to death.

The lieutenant looked hard at Gerrard for a moment and then grinned: "Not bad for starters."

The shop owner was dancing round the men, trying to express his thanks. "Oh, how simply marvellous, how terribly clever, what did you use? You must all come upstairs and have a drink."

The soldiers began to pack their gear together. As the lieutenant turned to move out, he glanced back at the shop owner and said, "Not tonight, Josephine."

During the weeks that followed, the production line at Polytad got fully under way producing the Aminostyrene with the added cyanide molecule. As the new material was completed it was rushed in an almost continuous succession of lorries to the periphery of the stricken area.

Troops moved in with spray units, and each time an outbreak of infected plastic was reported, they covered the area with the brown, sticky deposit of poisoned Aminostyrene. Gradually, the number of outbreaks diminished; gradually, Ainslie's bacillus gave up its struggle for supremacy, and the corroded heart of London started up into action.

During the whole of the period, Gerrard worked almost continuously. He found, to his astonishment, that the urgent, relentless work was to his taste. Field work against a known problem, rather than the long-term and often frustrating search for originality in the laboratory, gave a tremendous boost to his sagging sense of purpose.

On a number of occasions he had tried to reach

Anne, but each time he seemed just to have missed her, or she had left a rather unconvincing message saying she would be at a certain place at a certain time. And then when he rang, she was never there.

In the end he had made contact, but it had been cold and confined only to a discussion of the mutant problem.

As the situation gradually improved in Central London, he decided to get away from the stench and the desolation. His part was, in any case, finished.

He drove down to Eastbourne, walking over the downs and along the shore, gradually unwinding. Three days were enough. He was sitting in the torpor of the hotel lounge on the third day wondering whether or not to go back to London. The Kramer consultancy hadn't been in touch. He was obviously in high disfavour.

A waiter told him he was wanted on the phone. Immediately and with pleasure he recognized Buchan's rich Lowlands accent. The Kramer consultancy was in jeopardy. There were threats of bankruptcy, several claims had been made, and an extended legal battle seemed inevitable. Anne Kramer, now the majority shareholder, was back and wanted them to continue.

"Without me," Gerrard replied. "I'm cast as the arch traitor. They won't want me at any price. Anyway," he said, "I'm not sure I want to, frankly."

There was a long silence on the other end of the line. "I didn't think you went in for self-pity," said Buchan. "But if that's the way you feel, I'll do no more about it."

The remarks stung Gerrard and he began angrily defending himself and criticizing Kramer's previous attitude. He delivered a long attack on the changeover from responsibility to sheer profit-seeking. It was a long and rather over-moralistic homily, and Buchan on the other end of the phone quietly let it run on until Gerrard eventually paused for breath.

"Have you quite finished?" he finally asked.

"You're damn right I have. You can stuff it!"

"Because, if you'd allow me just to get a few words in edgeways, I was about to say that a lot of what you say seems good sense. I mebbe wouldn't have put it quite so emotionally."

Now it was the turn for a silence to fall on Gerrard's side of the line. "I don't understand. You agree?"

"In some ways," said Buchan. "That's why I'd rather like you to come to the meeting."

"What meeting?" said Gerrard. "You didn't say anything about a meeting."

"Did I not?" said Buchan. "Och, well, there's to be one tomorrow and, in fact, that's why I'm phoning. They asked me to."

"They actually want me to go to it?" asked Gerrard.

"I wouldn't say there was a great deal of enthusiasm, no red carpet or anything," said Buchan, "but you are a contracted member of the consultancy."

"Only just."

"We'll see," said Buchan. "Anyway, come. It's at the Connaught Room, Royal Yorkshire Hotel, at two forty-five p.m. tomorrow. Look forward to seeing you." Before Gerrard could answer, he hung up.

Gerrard went into the hotel restaurant, and almost in compensation for his doubts and anxieties, worked methodically through the most expensive dishes on the menu. Finally he sat staring moodily into a balloon of the best cognac, smoking an over-large cigar.

He mused over the structure of the group. Wright and Scanlon would almost certainly join forces to get him out. They wouldn't easily forget that he had been responsible for indicting the material of the bio-degradable bottle as a principal cause of the London disaster. He began to imagine the future course of the group. He himself had joined because, under Kramer, he believed that they would develop a policy of increasing social responsibility in science. Many of their projects had been clearly designed with the environment very much to the fore. There had been, for example, a contract with a North of England textile-dyeing firm to design pollution-free effluent traps.

But as Kramer had redirected his energies towards profit and expansion, many of the more socially valuable projects had been dropped as too costly. The group had been driven, purely by Kramer's drive, into accepting relatively easy projects with a high and quick financial yield.

In bed, in spite of the wine and brandy, his mind raced. What were the alternatives? A Ministry job—it was his if he wanted it—giving second-class advice to tenth-class politicians—doing dull research to provide political ammunition for men whose idea of intellectual honesty was to construct successful lies. Science in the cause of double-think.

Back to Canada? God, no. He remembered the faculty club, with its highly structured bonhomie and emptiness. The intelligent smiles on desiccated faces. And the five months of winter seemed an intolerable prospect.

As his anxiety and doubt increased, he finally realized that everything he thought of made his pulse race. Finally, with some sort of humour, he found himself worrying about whether he had a clean shirt for the morning.

As he fell asleep, Anne's face kept recurring. Half of him wanted her lying beside him, the other half rejected her intelligence and apparent coolness.

The next morning he drove up to town early. Back in his flat he shaved, bathed, changed, and, unable to face the thought of food, got back into his car and drove towards the hotel where the meeting was to be held.

As he drove, he tried to imagine the outcome of the meeting. Why a hotel, why not at the labs? His confidence ebbed. Buchan was a strange, complex man. Perhaps he was playing a game. Needling Wright by encouraging Gerrard to speak out.

If he kept quiet, what then? He wanted to go on working in the consultancy. For one thing it would keep him in contact with Anne. Was there any chance of coming to terms with Wright? Anger boiled up again. He would speak out and damn the consequences.

When he arrived at the hotel, his mood changed again. He had expected an armchair meeting in a small private lounge. Instead he found a small conference room had been booked. There were more members of the Kramer Board than he had realized.

To his annoyance he found he was early; the meeting was now scheduled for three p.m. So he had to hover round the table while the rest entered. Betty had arranged the table formally with glasses of water, pads, and pencils.

Eventually everyone but Anne took their place. She had phoned to say that she had been delayed and would they start without her.

Wright took the chair in Anne's absence. On his right was the financial backer of the group, Sir Harvey Phillips. On his left was Wright's own vacant chair, then Scanlon, and the firm's accountant, Simon Marks, a dark, youthful face with, Gerrard noticed, hard eyes.

Buchan sat next to Phillips with Gerrard beside him. At the far end of the table was the group's lawyer who also, it seemed, had invested in the group, Alistair Macdonald. He was a thin, foxy Highland Scot with a studiously polite manner. He also represented a merchant bank which had originally capitalized the group.

The meeting opened with an empty and formal speech of regret from Wright at Kramer's untimely death. Just as he finished, the door behind him opened and Anne came in. Everyone rose.

Gerrard watched her expressionless appraisal of the men round the table but her only reaction was a grave nod of thanks as she took Wright's seat, leaving him at the head of the table.

She still disturbed him. He had arrived angry enough to speak and now, in her presence, he felt he could hardly utter a word without stammering.

The meeting proceeded; condolences were extended to Anne Kramer and the events of the past few months reviewed and examined. Gerrard's chance came to speak. He felt a slight nudge from Buchan but he ignored it. The moment passed and he could feel the disgust of the older man as he drew back disappointed. The meeting went on to other matters. Macdonald, the lawyer, began to outline some suggested plans for extricating themselves from the dilemma created by the involvement of their product in the disaster.

After he had finished, Marks gave a flat but expert account of the financial position. They could certainly survive, it appeared.

Then it was Wright's turn. Gerrard listened incredulously. There was not one word of regret or self-recrimination at having indirectly been involved in the deaths of thousands. Nor was there the slightest awareness of how close the situation had come to total disaster.

As Wright unfolded his version of events, he made it appear as though the whole dreadful sequence was a minor setback for the group and their product. Gerrard became aware that Wright was getting at him in a roundabout way. There was a reference to their having been exposed to the results of activities which jeopardized their future.

Gerrard suddenly found himself on his feet. He looked around. Anne, apparently oblivious of his movement, was looking down, doodling. Buchan was conducting a bored examination of his pipe. Scanlon was smiling at his discomfort.

Gerrard's anger rose and set cold and hard. He found his voice: "I'd like to speak."

Wright looked at him coldly: "I'm afraid I haven't quite finished."

"You've said quite enough."

Wright flushed angrily: "This meeting will be . . ."

"What meeting, for God's sake? We're only eight people, we're supposed to be talking about the death of our founder—the half-destruction of a city. Now I'm going to speak."

Wright started to reply but Anne put a hand on his arm: "Please."

Wright hesitated, then subsided. "Go ahead, Dr. Gerrard."

Gerrard cleared his throat and looked around: "Well, I'm new here and it doesn't look as though I'll be around much longer so I'll start by saying that I've never seen such a bunch of complacent, self-seeking hypocrites in my entire life. I'm not going to dwell on the absolutely sickening string of half-truths from Dr. Wright or his attitude towards this whole affair which, in my view, fails entirely to consider our responsibility."

Wright rose to his feet, white-faced: "I protest. . . ."

"Please hear me out," Gerrard snapped. "I've waited for one word of regret or compunction from you. One word that tells me that you have learnt something from all this. That you accept some degree of social responsibility for your activities.

"When Kramer started this thing up, it was great, inspiring. He had ideas, he could make them work, and he was concerned. He cared about the appalling results of technology.

"O.K., call me a romantic, but when I first met Kramer he gave me a sense of idealism about science. He taught me that it's possible to use the special skills of science to help people. To get us out of the polluted mess we're all in. But his attitude changed, and we all know it did. Mine hasn't.

"In our group we can muster tremendous variety of special knowledge and expertise, we can use it, we can think creatively, and we could go to work now to design and fabricate on behalf of people. Not just to make a profit—obviously we've got to break even—but to direct everything we have towards society.

"No one will ever know just how much responsibility we will bear for this disaster. We made Degron, we designed the bottle. Nobody could have foreseen the bacteria which grew on it, but our product—the result of our thinking, our ingenuity—played an essential part. None of us set out to do anything more than be technically ingenious. We succeeded and London nearly died. Surely that's more than enough to make us redirect our activities. The next time it may be the whole world. If this group is going on—and I hope it will—it must decide right at the beginning exactly what it is doing and why. Obviously we're a limited company, and people want a yield on their investment. But, given that, we can surely find ways of being creative on behalf of society." He faltered for a moment. "That—that's all, I guess." He sat down.

When Gerrard had finished there was a long silence. He looked around the table. The only one who met his eye was Buchan, looking at him with a quizzical expression in which it was impossible to read either approval for the content of his speech, or reproach for his impassioned tone.

Anne was looking down. Wright, like Gerrard, was carefully scanning the reactions of the rest of the group and obviously finding a certain relief and satisfaction in the process. From any outward signs, Gerrard's speech had effectively done Wright's job for him—antagonized the entire Board.

Wright stood up. "Thank you, Dr. Gerrard. I'm sure we're all most intrigued with your ideas and suggestions. Has anyone any further comments on Dr. Gerrard's . . . homily?"

Gerrard looked over at him. If he had ever hated a man in his life, this man was Wright and all he stood for.

"I was hoping you had," he said. "It was directed at you."

"I rather gathered as much," Wright smiled thinly. "Perhaps we can have a debate about it some day—at Tower Hill or Speakers Corner, say—but you will forgive me if I now proceed to the main business of this meeting."

Nobody spoke. Scanlon was smiling, Buchan filling his pipe. The lawyer, Macdonald, was gazing up at the ceiling. Anne looked down at her pad and made a note.

"Thank you," Wright continued. "Now to the rather pressing business of electing a new chairman for the consultancy. I should like to take any nominations."

There was a pause, then Scanlon spoke: "There is only one person in my view—the senior member of this consultancy and the man who has made the biggest contribution to our work—yourself."

Sir Harvey nodded slowly: "I should like to second that."

"Thank you, gentlemen. Any further nominations?" Wright was pleased but determined not to show it.

Buchan put his pipe down on the table. "Aye, I'd like to nominate Dr. Gerrard."

"Dr. Gerrard?" Wright looked startled. "Are we to take this seriously?"

Buchan nodded: "Never more serious in my life. What he said made very good sense. That is the way I personally should like this consultancy to be run. I nominate Dr. Gerrard."

Wright flushed with anger: "I'm sorry, I can't accept this nomination, and I'm afraid I regard it as entirely frivolous. Dr. Gerrard has only been with us for a very short time. He knows nothing about our background, our work, or our set-up, and frankly I feel that the emotional outburst we have just endured makes him totally unsuitable to remain as a member of this consultancy, let alone as director."

Buchan drew on his pipe. "You're assuming you've taken over the whole works already. Ye've no right to be in that chair while your nomination is being decided."

Wright hesitated and looked at Anne.

Anne nodded at him: "Perhaps I'd better take the chair now, Dr. Wright."

They changed seats. Anne glanced round at Macdonald, the lawyer, at the end of the table: "Can we be advised, Mr. Macdonald? Is Dr. Gerrard's short length of time as a member a factor here?"

Macdonald shook his head decisively. "Not that I can see."

"Then can we proceed with nominations?"

Wright started to speak but Scanlon restrained him.

"Is there a seconder to Dr. Gerrard's nomination?" Anne looked around the table.

Finally, Macdonald spoke: "Yes, I should like to second Dr. Gerrard."

Wright looked inquiringly at him but the lawyer was looking down at his papers.

"Anyone else?" said Anne. There was a long silence.

"Right then, we'll proceed with the voting. I don't think we need any more than a show of hands here. Those for Dr. Wright's nomination, please raise your hand."

Scanlon and Sir Harvey raised their hands.

"Two," said Anne. "Those for Dr. Gerrard," she asked.

Buchan and Macdonald raised their hands.

Gerrard's mind was in a turmoil, hardly knowing the reason behind this sudden shift of fortune—still uncertain and suspicious of the motives of the other two.

Anne looked down at the accountant. "Mr. Marks?"

"I attend this Board purely in an advisory capacity, I have no voting rights." Marks's relief at being left out of the situation was apparent. The tension was affecting everyone.

"Two for each candidate," said Anne. "Then it seems I must exercise the casting vote."

Wright looked gratefully at her. A man of limited empathy, the sudden opposition to what he considered a rubber-stamp procedure had thrown him off his stride.

"Yes," said Anne. She carefully took her dark glasses off and folded them.

Damn you, thought Gerrard, you're really enjoying your little moment. Get on with it.

"After all we've heard here this afternoon," Anne said, "I feel that I must support the nomination of Dr. Gerrard."

In the silence which followed, Wright shook his head slightly, as if he couldn't trust his ears. Gerrard sat stunned.

Then Wright found his voice and rose to his feet: "I can't believe it . . . I can't accept this . . . for God's sake, why?"

Anne turned her head away from his gaze. All Wright's reserve had gone; he was almost in tears.

"Because I have an entirely different concept of the management of this consultancy from yours," she said.

"But in what way? I just don't understand . . ." Wright was shouting.

"My husband ran this consultancy as an autocracy.

That was all right for him. He was . . . Arnold Kramer. He founded it. But it had crippling disadvantages and I feel that Dr. Gerrard outlined the problem very well. We're just not doing what we set out to do. Our ideals have . . ."

"Ideals!"

"Yes, that's right. We had them at one time."

"I cannot accept this . . . nor can I work with . . ." Wright pointed a shaking finger at Gerrard: "that man. I warn you, Mrs. Kramer, you force me to resign, and as you well know the patents for Aminostyrene and Degron go with me."

Anne turned to face him. "Yes," she said quietly.

Wright faltered: "You're prepared to see them go?"

"I want them to go. They caused the death of my husband and nearly killed Dr. Gerrard and myself, and they have brought us nothing but discredit. I'd like to wipe the slate clean and start again."

"Well said," Buchan stared straight at Wright.

"But the financial support for the company comes almost entirely from these products," Scanlon leaned forward anxiously.

"Not so," Buchan continued. "The Degron licences are in fact in the name of the group, not yours, Wright."

Wright pushed back his chair: "I'd be interested to know what Sir Harvey has to say about this."

Sir Harvey shrugged his shoulders: "Mrs. Kramer is the majority shareholder, ultimately the decision is hers. My main brief here is to ensure the continuance of the yield from our investment."

"Then it is quite clear that I must go." Wright rose to his feet and looked across at Scanlon. But Scanlon was avoiding his gaze, looking intently at Sir Harvey. "If you desire any further communication with me, it must be through my solicitors."

Wright turned slowly with all the dignity he could muster, his back straight, his head held stiffly, and left the conference room. In that moment Gerrard almost felt sorry for the man. Despite his proud stance, or perhaps, because of it, Wright suddenly looked old. A broken man.

Anne spoke: "You have been nominated chairman of this company, Dr. Gerrard. Do you accept?"

There was a pause while he felt the attention of everyone in the room on him. "Well . . . yes, I guess I do." His acceptance sounded lame, even to him, and he saw a shade of disappointment cross Anne's face.

Then it really hit him. He was the new boss of Kramer's. Everyone was looking to him for a lead. Wright's departure had shaken them all. He must reassure them, give them a positive line of action to follow.

Anne rose from her chair: "Now that we've got a new chairman, I feel out of place sitting here. Would you take over the meeting, Dr. Gerrard?"

Gerrard nodded, rose, and trying to display a confidence he did not feel, took the chair.

He looked around the table: "Gentlemen, this has been a traumatic meeting. I see little purpose in continuing at the present time. I propose therefore to adjourn until next month." He looked down at the date indicator on his wrist watch, "The twentieth to be precise. At that time I shall hope to present to you a suggested plan for the future running of this company. Now, if there is no further business, I propose to close this meeting at," he glanced at his watch again, "five-thirty p.m."

The meeting broke up, Scanlon and Sir Harvey leaving the room in close, urgent consultation. There would be trouble from that source, thought Gerrard.

Buchan came up to congratulate him. "Ye'll have your work cut out, ye know that?"

"I'm sorry about Wright."

Buchan looked at him a little sardonically. "Really, I'm not. A little radical surgery is very healthy." He looked after Scanlon, who was following Sir Harvey out the door. "And I'm not sure the knife went far enough. Still," he smiled, " 'Sufficient unto the day is the evil thereof.' I'm away for a wee celebratory meal at Princes'. Care to join me?"

Gerrard looked over to where Anne was standing on the other side of the Board table talking to Marks and Macdonald.

"No thanks."

Buchan followed his gaze. "Aye, I see. Well, good luck, laddie. I've a feeling you're going to need it."

Buchan left. Shortly after, Marks and then Macdonald came up to congratulate him and assure their support.

Betty gathered up the papers and came up to him: "Can I go now, sir?"

He noted the change in tone with a certain dry relish. "Of course. I'll see you on Monday."

Betty left and he was finally alone with Anne. He came to a decision. He had won so much in a few short hours. A good gambler would take advantage of the situation when luck was running his way.

"Anne."

Anne turned. She had been sorting out the pile of papers and probate documents given her by Macdonald.

"Yes?" she said. She was still on the other side of the long table. He leant across it.

"Thank you. I mean that."

She looked at him coolly. "Not at all. I'm protecting my own interests. I merely selected the best man for the job, that's all."

"I'm not sure I can do it by myself."

"I'm sure everyone will help you once they've learnt to accept the new situation."

"That's not what I mean," he moved around the table towards her. "I want your help."

"Of course, I'll do what I can," she turned away from him, back to the table.

"You know what I mean."

She froze. He was now standing right behind her. She didn't answer.

"This is a hell of a job. Perhaps far too big for me. I can't do it without you. I need you there as a full partner."

"A partner! I rather thought I was already . . ."

He grabbed her by the arms and swung her round. "Don't fool with me. Maybe it's a bit early yet. But I want you. I can't do this job without you."

There was a pause. She still looked away from him.

"Please listen. I want this job, O.K.! But you're a hell of a lot more important to me. If there is no chance, then forget it, I can't stay here."

She did not reply. He slowly released his hold on her arms and walked across the room.

He had opened the door when she finally spoke: "Luke." He turned. "You'll have to give me time."

He looked back at her. "All the time in the world. In fact," he glanced at his watch, "five minutes. I'm taking you out to dinner."

She came up to him and raised her lips to his. Their kiss was long and gentle but gave a suggestion of infinite possibilities.

With difficulty, Gerrard kept his voice from shaking: "Let's go now, shall we?"

She looked up at him, her eyes softened with a trace of tears.

As they walked through the overheated foyer of the hotel into the winter air, it was already dark. The sky was cold and clear, the stars burned brilliantly. They both looked up at the icy panorama.

Mars showed clearly as a pale-red spicule of light. Neither of them had ever heard of Conrad's Plain.

It lay two hundred miles to the north of the Martian equator. First discovered in photographs taken on fly-past by an unmanned Mariner probe, its completely featureless surface had made it an ideal landing site for the first of the robot probes to make a soft landing.

On the Plain, a twenty-four-hour Martian day was coming to an end. The sun was a small blood-red disc sinking behind the craggy hills around a crater to the east, and violet shadows raced over the rocky sand dunes like giant fingers.

The only sound was the faint whistle of a light, chill breeze lifting small flurries of sand briefly into the air. Capping the hills, there was a greyish-white layer of hoar frost, and in some of the deeper crevices around the base of the crater there were small patches of strangely shaped lichen.

Overhead, a few wispy clouds drifted slowly across the deep-violet bowl of the sky, but no other movements disturbed the still scene. A panorama which had repeated itself year after year and century after century without change.

There were no eyes to register the colours, no ears to listen to the wind, no hands to fashion the rocks. Just the lichen scraping out an existence in the damp rocks.

Although it was unheard, a faint rumble began in the sky overhead. Then the rays of the setting sun picked out a tiny spot of light, moving across the unfamiliar pattern of stars.

Gradually, the distant sound increased in volume and changed to the crackling blast of a rocket motor as Argonaut One descended towards the surface, suspended on a tail of lashing flame.

As it approached, light sand kicked up in a boiling cloud, then heavier rocks spun into the air away from the flare of the rocket motor. Finally, the ungainly spider shape settled down on three hydraulic legs which bent and then straightened slowly under the impact. The motor snapped off, and the dust cloud slowly drifted away in the wind.

There were cracking sounds as the red-hot nozzle of the rocket motor cooled in the thin air.

Then, from the top of the insect-like craft, a servomotor whirred, a small hatch opened, and a complex radio antenna unfolded and clicked into an open, web-like pattern.

Automatic switching circuits began to activate the maze of intricate electronics in the body of the machine. Slowly the artificially made creature began its work. A small door opened at its base, and an extending arm holding a small shovel dug its way into the soft Martian sand and then withdrew with its load. Sensors began to measure temperature, wind velocity, radiation levels, and oxygen concentration.

Powerful transmitters gathered up the data, coded it

into radio-pulses, and flung it on its way back to Earth; back to the jubilant mission-control team at Cape Kennedy.

During the cold of the Martian night, Argonaut One steadily built up a radio-picture of the ancient planet. As it did so the tightly packed circuits gave out heat.

Heat which gradually stole its way into logic gate M.13.

Inside the metal casing of the gate, the frozen spores of Ainslie's fifty-ninth mutant responded to the warmth and began to germinate.

Two hours after sunrise the following morning, Argonaut One died abruptly.

Inside its shining body, plastic began to soften. . . .

ABOUT THE AUTHORS

DR. KIT PEDLER's accomplishments in medicine, experimental biology, and ophthalmic pathology are indicated on his letterhead, which reads: "Dr. Kit Pedler, M.B.B.S., Ph.D., M.C.P." A regular participant in BBC current affairs and science programs, he is also Reader and Head of the University of London's Department of Ophthalmology and involved in experimental vision research. He is currently working on what might be described as an electronic replacement for the damaged or diseased eye.

GERRY DAVIS, also a Londoner, has written copiously for both British and Canadian television and also spent several years working with the Canadian National Film Board as an assistant director and film editor. He returned to England as the editor of a drama series aired on an independent network. With Kit Pedler he completed the screen adaption of MUTANT 59, and the two are now engaged in writing a stage play commissioned for London's West End.